If You Only Knew

If You Only Knew

PRERNA PICKETT

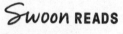

Swoon READS

New York

A Swoon Reads Book

An imprint of Feiwel and Friends and Macmillan Publishing Group, LLC

120 Broadway, New York, NY 10271

Our books may be purchased in bulk for promotional, educational, or business use. Please contact your local bookseller or the Macmillan Corporate and Premium Sales Department at (800) 221-7945 ext. 5442 or by email at MacmillanSpecialMarkets@macmillan.com.

Library of Congress Control Number: 2019940970

ISBN 9781250314468 (hardcover) / ISBN 9781250314475 (ebook)

Book design by Liz Dresner

First edition, 2020

10 9 8 7 6 5 4 3 2 1

swoonreads.com

Dedicated to MY Fab Five

COREY

For the last five years I'd lived by one simple rule: Stay alive.

I put that rule to the test by making one simple statement.

"This isn't a good idea."

Vance waited in the shadows, molding himself to them. The whites of his eyes narrowed. He clenched his jaw.

"I'm not asking for your opinion." He lifted the hem of his shirt and stuck his thumb into a belt loop. His piece glinted against the little bit of light filtering through the row of windows on the garage door.

I gripped the bat in my hand and gritted my teeth. Being in jail had rusted my instincts, short-circuited my sense of self-preservation. All I needed was the sight of Vance's gun to remind me of that.

"I know what I'm doing, Fowler. Right, boys?" His question echoed and fell around me as he nodded to Drew and Jaimie. They stood at the back of the detached garage in their matching black shirts and jeans, holding flashlights. Drew frowned, a grim line set across his mouth.

I cleared my face of all emotion, a blank canvas, tightening my hold on the bat in my hand, and tried to convince myself it wasn't created to hit baseballs, but rather elite sports cars.

"You know you want to. That lawyer deserves worse." Vance crept closer to my ear, egging me on with his jittery presence. "Just one swing, right there on the front windshield."

Hopper didn't deserve it. Not really. Especially not after everything he did to get my sentence reduced. Which wasn't part of his job, considering he was the prosecuting attorney.

"Not like he can't afford another one," Jaimie taunted.

The words didn't offer me any comfort. My hands kept sweating, making my hold on the bat slick. I forced myself to shut off the danger sign flashing at the back of my head. This wasn't exactly how I planned on paying back Hopper for his kindness.

I rolled the bat back and forth, tossed it in the air, and watched it twist, the black ingrained logo showing its face with every turn. Vance's wide grin reflected across the shining surface of the car.

"A year in that hell. And for what? Nothing you did."

I almost snorted at that one. Maybe I hadn't done *exactly* what I was charged with, but I still picked the path that led me to the dank and dark cell.

"Corey, do it."

This time, it wasn't a question. Jaimie and Drew had already dumped out all the garbage onto the patio, spray-painted the back and side of the house, and broken a couple of windows. All the commotion was blocked out by the house party next door. When the lawyer was away, the neighbors came out to play.

I gripped the bat tighter and ground my teeth as I pictured the look on Mom's face every time she came to visit me in prison.

What the hell was I doing here?

Playing chameleon. Shifting colors. Changing back into one of them. If I didn't, I'd end up dead. Or worse.

"I mean, I could always get your mommy or brother to take your place." Vance's threat rang in my ears.

The sorrowful picture of Mom was replaced with an image of bleeding cuts zigzagged across her skin. The picture kept my cowardice at bay. A silent motivator. I lifted the bat and pulled back my arms.

My first swing landed on the windshield with a sick crunch. The broken glass webbed out from the point of impact, caving in.

"That's my boy." Vance smacked my back like a proud father who just watched his kid hit a home run.

My gut tightened, like my stomach had taken the hit, not the car. Sweat dotted my skin, clinging to the back of my neck. What the hell was wrong with me? I needed to get my head back in the game.

Vance unzipped the backpack he'd thrown onto the concrete floor when we'd first broken into the garage. He lifted a can of spray paint and tossed it to me. I thought they'd used all of them on the house.

"And that's not all." He tipped over the bag to show me the other cans he'd brought along. "Do your thing, Picasso."

I should have known. Vance had let me stay back while Drew and Jaimie worked on spraying the house and breaking windows earlier. He'd led me into a false sense of security, and now I knew why.

This was the finale. And I was conducting it.

I slipped on the painting mask and took in a deep breath. The familiar shape of the can held easier in my hand than the bat. The metal ball bearing clanged as I shook the can and squatted down. A hiss and my hands glided against the side of the car as I directed the flow of the paint, shaping it, creating. I was the master and the paint was my bitch.

Jaimie and Drew tipped over the boxes sitting on the metal shelves, the sound ricocheting against the walls. Papers flew around me; one landed on my head before floating to the floor. But I couldn't be bothered. I was in the zone. This was my aerosol-ridden heaven.

Every now and then, a crunch or squeal of broken glass managed to disturb my work but not enough to knock me out of the high I felt when painting.

Vance pulled out a cigarette and lit it, the flame flickering in the dark, showcasing the scar that sank on his left cheek. He never got his hands dirty with stuff like this. He made sure it got done, that we didn't back down.

I ground my teeth and went back to work, spraying the finishing touches to my masterpiece.

An ache lanced along my muscles. I stood up and rubbed my shoulders, pulling my hoodie up over my head. June nights in Pennsylvania could be suffocating, but I didn't want to risk being recognized and my dark sweatshirt did the job.

I cleared my throat. "We should get out of here."

Vance eyed me for a second, predatory in the dark. He smirked and said, "Good idea. It is getting kinda late."

I turned around and surveyed the wreckage: the crushed wind-shield of the Porsche, the flames I'd drawn on the black paint, shining, ready to carry it away into the sky. Maybe the badass work would make up a little for the rest of the car.

Drew and Jaimie had been busy while I'd painted. The trophies on the shelves were bent and broken. The headlights were smashed, the sides of the car so fragmented it seemed like it was hunching in on itself. They'd also turned over one of the shelves. A paint puddle formed on the ground by the back of the garage.

A sharp smile edged on the side of Vance's mouth. "We did good." He rubbed his hands together. "I think Hopper will get the message."

With caution coating our movements, we pulled up the door of the detached garage, the only way out. When we'd first arrived, there was still enough noise to cover our entrance, but the party had died down and the night had stilled with the quiet ready to turn on us. We'd managed to get the door high enough for all of us to duck into the driveway when the sound of a motorcycle pulling in up front made us freeze.

"Shit, what's she doing here?" Vance muttered.

I yanked my eyes up to his, stomach plummeting. This was supposed to be an easy job, in and out. No witnesses. I should have known better. Fisting my hands, I squeezed until my arms shook, trying to calm the anxiety climbing higher.

The headlight bounced around as the girl maneuvered up the driveway and stopped in front of the garage, unaware of the mess surrounding her. A helmet hid her face behind the dark visor. She parked the motorcycle and turned it off. We ducked low as she slipped off the helmet and shook out her hair.

Vance gave the signal when she turned her back to us, and I blinked myself back to the damaged garage.

"Run!" I'd barely said the word when the girl twisted around and finally noticed us, her eyes widening.

"Hey! What the hell do you think you're doing?"

We scattered into the darkness. One of the guys slammed into my back while Jaimie ran into the girl, accidently knocking her down. My foot stuck against an uneven part of the pavement, and I struck concrete with a thud. I sprang up and ran to the fence separating the house from the woods behind it.

"Stop!" The girl screamed again. "Wha-wha-what did you do?" The horror in her voice grabbed ahold of my instinct to flee.

My hands were around the top of the fence.

"Ah!" A short, high-pitched scream made me falter. "Ow, ow, ow." The girl hissed in pain.

I stared at the fence in front of me. My heart rate steadied, and I gained control over my breathing. The girl let out another whimper, and my hands retreated to my sides.

Go. Just go.

Clenching my fists while fighting a snarl of annoyance with myself, I turned around and headed for her. Pulling my hoodie over my face, I hoped it would conceal me if I stuck to the shadows.

She held her leg while biting her lip, her jacket clinging to her curves. Her eyes narrowed and raked over me, the anger searing, making me forget for a second why I was there in the first place. Guilt held tightly to my stomach, but I pushed it away and held out my hands to let her know I wasn't planning on hurting her.

Vance and his guys were long gone. Reluctantly, I approached her. She scooted back on her butt.

"Don't even think about doing whatever you think you're going to do, because trust me when I say I know how to handle myself." She growled the words.

My steps faltered. *Shit.* I dropped my hand and realized how stupid I was being. Damn me for suddenly growing a conscience. Where had it been all those years before I went to jail?

"Are you okay?"

"Why the hell do you care?" She jumped up on her uninjured leg. She was several inches shorter than me but more than capable of glaring at me in a way that made me swallow hard.

She put some pressure on the injured leg as if daring me to challenge her words.

I moved my eyes to hers. "I'm sorry," I whispered before making a run for the fence again.

My hands scraped against the unvarnished wood. I gripped tightly, the splinters digging into my skin, braced a foot against the fence, and lifted myself up and over, landing with a thump on the hard ground.

"I'm going to kill you! There's no way you're going to get away with this!"

The fence jolted, and I jumped up. She was trying to climb over.

"Stop! You're going to hurt yourself." I hit the fence with my palm.

"Why do you care?" she yelled.

Holy hell. Was I seriously having a conversation with some girl through a fence after vandalizing her house?

"Just be careful. And ice your ankle." Apparently, yes.

"Anything else?" Her tone hadn't lost the highest level of pissed off.

"I—I . . . I'm sorry."

"Not as sorry as you're going to be!" The fence jolted again.

That's what I got for trying to help. I lifted my hoodie back onto my head and ran through the shadowed forest.

TESSA

eality crashed down on me in heavy waves. If I didn't surface soon, I might drown, so I forced myself to take a breath. Flipping on the light, I took an unsteady step to assess the damage. Our garage, which used to be immaculately laid out, sat in broken remnants—from the scattered pieces of paper and nails to the broken trophies sitting in glinting pieces. My eyes landed on Dad's Porsche, hunkered down like a deformed centerpiece.

I squeezed my eyes shut for a second, but when I opened them the car remained posed like a monument to the destruction. My belly did a flip, and I recognized that sinking sensation puddling around my feet because I had lived with it for the better part of a year. Guilt. I may not have been the one to break the car, but I couldn't help but blame myself for this somehow.

I stepped around the broken glass, and my heartbeat roared in my ears. The sight of the Porsche unburied memories I had tucked away, and I choked on my breath.

My body heated as the anger poured onto my skin. This wasn't happening. Slowly the ebbs of panic stopped pulsating, giving me room to push the memory where it belonged, deep within the past, into the furthest corner of my mind.

With a better grip on my reality, I dug out my phone. My fingers trembled. Dad's face hovered on the screen. He was at Graceland, the first vacation he'd taken since I could remember. I scrolled past him and found the number I needed, making the call.

"Tess, you okay?" Uncle Mike answered on the first ring.

"No. Someone broke into the garage and . . . you just need to get over here. Now."

"I'll be there right away."

Sometimes it paid to have an uncle who was also a detective.

I went over to the porch steps and sat down. The warmth of my jacket became unbearable, and I unzipped it and tossed it over the railing. In my head, I went over the details of the guy who stopped to make sure I was okay after one of his friends pushed me to the ground. It wasn't much because the shadows had covered his face, along with the ratty old hoodie he had worn, but I needed to do something until Uncle Mike got there.

I stared at what was left of the car. Dad's baby. He'd bought it after winning his first major case over a decade ago. Looking at it made the guilt bounce around like a Ping-Pong ball in my stomach, and I darted my eyes to the motorcycle.

Pushing myself up, I approached the motorcycle and ran a hand over the front. The metal sent a shiver up my arm despite the heat of the night. The pain in my ankle receded, and I managed to make it over without wincing. I lifted a leg over the side and sank into the seat, gripping the handles, letting the familiarity of it calm my heart.

Headlights wedged away the dark driveway and flashed across my face, into the damaged garage. Uncle Mike stepped out of the car, slamming the door behind him. In the passenger seat was his daughter, my cousin and best friend, Paige. I got off the bike, hands lingering on the handles, and headed for them.

"What happened?" Uncle Mike asked, smoothing a hand over his balding head.

Paige ran the length between us and pulled me into a hard hug. "Are you okay?" she asked. Her hazel eyes were wide when I stepped away from her. She didn't wait for my answer but instead hugged me again.

I let out a surprised wheeze.

"Paige, sweetheart, I think you're suffocating her." Uncle Mike put a hand on her shoulder and smiled, unable to hide the crease of worry between his brows. "She was right next to me when you called. I couldn't persuade her to stay home."

Paige finally let me go but kept an arm wrapped around my shoulders.

Uncle Mike sized up the damage. "Geez, this is crazy. I gotta call your dad."

"No!" I grabbed the phone out of his hand. Uncle Mike raised his brows. "He'll be home tomorrow. We'll deal with it then." I didn't want to interrupt his vacation.

Uncle Mike sighed and crossed his arms. "He'll kill me for it."

"You say that every time you keep something from him, but you're not dead yet." Uncle Mike was Dad's baby brother, and there was no way he'd ever hurt him. "It's my decision. I'll deal with the repercussions. Besides, you know how much he needs this."

"Are you sure, Tess?" Paige crossed her arms. Her dark-blond hair was up in a messy bun.

"Yes," I reassured them.

Uncle Mike glanced down at his phone. "I'll call the precinct and have someone come down and watch the house for the next couple of nights. I thought you were going for a short ride on the back road?"

"I came to check on Chewy." Paige was allergic to cats so I couldn't bring her along while I stayed over at their place while Dad was on his trip. Thankfully I'd been able to bring Jiminy, my dog, over.

"Did you see anything?" Uncle Mike asked.

"Yeah, there were four of them. All dressed in black. Black pants, black hoodies, black shoes."

"Did you see anyone's face?"

I rubbed my arms up and down, suddenly cold. "No."

"Can you remember anything at all?" Uncle Mike urged. He took out his pen and pad. He never left home without them.

I shook my head. "I talked to one guy, but it was too dark to see his face."

The boy, whoever he was, had surprised me with the apology that escaped his lips. That and the fact that he'd turned around and checked on me when he was so close to escaping. The other three deserted him. They all ran down the driveway, and a few seconds later the roar of an engine and tires peeling out hit the night.

"Anything missing?" Uncle Mike tucked away his notepad and started toward the inside of the garage.

I stepped over broken glass and tossed paper. Paint was splattered in the back—pale yellow, the same hue as my bedroom. Dad and I had painted it a couple of years ago.

We walked along the side of the car and I stopped. Graffitied flames roared along the driver's side, up the back to the tail. They rose up high toward the top of the car, oddly mesmerizing and beautiful. I reached out a hand and touched the still-wet paint, and my fingers came away orange.

"That's interesting." Uncle Mike knelt down.

"More like rude," Paige said, standing behind us.

I squeezed the bridge of my nose and shut my eyes.

A second later, a police cruiser pulled up behind Uncle Mike's

Crown Victoria. Officer Jenkins stepped out, and I had to force myself not to react. Paige and I exchanged worried glances. The last time we had seen Jenkins was a night both my cousin and I wanted to forget. Uncle Mike walked over to him.

"Do you think he'll say anything?" I whispered when Paige sidled up to me.

"No way. Not unless he wants to lose his job." Paige focused on the officer, who glanced at us with a grim expression before turning back to Uncle Mike.

That was answer enough for me. Jenkins didn't seem to want to be around as much as we didn't want him around.

"What about the inside of the house?" Uncle Mike called.

"I haven't checked."

Jenkins approached me. "Got the keys?"

I went to my jacket and took them out before handing them over. My fingers brushed his palm, and I suppressed a shudder.

Jenkins smirked at my glare and went up the stairs. We waited outside while he did a sweep of the house.

"It's all clear in there," Jenkins called before flipping on the back-yard floodlights.

I squinted from the glare, raising my arm to block the light.

"Wow," I heard Uncle Mike say behind me.

I blinked a few times to clear the spots behind my eyes and sucked in a breath when I finally saw what Uncle Mike had. Spray paint covered the siding, still wet and dripping. Unlike the flames on the car, which were almost beautiful and obviously done with some sort of talent, the vile language and symbols that covered the house were juvenile at best.

Letting out a slow breath, I unclenched my hands.

"There is damage inside as well," Jenkins said. "Tessa, you might want to take a look around to make sure nothing was stolen." I hated the way my name sounded when he said it.

"We'll come in with her," Paige piped up, grabbing my hand.

We walked inside with Jenkins leading the way. "Anything?" he asked, his dark blue uniform a contrast to the white walls of the house.

A uniformed officer hadn't been inside our home in years. Not since Uncle Mike got promoted. The reminder was a jolt running down my spine, causing me to freeze.

"Tess?" Paige encouraged.

I scanned the area. Nothing in the kitchen or living room looked out of place. I shook my head.

Jenkins raised a brow but didn't say anything before resuming his walk around our house. Our house. Not his. That was why it felt wrong. This was my space and him being here made it seem unfamiliar.

"Most of the damage is down this way," Jenkins said over his shoulder.

I pulled at the bottom of my shirt and followed him down the hall. We ended up outside my bedroom. The lights were already on, and I stood at the threshold staring at the glass scattered along my floor and the gaping hole that used to be my window. A brick lay on its side by my bed.

My throat closed, and I tried to swallow. I wanted to wash my skin of the whole night. I wanted to get back on Beauty and ride away from the sight in front of me, pretend like it never happened. Go back to that brief moment right before I got home when everything felt like it was finally right. Normal.

"Now are you ready to call Uncle Kent?" Paige rubbed my back up and down.

My phone chirped in my pocket before I could answer. Dad's face popped up on the screen.

"I guess that answers your question." I held it up for Paige to see.

Paige gave me a half-hearted smile before stepping away to give me some privacy. Jenkins only held his thumbs in his belt loops and stared at me. I turned away and prepared myself to answer the call. Dad would know right away that something was wrong, and I was going to have to be the one to ruin the trip of a lifetime.

I meant what I said to that kid before he jumped our fence. I wasn't going to give up. They weren't going to get away with what they did.

COREY

hree days later, I was still trying to convince myself nothing had happened on Friday. I never agreed to go out with Vance and his guys. I never broke into Hopper's garage. There wasn't some girl out there who wouldn't back down even after getting hurt. A girl who might have seen my face.

No. She didn't. She couldn't have. I was careful. The fact that the police hadn't shown up at my front door was a good sign. But the fear and doubt wouldn't stop warring in my head.

I flipped onto my back, my bed groaning in protest, and stared at the water-stained ceiling in my bedroom. The first few weeks after my release I'd slept on the floor because my bed felt too soft after a year on a mattress pad only a couple of inches thick. I had to train myself to sleep on what I used to think was the most uncomfortable bed in the world. Now it wasn't so bad. Weird how your view of the world changed like that when you spent time in a cage.

My phone buzzed underneath my pillow. I sat up and grabbed for it, glancing at the ID.

"Yeah?" No shaking in my voice. Control was always good when you were talking to the man in charge.

"Corey, I heard about Friday night."

I shifted in the bed, kicking the blankets off. "I'm not surprised." Nothing got past X. My dad's old boss. And mine since the age of fourteen.

I squeezed my eyes shut and covered them with my hand. "Did you know about his plan?" I asked.

Laughter streamed through the phone. I fisted the blanket. It wasn't so much hearing the proof that X got to live a normal life while I struggled to fix mine that got to me, but the fact that he had a family. People who loved him. Who knew him as someone other than the man that controlled Branson, Vance, and me.

"No. It's not my job to know. It's your job to find these things out and stop them before they escalate. Remember?"

I stiffened. How could I forget when the reminder followed me everywhere I went?

"I'm sorry, sir. I tried, but you know how Vance is when he gets those ideas in his head. He threatened my family's well-being so I followed along."

Vance always made sure I knew he held all the cards in his hand. Didn't used to be that way, but I didn't want to think about the past.

"Nevertheless, I'm worried about Hopper being an issue after that little stunt. He needs to stay in the dark about Vance's involvement."

Of course. It always came back to keeping Vance safe. X was big on protecting his family, including his idiotic nephew.

"How are you doing otherwise?" His stern tone turned warm suddenly. He knew how to get to me. "I haven't heard much from you since your release."

"I'm fine." My answer was more clipped. I didn't know how to talk to X after he abandoned me in that cell for a year. After everything.

"Good. I have to get going. Remember to rein in Vance."

"Yes. I will." I forced myself to keep breathing. Standing up, I started pacing my room. My heart hammered, and the walls swam sideways. An invisible hand squeezed my throat. I leaned against the door for support.

I tossed the phone to the bed and pushed away from the wall, stepping toward the small window in my room where the white clouds brightened against the morning light.

Rein in Vance. How the hell was I supposed to do that? The last time I tried I ended up in jail.

I crossed the small room, counting ten steps from the door to my bed, and sat down, covering my face with my hands.

"Corey, get up! I made breakfast!" Mom called from the kitchen, startling me out of the haze fogging up my brain.

The old lady I shared a wall with banged on it. For someone who looked like she'd keel over any minute, she sure had great hearing.

"All right, I heard you!" Mom swept into my room and banged back. "When is that old bat finally going to kick the bucket?" She shook her head and put her hands on her hips.

I held back a smile.

"You okay?" Mom asked, plopping down on the bed next to me.

"What makes you think something's wrong?" The hollow in my voice probably didn't do me any favors.

Mom patted my knee. "Usually you make a crack about me giving that biddy a heart attack."

Not in the mood, I wanted to say. Instead I shrugged. "I'm good."

Mom removed her hand and glanced around my room. "You need to clean. Today. You know the rules, Corey. As long as you're living under my roof, you need to help take care of it."

"I know. I'm sorry. I will." My stomach grumbled as the smell of bacon wafted into the room.

In the hall, I collided with my little brother, Tim. He glared at me before stomping into the kitchen. I wondered if I was that much of a douche when I was sixteen. Probably. Then again, at his age I was busy keeping tabs on Vance.

"Stan says he's coming over tomorrow to look at the air conditioner," Mom said.

I paused for a second. "That's nice of him."

Mom sighed. "The super is behind, and you know it would take at least another month for him to come by and fix it."

"I didn't say anything, Mom." I didn't want to argue with her.

"You know you're going to have to see him at some point."

I rubbed my shoulders and kept my mouth shut. Stan was an old friend of the family. I worked at his auto-body shop for a few years before my sentencing. Stan offered to look out for my mom and Tim afterward, and he kept his word. Coming by and bringing groceries, fixing Mom's car whenever it had problems, helping Tim with his homework. Things that I did before I got sent away. Since returning home, I struggled to find my place in the family.

Stan wasn't trying to push me out; he wanted to help. He cared about us. He cared about me even though I didn't deserve it, which was probably why I didn't want to see him. I was still ashamed of the things I had done. For using the job he gave me as a shield to hide my place in X's crew from my mom. For helping Vance by getting details on the cars Stan worked on for Vance's chop-shop scheme. The look on Mom's face when she came to the station after my arrest still haunted me.

"Did you hear about Mr. Hopper?" Mom asked, following me down the hall to our tiny kitchen.

I flinched. I hoped she didn't notice.

"What about him?"

Mom planted a kiss on Tim's cheek as he ate out of the pan.

"Dude, get a plate. You're not an animal," I said, handing him one. Tim wasn't amused and snatched at it.

"Apparently his home was vandalized Friday night. You wouldn't know anything about that, would you?"

My stomach jumped, and I piled on the eggs.

"Corey." The firmness in her tone brought back too many memories. Ones I liked to forget. "Where were you Friday night?"

I turned to meet her gaze. "Nowhere. I was here."

Tim's brows pulled together. He shook his head and went back to eating.

I glanced one more time at my little brother, busy scarfing down breakfast. Tim was at home, but out cold, when I left the other night. From the expression on his face, he must have woken up at some point and found me gone.

"Mom, I was here." The food in my mouth turned bitter, and I kept my eyes focused on the plate.

"Are you sure?"

I chewed slowly, my shoulders tensing, trying to figure out what to say next.

"He was," Tim backed me up, mouth full.

My fork froze midbite. I didn't want Tim involved, which was why I hadn't deflected to him earlier. "Tim," I gave a low warning.

Tim didn't get the cue and took a swig of orange juice before continuing. "What? You were. I remember because we stayed up playing Xbox."

I ground my teeth together and dropped my fork. This was going too far. I didn't need my brother lying to my mom, too. Not that he had much of an example when it came to people being honest.

"Okay. If you say so. But if you know anything about what happened, you need to do the right thing."

Do the right thing. Mom spoke those words so often they were a part of her, streaming in my conscience whenever uncertainty coated a situation. Those were the words in my head when the police officer cuffed me and took me to the station.

Do the right thing. Do the right thing. The words rang in my ears, bubbling inside my head until it felt like it would pop off.

"Mom." I grabbed her wrist with a gentle tug. "I wasn't here Friday." I let out a breath and shut my eyes for a few seconds. It was time to be honest.

"What the hell, Core?" Tim glared at me.

Mom plopped back down on the seat. "What?" Her whispered word was covered in hurt.

I finally looked at her, and my ribs constricted and took a pounding with the disappointment hanging in her eyes.

"I'm sorry."

I *was* sorry. All the damn time. For the year in jail. Sorry for what I did at Hopper's. Sorry for what I put Mom and Tim through. Sorry for falling into the same trap as my dad. My heart hit against my chest hard, and my skin felt too tight, just like always whenever I thought about *him*.

When I got out of jail, I vowed to do right by my family, to make up for my mistakes. Instead I was doing exactly what I had done before: following orders. It clicked into place then, what I needed to do. How to make things right. How to protect my family. How to show my brother that I was better than he thought. How to save what little sliver of dignity that hadn't been stripped away.

How to escape Vance's control.

I cleared my throat. "I'll make it right. I promise."

I never stopped thinking about Mom and Tim while in jail. It was hard not to let my mistakes fester, to kick myself for letting them down when I was surrounded by the reminders of my shortcomings on a daily basis. I couldn't take those things back, but maybe I could give them a clean slate. Away from me.

Tim stood up and walked over to the sliding door where our tiny balcony stood. The view wasn't much. Just gray buildings and a parking lot full of rusted and broken-down cars.

I stared at the squared shoulders and clenched fists of my brother, and I knew I was just like my father—a disappointment. It cemented my decision.

Mom pushed back her chair, face contorted in anger. "What were you thinking?" she hissed.

I pulled my arms back from the table and stared at the roll of paper towels at the center, preparing myself for the onslaught coming my way.

"After everything? How could you? You said you were out, Corey!" Mom raged. "What would your nana think?"

I closed my eyes at the mention of my grandfather, Mom's dad. The man who tried to do his best by us after Dad died. Nana passed away when I was twelve, before I went to X for a job. And I was glad he wasn't alive, because sometimes I thought that if he had lived to see what I had become it might have been the death of him.

"Don't." I ground out the words, "Don't bring him into this. I was only thinking about keeping you alive, Mom. That's all I ever think about." I pushed away from the table, chair scraping against the floor. I grabbed my plate and walked it to the kitchen sink, hands shaking. "It'll be fine. Don't worry." I placed the plate down and grabbed ahold of the counter and focused on breathing.

I turned around and stared at my brother, his eyes wide with fear and sadness, and Mom's shaking shoulders. This was my life. From the outside it didn't appear to be a lot, but it was all I had and I'd be damned if I let anything happen to what little I had left.

I could handle going back to jail and sitting in a cell that was so cold it dug into my bones. The one that smelled like wet concrete and mold, where the only comfort I found was in knowing my family was safe.

"What do we do if you can't fix this?" Mom wiped her eyes with the back of her hand and finally faced me.

"You will be taken care of, Mom. No matter what. I'll make sure of it."

I grabbed my bike and exited the apartment. Mom and Tim didn't try to stop me. They'd be okay. They had Stan now. That gave me some solace.

Everything comes with a price. It took longer for me than most to realize the cost: freedom.

We struggled after Dad died. We had nothing, and the bills started to pile too high. So I did the only thing I could think of—I went to my dad's old boss for a job. Even at fourteen, I didn't take my responsibilities lightly. I knew in order to keep my family afloat I needed the job. I would succeed, unlike my father. And I did, for a while anyway.

I got comfortable with my way of life. That's when the trouble began.

I rode my bike with heavy legs, making it hard to pedal. I hated riding the thing around, but after I went to jail I made my mom sell my car and use the money to help pay for the lawyer's fees and other bills.

I took my time making my way around town, taking in the scents, the glare of the sun, letting myself feel all of it before it was too late. I stopped at the park and breathed in and out. Stared at the green, soaking it all in. Trying to memorize it all for later. By the time I was done, the sun was high in the sky and the heat of the afternoon made my sweatshirt cling to my back. I had to get going.

I pedaled faster, the wind whipping at my face, wanting to get it over with already. The closer I got, the more the fear made me numb against the decision I had made. That happened sometimes when I got scared. Instead of making me freeze, it propelled me forward, further into the darkness, digging me deeper into the hole of bad choices.

When I got to the slanted driveway, the fear was what I leaned on to give me the courage for what I had to do next.

TESSA

My feet ached after hours of standing. My shift at Dr. Ford's vet office neared its end. I sat at the front counter, tapping my pen against the check-in clipboard, watching the clock on the wall. I needed to get home and help Dad with the house damage. I managed to convince him not to cancel the rest of his trip. He made me promise to stay away from the house until he got back last night so he could assess the damage for himself. I hated leaving him that morning to do it all on his own, but he insisted that he was fine and that I shouldn't call in sick.

"How you holding up?" Paige walked down from the back room where the animals were kept. She had doodie duty.

Paige gave me a look. "You were thinking doodie duty, weren't you?" Her flat expression only made the laughter bubbling in my chest pop out of my mouth. Paige rolled her eyes. "You are such a child sometimes," she huffed.

I held the clipboard up against my mouth, hiding my wide smile. "Oh, please, don't act like you weren't the one who came up with it."

Placing an elbow on the counter, I shifted my weight to my left leg because my right ankle was still a little sore from the other night.

Paige walked back to the sink and washed her hands, and I went to the computer to check our patient list for tomorrow. I'd already called in reminders to everyone, but Paige had to send out texts to those who had signed up to receive them.

After I got done with the checklist, I went back to staring at the front door and rolling a pen back and forth on the counter. I couldn't wait to get home and shower and wash the smell of wet dog off my skin. Not that I was complaining—I loved working at the vet office. It gave me the opportunity to interact with animals, my main passion after biking, and to learn more about being a veterinarian. Sheila Ford was an excellent mentor. Her love for her job got me excited about my own future.

Grabbing my phone out of my pants pocket, I checked my messages for the umpteenth time.

No text from Dad. I had asked him if I could bring anything home to eat for lunch and he hadn't responded. I fidgeted with the screen before typing out another message.

Dad???? FOOD???

It was very unlike him to not respond when the possibility of takeout was an option.

A soft meow caught my attention, and I glanced down the hall to the row of patient rooms in time to catch Mr. Morrison walking out with his fat gray cat, Barry. Dr. Ford trailed out behind him, her black dreads up in a ponytail.

"Make sure to give him the worm medication, and he will be just fine."

"Thank you, Doc." Mr. Morrison wobbled with Barry under his arm and lifted the cat up to his face. "You hear that, buddy? You're going to be fine."

I stifled a smile. Mr. Morrison came in often with Barry. He was a bit of a hypochondriac when it came to his cat. After Mr. Morrison checked out and paid for Barry's medicine, I officially clocked out.

"Tessa, you know you can take as much time off as you need if things at home need more attention." Dr. Ford picked up a chart, a mug full of sludge coffee in the other hand. She took a sip and the mug came away with a red lip stain.

"Thanks, Sheila. I'll let you know."

I grabbed my bag from under the counter and headed out the door, squinting against the bright sunlight. I walked to the car, head bent as I unzipped my bag to find my keys, when someone collided against my shoulder, jostling my movements.

"Whoa, Hopper. Watch where you're going much?"

I froze and my heart took stuttered beats. Sweat broke along the back of my neck. "Jared." I pursed my lips and met the familiar blue eyes. "What are you doing here?"

The sun glinted off Jared's streaked-blond hair. He wore his usual preppy style button-up and bro-shorts, as Paige referred to them.

"Looking for you, of course." His cocky smile made my stomach writhe, and not in a sexy way.

I grabbed my keys out of my bag and walked around him. "I told you to stop doing that." He quickly blocked my path to the car.

I threw my head back and groaned. "Would you please stop? This"—I pointed to him and then back to myself—"isn't going to happen. Not again."

Jared held up his hands in surrender. "Look, I'm sorry. Please, hear me out, Tessa. I'm not that guy anymore."

I gave him my best skeptical stare. "Move."

"Tess, please." He palmed his hands in a prayer position. No one was going to answer that prayer, least of all me. "You always said people deserve a second chance."

A shot of anger hit my veins, but I resisted getting drunk on it. "Second chances are for people who own up to their mistakes." I kept my voice level.

Jared's face turned ten shades redder, and I knew I had struck a nerve. But he deserved it after using my own words against me to justify his actions.

"You know who my family is." He stepped closer. "I panicked. I'm sorry."

I placed my palm on his chest and pushed him away. I hated when he invaded my space like that. It was his go-to intimidation tactic. "You left me in the car, Jared! I woke up alone. Do you have any idea how scary that was? No, you don't, because you've never thought about anyone but yourself."

I stomped past him and yanked open the car door. "It's over, Jared," I tossed over my shoulder. "It was over the minute you decided to abandon me after you screwed up."

Sliding into the driver's seat, I slammed the door shut and turned on the ignition, driving out of the strip mall, tires squealing in protest.

By the time I got home, I'd forgotten all about lunch, still reeling from the run-in with my ex.

It turned out I didn't have anything to worry about. Uncle Mike and his husband, my uncle Steven, had brought over some pho from our favorite place, and there was enough left over for me as well. My appetite had taken a nosedive after seeing Jared, but I forced myself to eat and eventually the aromatic, spicy broth worked its magic, and I felt stable enough to help Dad.

Jiminy whined by the back door when I finished changing, and I pulled it open to let him out before running down the steps to where Dad stood in front of the open garage. Sweat dripped down his face. He'd gone on a run to calm himself down, but it appeared to have done little in that department. Instead, he seemed more agitated than before, pacing back and forth, rubbing the back of his neck, muttering to himself about some case he needed to get to and how he didn't have time for this BS.

I grabbed a trash bag and started working, hoping it would give him the push he needed to focus on the task at hand. The anxiety built higher along my nerves. It made it difficult to force past my own fears. The idea of Dad having another heart attack put my life into a crystalline resolution, highlighting all my mistakes, the ugly truths, and the guilt that floated right below the surface of my skin.

I chewed on my lip. The box fan Dad had set up inside the garage leveled out the temperature wavering inside of me. Small ripples of dread shuddered on my skin. I hadn't been inside the garage since the other night. I glanced at Dad quickly; the bags under his eyes were dark and his shoulders hunched over. Worry crested in my chest. I hated how much this weighed on him. I pictured him with the tubes that went through him last year at the hospital after he had his heart attack and fought back the tears clinging to the surface of my eyes.

Grabbing a broken trophy, I stuffed it into a garbage bag, ignoring the pain tracing circles around my chest whenever my eyes passed over Dad's Porsche.

"You don't have to do that, Tess," Dad said, his voice strained. His eyes didn't move away from the car.

I slipped the plastic bag in between my fingers, the elastic stretching against my skin, hoping the touch would help me forget that some idiots had dared to break into our place.

"It's okay, Dad. I don't mind."

He rubbed his head, breathing in and out of his nose, and finally pivoted to me. "You shouldn't be doing that. You act like you're not scared by what happened, kiddo, but I know it bothers you."

I spent last night jerking awake at phantom noises and then pacing the house with my baseball bat for any returning thugs. Not exactly sure what I would have done if the offenders had returned. I liked to think I picked up a thing or two watching way too many kung fu movies with Paige and her boyfriend, Alex, but I most likely would have ended up flailing around like a jellyfish.

"You don't have to be brave for my sake," Dad said.

"Says the man who sleeps with a gun under his pillow." A small corner of his lip twitched. I almost got him to smile. Since coming home, he'd mostly frowned and flared his nostrils. Dad was supposed to go back to work today, but he had let the office know he was taking one more day.

The back of Dad's shirt was drenched in sweat so I grabbed the bottle of water sitting on the workbench, handing it to him.

"Thanks," he mumbled before getting back to work.

I frowned at his inability to take a break and simply rest for more than a few seconds. Jiminy whined by my side, waiting for a pat. I bent down and hugged his black coat. The phone in my pocket buzzed.

Wanna go for a ride later? Alex is getting antsy being cooped up at work all the time.

I read over the text from Paige. I held back a laugh. Like they needed to even ask—I was always down for a ride.

"That Paige?" Dad asked, noticing the smile on my face. He took the garbage bag out of my hand. I nodded. "You should go inside and give her a call."

I tilted my head to the side and crossed my arms. "I can work, Dad. You can't get rid of me."

He shook his head. "Do whatever you want, sweetie. You always have," he said with a laugh.

Taking the bag back, I said, "Maybe you shouldn't have raised me to be so independent, then."

The words left a hole that wanted to expand into my chest. He was right. I did do what I wanted. All the time. At the cost of the ones I loved.

I closed my eyes and tried to fight the image floating in my head from the night of the crash. The sound of glass breaking, the unnatural way the car had turned, the look on Paige's face when she showed up—part fear, part disappointment.

Secrets brimmed and I was afraid they were going to start leaking out of me. Pain and rage radiated from my pores.

I gathered the rage and cradled in against my chest to help me get through the other feeling sitting right under it. Because anger I could do. Anger I could work with. It started when Mom left and connected all the way to the night of the accident. Always there, right at the top of the pyramid of emotions, the tip of the iceberg, so to speak. It was everything else, below the surface, I had a hard time with.

Dad and I worked in silence even though all I wanted was to come clean about the accident. But then I'd have to throw Paige under the bus, too. My mind kept going back to my guilt even though I tried to fight it with my anger, eating and digging deeper and deeper into my muscles. By the end of it, I would simply be bones and organs with the guilt keeping me standing.

It had to end at some point. Didn't it? I had to move on.

When I was about halfway through cleaning the garage, the sound of tires skidding against pavement caught my ears. I looked down the driveway in time to catch a kid in a familiar dark sweatshirt come walking up to us.

"You have got to be kidding me." Also, a sweatshirt. In June. The guy was asking for a heatstroke.

He approached where I stood. Dad was busy in the back of the garage and had yet to notice him. His steps were cautious and hesitant, hands in pockets, no swagger in his walk. He stopped his approach and our eyes connected. I held in a breath and forced myself to blink, hoping I imagined the whole scenario. But there he stood, and my heart skipped in an agitated beat. I hadn't seen his face that night, but I recognized him anyway. From his walk, the length of his body, the curve of his shoulders.

He cleared his throat. "Mr. Hopper," he said, trying to catch Dad's attention. Jiminy barked a couple of times.

Dad had his arm raised, placing a bucket back on a high shelf. He turned his head and froze when he saw the guy standing in the sunlight while we remained in the shadowed garage.

My heart pounded, the feeling of unease settling between my ribs.

"Corey? What are you doing here?"

My whole body froze. "Wait. Dad, you know this guy?" I looked back and forth between the two of them.

Dad wiped his brow. "Yeah. Corey's the kid I told you about. The one I prosecuted last summer?" Dad's brows wrinkled. "Are you here to take me up on that offer?"

Last summer. Right. Last year Dad sent an eighteen-year-old kid to jail for drug possession. Nothing new—in fact the case was pretty cut-and-dried. Except Dad didn't think the kid was guilty. He thought this guy, Corey, took the fall for someone else and tried to cut him a deal. Corey refused to budge. Claimed he was guilty. Dad, the human lie detector as I liked to call him, didn't believe him. They were at an impasse.

I remembered how frustrated Dad was, how it ate away at him. And then the heart attack happened and I forgot about the case; it got buried beneath the memories of fear and pain. Apparently, Dad hadn't forgotten.

Corey pocketed his hands. "No, sir. I'm here to turn myself in."

Dad stared, the silence cutting the space between them. "What do you mean?"

"It was me. I was the one who vandalized your home."

I took a moment to get a good look at Corey, anger filtering my vision. "What are you doing?" I asked. Why was he doing this? He could have easily gotten away with what he had done the other night. I never saw his face; there were no other leads.

Dad shook his head. "You did this?" He swept an arm across the open garage.

Corey nodded.

Dad's hands were in fists by his side. I could sense the rage building inside of him. He flared his nostrils. "Why?" he said through clenched teeth, stepping toward Corey.

My heart started to kick harder, and I dropped my arms to my sides, preparing myself for his next move.

Corey shrugged. "Because I was angry. Because I felt like it." There was no resolve behind his words.

Dad flew across the space between them and grabbed Corey by the collar, startling both of us. "Do you have any idea the kind of danger you put my daughter in?"

"Dad!" I tried to deter him from the direction he headed. Which was straight to Pissed-Off Town, one exit away from I'm-Going-to-Kill-You Ville.

"Tell me who else was involved."

Corey's face flushed red; his eyes contained a panic I'd seen a few times in my life. All from boys who'd come over to pick me up for a date. Fear. He looked so scared and young. He was simply a boy. A boy dumb enough to return to the scene of the crime.

I shook my head and tried to get rid of those thoughts. Corey should be scared after what he did. "Dad." I lifted my hand and placed it on his shoulder. "Calm down."

Beneath my fingers, the tension in Dad's body flexed in his muscles. "No, he needs to answer the question first." Everything he'd kept in the last forty-eight hours slowly came undone, all the frustration and anger and hurt.

"Dad, please," I pleaded. But he wasn't listening. "You have to. He's never going to talk when you're attempting to kill him. You're going to give yourself another heart attack." The panic in my voice shook through the grasp I had on it as I whispered in a harsh tone.

Dad turned to me, his face softening. His body relaxed, and I removed my hand from his shoulder.

"Is this how you pay me back for what I did for you?" Dad's body sagged in defeat. "Destroy my home, my sense of security, put my daughter at risk? You better tell me about the others before I take you down."

And there it was. Dad and his threats were as familiar as the freckles on my left forearm. The guy straightened, and his eyes roamed my face in a flash, then went back to Dad's. What was he doing here? Why wasn't he at home?

Whatever the reason, I knew one thing—it probably wasn't going to end well for either of us.

COREY

My throat squeezed tight, and I breathed through my nose. Hopper removed his hands from the collar of my sweatshirt, and I swallowed the pain before taking a full breath. My chest heaved heavy while Hopper and I eyed each other. I rubbed the back of my neck.

The girl, Tessa, kept staring at me. Her lips set in a straight, grim line.

"They cut your tongue out in jail?" Hopper's nostrils flared.

I shifted my gaze back to Hopper and fought the urge to turn around and run back home. I could go back and pretend like nothing happened. Continue following X's orders, continue being leashed to Vance, continue to try to calm him when he came up with some crazy scheme and then pay for it when I did. But I didn't want to spend what time I had being someone else's pawn anymore. I wanted to make one decision for myself. Even if it cost me my freedom, at least I had a say in it.

"It got out of hand, and that's my fault, sir. I came here because I want—no, I need—to make things right."

Hopper crossed his arms and stared me down. It reminded me of the first time we met at court. The intense way he held himself, how he refused to drop his gaze. My quiet affirmation to the crime. I forced myself to pull my shoulders back and stand up straight. Hopper continued to size me up while I tried not to sweat bullets.

"Is this the guy you saw the other night, Tess?"

Tessa wrung her hands.

"Tessa?" Hopper urged.

I couldn't rip my gaze away from hers. My body fought the edgy adrenaline pushing sweat onto my skin.

"I'm sorry." What was it about the girl that made me constantly apologize?

"Yeah," she answered, clenching her jaw. "You've already said that. It's him."

"I'm sorry for how far it went. I'll pay you back for the damage, go to jail for it. It's fine. I deserve it."

Hopper let out a laugh. "Pay me back? You have any clue how much money it's going to cost to fix that car? Thousands of dollars. You got that kind of money?"

No, I didn't. I had some scraped together to keep our family afloat before I went to jail. Now I had next to nothing. The thought didn't bring that resounding sense of calm I needed; instead, it made my sweat stick to my clothes.

"I didn't think so." Hopper took a step forward. "Are you still involved with the same people as before?"

A peace offering. That was what he was giving me. If only I could partake. "It doesn't matter. It was my idea to begin with. The other guys were following my orders. Call the cops. Put me away. I can handle that, but I'm not ratting anyone out for my mistakes."

There it was. The confession to seal the deal. Now I had to wait to find out my fate. My hands grew unsteady, the reminder of the cold I could never shake loose in that jail cell creeping up on me. I clenched them, tensing my arms to keep the shakes away.

"Corey?" Hopper's voice was pleading.

I flicked my eyes away from him to the garage.

Mistake.

The car was a tragedy. I couldn't see my paint job from where I stood. The house itself was a mess. They'd picked up most of the trash the guys dumped everywhere, but the spray-paint job would take a while to paint over.

"Do you know what's going to happen if you plead guilty to this? You already have a felony drug charge on your record. There's no coming back from this. If you're confessing for someone else, you need to tell me. I can cut you a deal. No time served."

My nonanswer was answer enough. I didn't understand him. He was pissed earlier, wanted-to-kill-me pissed, but now he seemed almost reluctant to call it in.

I didn't want to go back to jail, but if it meant I got away from Vance and kept my family safe, then I could do it.

"Dad." Tessa's voice cut through my thoughts. It was loud, but soft. The other night when she yelled at us, it boomed, carried the fear of God in it, I swear. It was still there—that sense of authority, self-assurance. "Can I talk to you for a minute?"

Hopper gave me a quick, pitying glance. He studied me like I was some pathetic beaten dog that followed him home, one he didn't want to turn away, one he wanted to invite in and take care of. Maybe I was that pathetic dog, but I could take care of myself.

Hopper and Tessa went into the garage. Their whispered conversation carried over to me.

"I can see the wheels turning in your head, Dad." Tessa shot me a furrowed expression. "What are you thinking?"

I turned my back to them to give them some privacy. Their dog sat by my feet, his big brown eyes studying me. He whined and scooted closer to me, seeking a pat or belly rub. Snatches of whispered conversation caught my ears. One question in particular snagged there.

"Do you trust him?" Tessa's question made me flinch.

Did Hopper trust me? At some point while he visited me in jail our relationship started to grow into some form of it, but I all but destroyed that on Friday night. I turned back to the garage. Whatever they were discussing started to take too long, and I needed to get out of there. I had a few things to take care of before I headed back to prison. I had to call my mom, tell her what was going on. I had to apologize to Tim and let him know that I loved him, encourage him to keep trying at school. Then there was Stan. I needed to make sure he'd continue to take care of my family in my absence.

Hopper placed a hand on his hip and took a turn around the garage. His eyes met mine. The back of my neck prickled, and I turned my gaze to Tessa, who stood staring at me with not only a steady fierceness but also an unfamiliar expression. Part of me thought it was doubt or maybe even guilt. But I had no idea what she had to doubt about me; I confessed. And she sure as hell didn't have anything to feel guilty about.

She chewed on her lower lip and lifted a shoulder. "Okay."

Hopper pulled his daughter in for a short hug and retraced his steps to me. The heat of the day rose, and the sun became a glare in my line of vision. I blinked a few times and forced myself to swallow the bile threatening to rise up my throat.

"Can you wait a few minutes before making the call? I have some things to take care of before they take me away." I turned around and started to make my way to the bike.

"Corey, I'm not turning you in."

Hopper's words sliced through my movements.

"What?" I forced myself to turn back around. The question hung in the air, and it tightened its hold on my chest.

"This isn't you, Corey. I don't believe for one second the kid I got to know while he was in prison is capable of this kind of malice. Not unless someone else is calling the shots."

Shit. This wasn't going how I thought it would go at all. Hopper was throwing my whole plan in the trash with his bleeding heart.

"You're going to fix this." Hopper gestured to the house. "Like community service."

"And what does your daughter think of this idea?"

Tessa studied her nails. "I don't trust you, but I do trust my dad." She dropped her hand and finally met my gaze.

I stood near them but still on the outside, contemplating whether I should jump on my bicycle and make my escape or whether I should stay and hear Hopper out on his insane idea.

"What do you say, Corey? Unless you want me to call the cops. I can do that, too. If that's what you really want."

What did I really want?

A tremor climbed up my legs. Maybe it was hope. I couldn't remember the last time that sensation took place. Probably before my dad died. Back when things were simple and all I really wanted was to paint every day. Hopper and his daughter waited, expectation and doubt molding their stances.

I thought about my mom, Tim; I thought about new beginnings and doing something for myself for the first time in a long time. I thought about finally taking my destiny back into my hands.

"Okay. Yeah. I'll do it."

TESSA

Jiminy's tail wagged back and forth. He barked happily a few times. Little traitor. Corey bent down and patted him quickly before standing back up. His lip twitched but he held back the smile and I studied him. His black hair hung loose around his ears, falling over his dark eyes. I made my way down to his nose, slightly crooked, probably from having it broken. His tan skin shimmered in the light and some scruff covered his jawline. I didn't know what to make of him—a guy who came to confess his sins, to take responsibility for his actions despite the consequences.

My stomach twisted with the familiar aching of guilt. Brushing away a loose tendril of my hair, I shifted my focus to Dad. He stood a few feet away from Corey with his arms crossed, wearing an expression caught between relief and worry. I knew the moment he offered to cut Corey a deal that he wasn't going to turn him in. Giving people second chances was Dad's thing. I pushed away memories of my mom and the many times she spiraled.

The guilt harrowed into me because Mom wasn't the only one who spiraled at one time. My own mistakes filled up pages.

I wanted a different me to step up and take responsibility for my actions, to make things right. Then there stood this guy, Corey, who had already paid for his wrongs and had willingly come back to do so again. He was brave. Braver than I could ever be, I admitted reluctantly.

Corey did the one thing I had yet to: confess. And that had to count for something. When he first arrived, I wanted nothing more than for the police to throw him in a cell and toss away the key, but spending even a few minutes with him made me realize things were more complicated than what they appeared on the surface.

Wasn't I evidence of that?

That was when the idea for the community service had formed in my head. Maybe helping Corey would help free me from the mistakes of my own past. Getting Dad to agree hadn't taken much persuasion on my part.

Corey, of course, didn't need to know any of that. I didn't want him to. We didn't owe anything to each other, and I planned on avoiding him as much as possible while he did his community service.

Corey shifted his weight and pocketed his hands. "When do I start?"

"Tomorrow." Dad held out his hand for a shake. Corey stared, wide-eyed, but shook it.

Dad went back to grab the bag of garbage from earlier and proceeded to dump out the contents.

"Dad, what are you—"

He pointed a finger at Corey. "Part of our agreement is that you have to clean up all of this."

I held back an eye roll.

Corey's stance was a complete one-eighty from earlier. Less afraid and more . . . not confident, but as if he had been standing farther away from us, a dark smudge in the distance, and we were finally closing in on him, the vision clearing.

"I'll be here. And I know you said I can't help with the car, but I'd like to try." Corey cleared his throat. "I have a friend, Stan; he owns a body shop."

Dad raised a brow at me. I raised mine to him. A slight shake to his head and Dad turned his attention back to Corey. "Okay. Thanks for the referral. Also, I will be here with you at all times. Those are the conditions. Do you agree to them?"

Corey nodded. "Yes, sir."

There was that *sir* again. I didn't even call my own father *sir*. It was weird to align my previous image of Corey with the one he presented to us now. The kid who vandalized our home and had a police record to the one who referred to my father as *sir*.

"Good."

Corey's lips lifted into a small smile, and his whole face changed. I stared at him for a second, taken aback. He glanced at me with a question in his raised brow.

"Come on, let's get inside." Dad started walking away.

"Just a minute." I made a face at Dad when he hesitated.

He rolled his eyes. "Come on, Jiminy," he said, before walking into the house with Jiminy trailing after him.

"Thank you for agreeing to this." Corey's cheeks were red. He scratched the back of his head and pulled the string around his neck tighter, as if to hide himself within the hoodie. But it was too late—I saw him, and he wasn't fooling anyone with that crap.

"There's really no need." The hood fell back, no longer shadowing his face. "My dad can't do all the work by himself. My uncles would help, but he'd never accept it. And I didn't want whatever would have happened to you on his conscience. He already has enough to lose sleep over."

"I understand." He ran a hand through his hair, and the scar on his brow came into view.

I scrutinized Corey. He didn't back down from my stare. A small wisp of a breeze blew through the backyard, alleviating some of the pressure from the heat bearing down on us. After a minute, the intensity grew, warmth flushing along my body. I forced myself to look away. The first thing that caught my eye was the Porsche. I closed my eyes for a second.

When I opened them, Corey stared at me like he was trying to figure out a puzzle. I remembered suddenly that this was the guy who ruined my dad's car with his gang. I stiffened when the realization of what I had done hit me. Corey was in a gang. A gang he still associated with. And my dad and I had just given him an open invitation into our house.

My stomach flipped uneasily. "What?" I snarled.

A wounded expression crossed his face, but it cleared quickly and that barrier he seemed to have built around himself came into full view.

"Nothing. I guess I'll see you around." Corey lifted up his bike and rode off.

I ran up the porch steps and into the house as soon as the bike disappeared around the corner of our driveway. Dad stood by the kitchen sink, taking a long gulp of water.

"Why didn't you try to talk me out of that crazy idea?" I slammed the door behind me.

Dad gave me a look. "Did you really want to see him get carted away to jail?"

"It's not like he hasn't been through it before," I muttered.

Dad placed his cup in the sink and walked over to the freezer. I stood in silence while he took out a carton of ice cream.

"Dad, you know that's not a good idea." I hurried over to him to grab the carton, but he slipped it under his arm like it was a football and dodged my attempts.

"After the last couple of days, I think I deserve some ice cream, kiddo." He shuffled around the kitchen and grabbed a spoon before dropping down onto a seat at the kitchen table.

"To answer your previous question, no, I didn't want to watch Corey get carted away to jail. But I just realized that we have no idea what we got ourselves into. Like at all. I mean, why didn't you want to turn him over in the first place?" I started tugging at my shirt, then tapping my foot.

"Having second thoughts?" Dad said, looking at my foot.

I let out a breath. "Yeah. Kind of. Please help me not completely freak out."

Dad took a bite of the almond praline, his favorite flavor.

"Tessa, I can't help who I am. Corey did what he did because of the people he hangs out with."

He'd voiced my objections. The ones that had been inconveniently absent when I talked to my dad earlier.

I swung an arm up in the air. "You're not helping. What makes you think they're not going to come after us? Dad, that is a very real possibility. If Corey is lying about being the one who went after you, then someone else was pulling the strings."

Dad paused. "You're right. I didn't think that part through."

"Wow, are you admitting you're wrong? That's new. Wait, has hell frozen over? Am I dead?" I hadn't thought it through, either, but I wasn't going to admit it to him when he had so willingly owned up to it for both of us.

Dad shook his head. "Stop it, Tessa Marie. We'll figure this out when he comes over tomorrow. I resent that you don't think I can protect you."

I snorted. "Dad, seriously? You do realize a bunch of goons vandalized our home just the other day."

Dad placed his spoon in the carton. "Look, this neighborhood is safe. This is the first time anything like this has happened here. It's shaken up a lot of people. There's a neighborhood watch already being organized, and the police are increasing their presence in the area. They would have to be completely stupid to come back. But you're right, I need to discuss this with Corey. If there's any danger of his friends coming back here, then I'll call the whole thing off."

"And call the cops on him?"

Dad shook his head. "No. I don't think I can do that. You saw him, Tess. That kid is not some hardened criminal. He's trying to fix his mistakes. I'll figure something out."

I worried my lower lip and tapped my foot again.

"Whatever you have to say, say it now, Tess." Dad folded his hands.

"Can you tell me more about his case like you said you would?"

"What do you want to know?"

I groaned and walked over to the table, taking the seat next to his. "Everything."

Dad nodded thoughtfully. He took another bite of ice cream, and I fought the impatience weaving into my movements, making me shake my leg. I knew better than to push my dad when he was having a moment with his ice cream. It would only backfire.

"The police station got an anonymous phone call last spring. Someone had a tip about a guy selling drugs. He provided the license plate and make of the car for the officers. It was Corey's car. They pulled him over and searched the vehicle."

"What did they find?" I urged.

"A couple of ounces of pot. Even though it's been decriminalized in certain parts of the state, it's still illegal in Branson and that was all the cops needed to take him in. With kids like Corey, it really doesn't take much."

My heart sank. Dad knew what he was talking about because he'd lived through it himself when he was younger. He and Uncle Mike grew up with next to nothing. They built new lives and left the old ones behind. Dad always said it was because of perseverance and a whole lot of luck. This was one of the reasons he tried to help out kids in similar circumstances as much as he could. Not that he went easy on everyone, but when he spotted a chance to better a person's life, he took it.

"And why exactly don't you think Corey's guilty?"

Dad pushed the ice-cream carton to the middle of the table. I grabbed the spoon and took a bite.

"When the officers pulled him over, Corey didn't even hesitate and followed instructions. He's probably familiar with what happens to kids like him if they show even a little bit of resistance, unfortunately. He didn't say a word on the way to the station. He confessed to possession before questioning even began. When I saw him for the first time in the courtroom, he looked like the kind of kid that had already accepted that life wasn't going to deal him any easy hands."

Dad swallowed. I reached over and touched his hand. He pursed his lips in a sad smile.

"I know what that's like. How it feels to be so hopeless. So I decided to talk to him, see if there was any way I could help him. But he was resigned to his fate. I did what I could, spoke with the judge about a reduced sentence. Seeing as how it was his first offense, it wasn't too difficult."

"And you visited him in jail."

He lifted a shoulder. "A few times. After I got out of the hospital, I wanted to check on him. I offered him a job when he got out. He didn't seem interested, but he was polite and didn't refuse my visits. He even showed me some of his artwork."

I leaned back against my chair. "Is he the one that painted those flames on the car?"

"I'm sure. I didn't put it together until he got here. But it was definitely him. Corey has a lot of potential, and it shouldn't be wasted just because of the circumstances he was born into."

I let out a breath, processing the information Dad had shared about Corey. I thought hearing about Corey's history would help ease my mind. It had. I trusted Dad, and once he got the answer from Corey about his gang tomorrow, I would put him out of my mind.

I had other things to focus on. Like trying to figure out how to live with my secret with only a couple of months left before college. The one that wouldn't let go of its hold on me no matter how hard I tried to forget. I thought I had put it behind me, but now with the break-in, it was resurging, threatening to pull me under. I needed to get a grip. Otherwise the walls I had carefully crafted along my heart would collapse, and I didn't know if I could survive what happened after.

COREY

I biked home with a little less weight on my shoulders. What happened at Hopper's didn't seem real or possible. Stuff like that didn't happen to people like me. Except it just had. Hopper gave me another chance, which meant I still had to deal with Vance and X.

I had to get my head back in the game.

My first priority was informing X. If he found out that I was hanging out at Hopper's without his consent, it would end badly.

After that, I had to deal with Vance. Make sure I wasn't slacking anymore when it came to my job. I'd avoided getting too involved since getting out because I didn't care, didn't feel like dealing with Vance. But now I had no other choice. If I was going to survive, I had to know what was going on.

I texted Drew. I needed to meet up with him later to catch up on what I had missed while in jail. Like he'd heard me cursing his name, a text from Vance waited for me.

My place tonight at 11. Don't be late.

I pocketed my phone, mumbling a string of curse words when I entered the dark apartment. Tim was hanging out at a friend's place, and Mom had a double shift. I had texted her earlier, letting her know not to worry about Hopper. She might get some sense of security by knowing I wasn't going back to jail. I took off my sweatshirt and tossed it on the floor of my room before locking myself in there to call X.

"Corey?" X exuded a cool indifference to most people, and it came through in his voice. I kicked off my shoes and resisted throwing them against the wall.

"I confessed to the vandalism, said it was my idea."

Silence greeted me on the other side. Only the sound of X's breathing informed me he was still there. "Why would you do that?"

"To get the scent off Vance."

"And?" he urged.

"Hopper believed me, but he's not throwing me in jail."

The line went quiet. "I'm guessing this has to do with the visits you had with him in prison." It was a statement, not a question. X knowing about my visitation log shouldn't have surprised me—he had eyes everywhere—but it still left me uneasy and feeling dirty.

I rubbed my palm on my pants. "Yes. He thinks he can help reform me."

A soft laugh hit my ears. "How intriguing. Well, that is a very lucky break."

I gritted my teeth. The condescension in his voice almost undid the little bit of calm I managed to hold on to. I was coming apart, slowly, painfully, and he was laughing at me. "What do you want me to do?"

More silence. Sweat formed on my forehead.

"Whatever you must to keep Hopper in the dark. Do the work; keep your head low."

"Of course."

X cleared his throat. "Make sure to keep up your guard around Hopper and his daughter. Don't get too close. None of us want anything happening to them. This also means we will not have as much contact as before. I can't have my name associated with this. You're on your own for now, Corey."

"What do you mean?"

X sighed on the other side. "It means that I trust you to take care of this without my help. It's time you started taking on more responsibility with the business, and this is the perfect opportunity."

I wanted to remind him that wasn't the deal when I first got out of jail. That he had promised he would let me out. But no. That was a pipe dream. I would never be able to escape.

"You are in charge of Vance. If things go awry, contact me then and only then. For now, this is goodbye. Stay safe, Corey."

I stood up and opened my window, letting the fresh air in. "Right. I understand." Although I didn't. On my own. Right. Why did it feel like he had abandoned me and not given me a way to prove myself even more?

X hung up, and I leaned against the windowsill. The idea of anything happening to Hopper or his daughter made my body shake. After a few minutes of practiced breathing, I pushed away from the window and headed to the kitchen. I hadn't eaten since this morning, and I needed to refuel. I grabbed a bag of grapes from the freezer and munched on them. The cold crunch helped calm the heat rising in my chest.

X wanted me to keep Hopper in the dark, which meant I had to keep a professional distance between us while doing my job and fixing up his house. No matter the pressure of X, gratitude still clung to the back of my mind. Hopper cut me a break; I wasn't going to jail; I could breathe again. It became harder this morning after I made up my mind to confess, when the prospect of heading back made it impossible to focus on much of anything else.

Hopper didn't have to do that—neither did his daughter—and I owed them.

Mom kept a notebook and pen in the junk drawer next to the fridge. I headed over to it and pulled it open. A mix of pens, papers, paper clips, coupons, and old mail covered the small space. I was shuffling things aside to find what I needed when a mess of objects fell to the ground. Grumbling, I bent over and picked it all up. A paper caught my eye. Partially folded, I opened it, standing up straight.

An application.

I read over the job description. It was for head nurse at the hospital. Mom had filled out about half of it; the rest remained uncompleted. I turned over the page and read it again. I took it with me to the table and placed my head in my hands. Mom had started to fill out the application at some point but changed her mind. Why? Because of me? Tim? Whatever the reason, I needed to talk to her about it because it could change things for the better. For her and Tim. And that was all I really wanted.

I went to the drawer and put back the application, folding it carefully, then grabbed a piece of paper and a pen, and began working on a budget for the next little while.

X paid me to keep an eye on Vance, but it wasn't much since I stayed away from the seedier side of his business. I kept Mom's monthly income out of it, because that was her money and I wasn't going to let her pay for my mistakes ever again. With enough time and effort, I could pay back Hopper for helping me out. I would pay him back for his generosity.

Hopper was a good lawyer, or so I'd gathered from the previous cases he'd tried. Cases of men that worked for X. He never relented on any of them, but he'd taken it easy on me. Maybe he saw the truth behind my eyes. Maybe it was the looks on my brother's and mother's faces. Or maybe he knew I really wasn't guilty and was taking the fall for someone else. Whatever the reason, he offered me a deal that most never got when they were in my position. I took it without hesitation.

It could have ended there. Instead, he came to see me in jail. Asked about my artwork. Even offered me a job. He went above and beyond for someone like me.

I tapped the pen on the table, thinking over the events in my life that led me to where I ended up. It was unfair, it sucked, but it was all I had to work with. Paying back the people I'd wronged over the years was the only way I could ever find true redemption.

The sun set, and I sat in the dark while the clock kept adding minutes. Tim texted to let me know he was sleeping over at his friend's place. I sighed, relieved, not ready to face his judgments. I pushed back the dining chair and headed out. I had things to take care of and couldn't be late.

Vance's place of business stood outside of town in the middle of the densest part of the forest. The police had no idea it was there. It was an even bigger dump than the one I lived in, but it was the only place big enough to run things through, and it was inconspicuous.

The only reason Vance even knew about it was because of me. Back before my dad got put away, I did a lot of exploring in the woods. Mom didn't want us around Dad's friends when they came over.

Mom would tell me to take Tim out and keep busy. That was how I found the building. The factory used to produce candy before burning down in the early 1900s. It was a part of history Branson had forgotten. When X told me to keep an eye on Vance, I knew it was the perfect spot to get the job done.

Approaching the hideout made my blood run cold. My palms sweat against the grip on the bike handles. That building used to belong to Tim and me, full of memories of the two of us creating our own adventures. I'd given those up for a few bucks. Now it held darker things. The top floor hosted the drugs Vance dealt and the stolen goods he sold. Nothing decent remained in there, not even the fading laughter of two boys passing the time or the bitter smell of burning sugar.

I maneuvered around the broken trails in the forest, taking the back way there. It was a catacomb of dead leaves, fallen trees, overgrown grass, and dirt paths that I barely made it through.

The darkness of the forest closed in all around. Half-dead cars with smashed sides and stinking engines lined the outskirts of the property. Stealing car parts was Vance's old business. Three years ago, he would have stolen Hopper's Porsche and made money off it.

Vance and his guys waited by a black SUV I'd never seen before. I slowed and leaned my bike against a tree before heading for them. They nodded their acknowledgment. Ever since taking the fall for Vance more than a year ago and getting out a couple of months back, I'd earned a badge of honor I never wanted. One where I followed orders without any questions.

Drew stood back with them, Jaimie, his cousin, close by like always. The two of them were practically attached at the hip. Drew tossed his cigarette to the ground and stomped it out, giving me a subtle nod.

"Ready, Fowler?" Vance puffed smoke in my face and handed me the keys.

I turned away from the worst of it and managed not to cough. My dad smoked a pack a day. That smell made me sick.

Instead of answering, I headed for the SUV. "What are we doing?"

"Have to take care of some business with an associate. We're heading to Casa Blanca," Vance replied, taking his place in the passenger seat.

I put the key in the ignition and prayed that I would make it home to my family tonight.

"That girl Gina won't stop calling me." Mitch, one of Vance's guys, wouldn't shut up in the back about all the women in his life. He was on the short side but built like a wrestler with a face not even a mother could love.

"Don't even get me started on clingy chicks."

I rolled my eyes when Jaimie started in. He had no idea what he was doing when it came to women.

"Jaimie, the only way any girl would cling to you is if she were falling off the side of a building. And even then she might take her chances with the asphalt," Drew said, teasing his cousin.

Jaimie's face flushed. "Whatever. You don't know what you're talking about."

The other guys laughed, and I felt a tug at my own mouth.

"What was that girl's name you used to see, Fowler?" Mitch asked.

I flashed my eyes to his in the rearview mirror for a brief second. "Taylor."

Mitch laughed. "Taylor. Right. She was cute. Whatever happened with her?"

"She dumped his ass before he got sentenced," Vance cut in, cackling.

He probably thought it would hurt me bringing her up like that. But no. I made peace with my ex. Taylor and I were on good terms. We dated for six months before things went to shit. I wasn't surprised when she broke up with me. Taylor had a future; she was smart and beautiful, full of hopes and dreams. Last I heard, she'd graduated and moved to California for college. I was happy for her. Happy that she got to have a fresh start.

Jaimie snorted. "Man, I have no idea how you got a girl like her. You gotta share your secret with me."

"Maybe don't tell women that they're soft enough to spread on toast," I answered. That was a line I heard Jaimie use at a party a while back, before prison. "And definitely don't ask waitresses if they're on the menu, too." Another line from Jaimie. That one to a waitress at a twenty-four-hour diner we used to hit up.

The rest of the guys snickered.

"It's cuz he's sensitive," Mitch butted in. "Girls love that shit."

"If you mean I listen when a girl talks, take a vested interest in things she likes, take her out to eat at places other than McDonald's and Burger King, and treat her well, then call me Mr. Sensitive."

"Man, whatever." Mitch waved a hand, brushing away my comment. Then he started complaining about women being too sensitive and went off on a tangent about feminism and the death of the alpha male. This was his fallback whenever he got called out on his shitty treatment of women.

The string slowly unraveling the memories of my past came to an abrupt stop. I squeezed the steering wheel and drove around the streets of Branson. I used to be close to these guys. They were as big a part of my life as Mom and Tim. Things were different now. Not one of them, besides Drew, came to visit when I was behind bars. They treated me like a friend, sometimes even a brother, but I learned quickly that in the world we lived in none of us could afford to actually care about anyone but ourselves.

I let the voices of Vance's guys drift to the background while I drove us to our destination. Vance continued to smoke next to me while my insides squirmed. The looming and shadowed buildings of the housing complex emerged ahead of us. I pulled into the parking lot while Vance directed me to the side of the squat apartments.

I turned off the ignition. Quiet descended in the car, tension stirred, and I rolled down my window, needing fresh air. My stomach roiled, nauseated from the smell of the cigarette.

"What are we doing here, Vance?"

"You have any idea how hard it is to run a business, Fowler?" He tipped his head to the side and eyed me.

I turned away and stared out the front windshield.

"It's all about supply and demand. You give the people what they want, and they come back for more. Easy enough, right?"

I tapped the wheel with my thumb.

"But then you have to keep track of who wants what, which guy is selling what, how much they're selling, how much they're collecting. It gets a little confusing at times. But that's not enough. You also have to remember that loyalty is a big part of the game. And if you don't have loyalty from your guys, then you're nothing. You know how you show your loyalty?" he asked, flicking his cigarette out the window.

I kept grinding my teeth, listening to his little speech. I knew how to show loyalty. Hadn't I spent a year of my life proving it to him and X?

"They pay you what they owe you. And when they don't, you *make* them pay."

I flicked my gaze to the darkness in front of us. The streetlight offered a sick yellow glow to cut the black into pieces. I didn't know what to say to Vance after he got done with his speech. All I knew was I didn't want to be there.

Vance pushed open the door and stepped out, straightening his leather jacket as he looked around the complex. The guys in the back followed suit.

"Damn it," I muttered under my breath.

This part was familiar. Too familiar. I'd witnessed others getting hurt for crossing Vance, but it didn't get easier. In the beginning, I told myself not to care about any of those people, told myself they deserved it for not following orders. Then I went to jail and had too much time to think. Those people were just like me. I wasn't any better than them. Desperation connected all of us.

The guys started walking toward apartment 104. One knock and a blond kid, couldn't be more than my age, answered. Fear sprang in his eyes, and he turned to make a run for it. But those guys were faster, bigger. He was a scrawny thing with a pathetic goatee and a Phillies hat. They dragged him outside, the dark molding against them.

The muffled sound of his pleading reached me as he held his hands up and tried to back away.

I turned away before the first hit landed. Each time this kid cried out, I felt it in my stomach. And I hated it. Hated feeling the guilt. Hated feeling trapped.

The kid kept crying, and I couldn't take it anymore. I pushed open the door and walked over to where Vance leaned against the side of the building, smoking.

"That's enough. I think he gets the point, Vance."

He squinted his eyes at me.

"You grow soft in that cell of yours, Fowler?"

"You aren't going to get back your money if he ends up dead." Rein in Vance. X knew this was part of the business. So did I. Vance's brutality sometimes got out of hand and that was when I came in—to keep things from escalating.

Vance stared me down while the cries of the kid getting beaten made me tense. He threw his cigarette to the ground.

"We're good, boys. Let's go," he said, refusing to look away from me. I ground my teeth together, unflinching.

The crew stepped away from the kid on the ground. I barely recognized him. Blood dripped down the front of his sweatshirt and jeans. He lay on his side. His chest moved with stolen breaths, slowly and painfully. The rest of the crew walked back to the car while I crouched low next to the kid.

"You have anybody here to help you?" I asked, placing his arm around my shoulder and helping him stand.

"Yeah. My girl's inside."

At the mention of this girl, the front door opened. A girl around the same age as the kid ran out. Tears streamed down her face. I handed him off to her and walked away. The car stayed quiet on the drive back. It always did after an order was carried out. I pictured that kid, the way his spine curved with the pain they'd caused. I needed to keep that image in my head. Picture my little brother in his place. Because that was why I did what I did. To keep him and my mom safe.

TESSA

I craved the ride, and I needed to get out on Beauty.

Dad left for the office, saying he had some things to take care of, but we both knew he was too much of a workaholic to stay away for too long.

Black Beauty, my motorcycle, waited for me in the garage. I zipped up my racing jacket, pulled on my gloves, and secured the helmet as I slipped onto her, a calm washing over my skin. I turned the ignition, revved the bike, and let her soothe the frayed edges of the nerves that still stung. I kicked the stand back as Beauty and I started our descent down the driveway. Her engine growled between my thighs, freeing me of the past—for a little while anyway.

By the time I arrived at the rarely used back highway, Alex and Paige were waiting for me along with a group of kids from school. Not everyone rode a bike. Alex and I were the only ones. The others brought their fancy Mustangs and Camaros. Since school got out, the number of us who liked to drive around the back road had grown. We only did it for fun, to help release some of the tension that built inside all of us stuck in a small town with no other way to do so.

Philly was two hours away, so we could only drive there every once in a while. Peyson, the closest thing we had to a city, was an hour west and much smaller than Philly. I drove to Peyson whenever I grew too restless and the heat became oppressive. They ran illegal underground drag races that held a lot of memories for me. My heart started to beat faster at the thought of racing. We did our own miniraces here. No betting involved, and it was fun, but nothing like the ones I'd participated in in Peyson.

I slowed my bike and pulled into the open field skirting the road. No one knew who the land belonged to. There were acres full of overgrown grass that reached my waist and then the forest several yards in, looming over it. When the highway was built, the road stopped being used by most drivers. My dad and his friends drove it for the same reasons every generation before and after did, to have fun away from the prying eyes of nosy neighbors and cops with too much time.

My mom used to bring me here when I was younger. I would cling to her back, the helmet protecting my face from the wind tearing at us. I'd giggle uncontrollably when she'd pull over and let me down. We'd eat a picnic of greasy burgers and fries in the wide field. Sometimes we'd lay on the grass and stare at the bright blue sky full of a majestic hope that would slip low into my belly and flutter along my rib cage.

Beauty was a goodbye gift from my mom. She left her to me before taking off, along with a note asking me to remember her whenever I rode.

And it worked. It did help me remember. My memories were a haze filled with the scent of fresh-baked cookies, the sound of her screaming at my dad, the alcohol making her movements slow and shaky. Then the feel of her soft hair against my cheek as she pressed her lips on my forehead and her tears dripped along the top of my head.

I parked the bike and took off my helmet, placing it under my arm when I slid off, approaching Paige and Alex. They leaned against

Paige's Prius, bottles of beer in their hands. There were about thirty of us altogether. I gazed over the familiar faces, a few new seniors, some from our graduating class. I nodded at them.

"Did someone really break into your place?" I stopped short of my trek to Paige. In front of me stood Randy Peterson, his red hair curled tightly against his scalp. I gazed up at his pale green eyes.

I sighed and shifted my weight onto my left leg. My right ankle was still a little sore.

"Maybe." My answer, curt and a little annoyed, didn't deter Randy. He was immune to my moody interactions.

I tilted my head and looked over his shoulder at Paige, who was busy miming suggestive sexual acts. I sucked in my lips to keep from laughing. I was never going to live down that one time Randy and I kissed earlier in the school year. It was a moment of weakness. My dad was still in the hospital, and I was depressed and afraid of losing him and maybe drinking a little too much, and Randy had been there. Jared had run off to whatever private school his parents had found for him, and I felt completely alone.

I probably would have hooked up with whoever was available at the time, to be honest. Thankfully, Randy was a gentleman. He'd pushed me away and asked if I was okay. Asked about my dad. That sobered me up pretty quick.

"Do they know who did it?" Suddenly Mindy Carlton was standing next to Randy.

"No. We don't."

I noticed Randy's hand in Mindy's. That was a new development. Randy was going to Penn State in the fall, and Mindy was going into senior year. They definitely hadn't been at prom together. I cringed at the memory of prom. I flew solo. Paige, Alex, and I had a blast dancing together, but I still felt like a third wheel to their duo.

"Now if you will excuse me, I have somewhere to be." I pushed between the two of them and finally reached Paige and Alex.

"That looked cozy. Did Randy ask you to do a threesome with him and Mindy?" Paige asked with a mischievous glint in her eyes.

I made a face. "Ew. No. And when did that happen?" I turned and used my helmet to point at the new couple, who were making out by Mindy's truck.

Alex gave me a hug before answering. That was his thing. He always hugged his friends when greeting them. I personally hated hugging but made an exception for my other BFF. He readjusted the thick black frames of his glasses, then took them off and wiped them down with the back of his Star Trek T-shirt.

"Last week, maybe?" Paige mused. "Who knows. And since when do you care?"

I shrugged. "I don't." Not really.

"I heard there's a criminal hanging around your house now." Paige's eyes twinkled.

Alex pinched her side. Paige yelped and jumped away. "I thought you were going to give her some time to come clean," he said.

"What? I couldn't wait. You know I'm not a very patient person, Alex."

"He's not a criminal," I said. "I mean, he is, but it's not what you think. And how did you find out? He hasn't even started working yet."

Paige took a sip of her drink and walked over to open the trunk of her car. Inside was a cooler full of drinks and snacks. Paige never left the house without food supplies. She handed me a bottle of water, and I took a piece of the ice filling in the spaces between drinks and chewed on it.

"Your dad called my dad. My dad told my other dad, and I over-heard them talking."

Alex waved a finger at Paige. "Paige, I thought we talked about you and your eavesdropping problem?"

Paige groaned. "Sorry, I won't do it anymore."

"That's all I ask. And, Paige." Alex took a step closer to her until they were nose to nose. "Do it again and I will make you watch all eight Harry Potter movies." He proceeded to rub his nose against hers.

"Yes, dear," Paige replied.

Sometimes those two were so cute it made me want to gag. And I was going to miss the hell out of them when we all split up in the fall for college.

The revving of an engine echoed into the dark night, and I turned to the cars taking their places on the road. A Mustang and an Impala. And a red BMW eerily similar to Jared's old car. The door opened and out stepped my ex. Great. Twice in one day. Exactly what I needed. Reminders of my past were suddenly trying to force themselves to the forefront of my mind, and I really did not appreciate it.

"What the hell is he doing here?" I said, gritting my teeth.

Jared pressed his fob, and the car beeped before he stepped toward the three of us. I stood immobilized by his approach. His walk, the confidence he exuded, the way his hair spiked just enough at the top, used to get me every time. Now all it did was remind me of how quickly he turned on me when even the possibility of him getting in trouble came about.

"Want me to cut him?" Paige dropped her beer bottle into the trunk and put her arm through mine.

"I can be your alibi," Alex chimed in.

I shook my head. "No. I can handle this. But thanks for the offer."

I stalked up to Jared, ready for a fight. "I thought I said to leave me alone," I growled at him.

Jared wore his usual preppy-boy attire: designer jeans and shoes, along with a plain, designer shirt. The whole getup put off a vibe that said *I'm better than you* but was not altogether that threatening. A complete illusion covering up the real Jared. The Jared who drank too much, did drugs when he felt like it, and cheated most of his way through school.

I fell for the illusion.

In the beginning, anyway. People warned me, but he had this air around him—it was like this vortex of charm that sucked you in and wouldn't let go. I had needed to get lost in those blue eyes and his easy smile. We started dating not long after Mom left, and he was the perfect break from reality. Then it all came crashing down around me.

"I'm here to see my friends," he said, indicating a few of his old buddies parked at the back of the field.

The soft breeze of the night did little to stamp down the anger rising to the surface. "Fine. But stay away from my friends. Their opinion of you has dropped slightly since the accident."

His eyes softened. I didn't fall for that false sense of concern. "I'm sorry, Tess. I will give you space until you're ready to finally talk."

"I'm done talking, Jared. There's nothing left to say."

Jared lifted a perfectly shaped brow. He had more eyebrow game than me, and he took a lot of pride in his grooming skills. "I think there's still plenty left to say, Tessa."

"I'm not sure if you remember, but we aren't together anymore. You know, because you almost got me killed?" I said with a sickly sweet voice and fake smile. "Oh look, you were right; there was still something left to say."

That did the job and wiped the cocky expression right off his face. "Right. Don't worry, I'll leave you guys alone. See you around, Hopper." He walked away, but I couldn't relax.

Him being in such close proximity put me on edge. Two more cars took off on the road for a short race, and I made my way back to Paige and Alex. The restlessness wouldn't let go, and I needed to get it off my limbs.

"You want to ride next?" I asked Alex.

"Hell yes," he answered.

Alex ran over to his bike, and I went over to mine. He'd checked it out last week to make sure it was in good shape, and I had recently replaced the old tires. I didn't trust anyone else to take care of my Black Beauty. We both rode over to the designated starting point, the end of a half-broken fence around the field. I put on my helmet, and Alex did the same before blowing a kiss to Paige, who pretended to catch it. So. Gross.

We waited until the cars got back before taking off. My heart pounded hard while I rode next to Alex, increasing our speed at a steady pace. The adrenaline skyrocketed through my body, and I wanted to shoot away with it. The speed wasn't exactly what I craved, but it was just enough to calm the overwhelming desire to race into the dark running through my bones.

When I was out there riding the pavement, gliding against the air on my bike, my mind calmed and I could forget my worries long enough to keep the ruse going. Otherwise it would all collapse over my head, and I wouldn't be able to dig myself out of the mess.

COREY

Hopper said I didn't need to come by until about three because he couldn't get away from work until then. I kept checking my watch, anxious to see what waited for me.

Mom walked down the hall, back from her shift at the hospital, as I stepped out of the bathroom, showered and smelling clean. Tim was out on another date. It was weird to think about my little brother suddenly getting action from girls. He was too busy with Star Wars to notice them before.

"Hey, feels like I haven't seen you in forever, stranger," she said, pulling me into a hug.

"It's only been one day, Ma." I let her go and noticed the looming shadow behind her.

"Hi, Corey." Stan stepped forward, revealing his face, and gave me a little nod. His dark eyes were shadowed underneath the dim hallway light. I felt Mom's eyes on me, making my muscles tense. "I'm here to look at the air conditioner." He held up a toolbox.

I nodded. "Thanks. We appreciate the help." The rocks in my throat made it hard to talk.

Stan was a little taller than me, slim, with graying dark-brown hair. He hadn't aged much over the years except for the lines around his eyes and mouth. He used to spend almost every weekend here when Dad was alive.

I gave him a brief nod before heading for my bedroom. Mom followed.

"You okay?" Mom shut the door behind her.

I plopped down on my bed and let out a breath. "Yeah."

"Stan's been asking about you a lot, and the air conditioner really needs to get fixed."

"You don't have to explain, Mom. I get it."

"What's this?" Mom grabbed my sketch pad off the desk while I pulled on my shirt.

Jumping across the room, I grabbed it out of her hand. "Nothing."

She hitched a brow, smiling that knowing smile only moms could pull off. "Nothing, huh? She's pretty." She crossed her arms and studied me.

What did Mom see when she looked at her ex-con son standing in front of her. Disappointment? Regret? I stared at my feet. I'd let her down more than once, and I thought about it every day.

"Everything okay?" she asked, placing her hands on my shoulders as if to steady me.

No. It hadn't been since I first went to work for X. My mom had taught me better. After Dad died, she did everything she could to provide for us. Worked her way through nursing school. Taught us right from wrong, tried to correct everything my father had drilled into our heads about life owing us because we thought it did. Too bad it wasn't enough. But there was still a chance for my mom and Tim.

"I wanted to talk to you about the job application in the drawer," I said.

Mom froze. "You saw that, huh?" She walked over to my desk and took a seat in the chair, shoulders low.

I sat on the edge of my bed, clasping my hands in front of me. "Why didn't you finish filling it out?"

Mom took in a deep breath and let it out. "Because I didn't think I'd get it." Her voice wobbled.

I wanted to pull her into a hug. She had no idea how much they relied on her at work. She didn't want Tim and me hanging out at the hospital, too many bad memories, but the few times I had been able to make it over I'd witnessed Mom's work ethic. She kept that place running like a well-oiled machine, and they would fall apart without her.

"Is it too late?" I asked.

She shook her head and squeezed her eyes shut for a moment. "No. They did a round of interviews but couldn't find anyone they liked. They opened it back up a week ago."

I ruffled my wet hair and pulled at the strands. "Is it because of me? Is that why you didn't apply? Because you were worried I'd screw it up for you? You know, because of my record?"

Mom shook her head, her brows and mouth frowning. "Of course not, Corey. It has nothing to do with you." She rubbed her arms up and down, casting her eyes around the room like she was trying to catch her thoughts.

"Mom?" She seemed distracted; her face was flushed.

She stood up and walked over to me, taking a seat beside me. The bed shifted slightly under her weight. Her arm went around my shoulders. "I doubt myself constantly, Corey. I worry that I'm not good enough, that I'm not qualified. That if I do get it, I'll end up failing." Mom voiced my own fears. We were more alike than I assumed. "Your dad didn't think I could do it. Maybe that's why I have so many doubts."

Mom tried to go back to school a few times when my dad was

alive. He always shot her down. Told her that he could take care of them, that she didn't need to work. I had no idea he made her feel like she wasn't good or smart enough. I wanted to go back in time and throttle my old man for the pain he continued to inflict on our family.

"I get it, Mom. Believe me, I do. But don't let that fear hold you back." Mom deserved to succeed after all her hard work. "You should go for it, Mom. Even if you don't end up getting the position, at least you can say you tried. You'll end up regretting it if you don't."

Mom pulled me in and kissed the top of my head. "Thank you, Corey. Your support means the world to me."

Mom allowed herself to smile. Her eyes misted over, and I glanced away. She stood up but stopped shy of the door.

"You're a talented kid, you know that?"

I met her gaze. The dark circles under her eyes were bruises against her tan face. The gray in her raven-black hair had spread in the last several months, but she refused to dye it.

"What's the point of hiding the fact I'm getting older? There's nothing wrong with it. It shows I'm getting wiser," she argued when I brought it up.

"Thanks, Mom."

"No, really. I need you to know that. I'm proud of the things you can do."

"You're talented, too." Mom half smiled. Sometimes she looked fragile in her pale green nurse's scrubs and Crocs. They hung off her, making her look even smaller than her five-foot-five frame.

"Carrying a tune does not equate to talent. Lots of folks can sing."

"And lots of folks can draw."

"Not like you. You've got what it takes to make it far. I just wish you believed in yourself more. You should take your own advice and try."

Her words made me flinch.

"You're going to go places, kid. You'll see."

I wanted to believe her. But I didn't.

Hopper waited for me in front of the garage. Still in a suit. He had a beige-and-orange lawn chair set up by the porch steps and his dog by his side.

"You're here." He flicked his wrist and checked the time. It was five before three. "And early." He shot me a look that made me straighten my shoulders.

"Where do you want me to start?" I asked, taking a look over the debris still scattered everywhere. Hopper meant what he said about me cleaning it all up.

He bent over and picked up the tablet in his briefcase. "Wherever you'd like. I have some work to do so I won't get in your way," he said, waving his tablet. "Pretend like I'm not even here."

Right. I could do that. I learned to ignore people every day in jail.

I turned to the task at hand. Most of the files were put back in place, probably the personal ones Hopper didn't want anyone seeing. Pieces of trash shifted across the ground as the wind picked up. Tools lay on their sides in the back. Nails littered the floor like a minefield. One wrong step, and I'd get one in my foot.

First thing I did was pick up the garbage. After that, I grabbed an empty cardboard box and started gathering up the broken trophies scattered along the bare concrete floor. They were sports-related. Some were for bowling; others were much older and had an unfamiliar name etched on them. Same last name, Hopper, but a woman's first name.

"You don't want to keep these?" I showed him a trophy.

Hopper's eyes hooded over. "No. Those can go in the garbage." He went back to the tablet.

I didn't know what to make of his dismissive response and went back to work. When I was done with the trophies, I began picking up the scattered tools. A cat meandered out of the trees and went over to Hopper, rubbing up against his leg, before running off again.

"Make sure those go back into their designated drawers," Hopper spoke up while I held a screwdriver in my hand. "They go in there," he said, pointing to the giant storage box.

"Any other specific instructions?" I asked. Hopper raised his eyes to mine, frowning. "Not trying to be a jerk. I promise. I want to make sure I don't screw it up."

Hopper placed his tablet on his lap. Jiminy wandered over to the side of the backyard to take a piss. "No. That's about it. You've done a good job so far, Corey."

I swallowed. "Thanks. I'll get back to it, then." I walked over to the utility box and placed the screwdriver in the correct drawer.

It took at least a half hour of sorting through the nails and screws to put them into the corresponding boxes. I had no idea there was more than one type of screw. There was machine, flat head, round head—more than I cared to remember. Hopper was a neat freak. More organized than most people I knew.

It took a couple of hours to get it done, but I did it.

"Is there anything else?" I asked, wiping my hands on my pants.

Hopper placed his tablet in its case and stood up. "Actually, there is one thing I'd like to discuss. It's about your crew."

I stood still, waiting for him to get out the question he hadn't asked yet.

"Are they coming back? Are my daughter and I safe?"

I cleared my throat. "Yes, sir. They won't come back here. I'll make sure of it."

"I can't ask you to do that, Corey. If it's too dangerous for you to be here, then maybe we should figure something else out."

Were they safe? X had no interest in making a move against Hopper unless I slipped up, which I wasn't planning on doing.

"You're safe. If anything changes, then I'll let you know."

Hopper gave me a stiff nod. "Okay. I'll see you next time."

I grabbed my bicycle and headed down the driveway. All I wanted to do was to sleep until my mind no longer felt tired. But I had one more task for the day.

I sent a quick text to Drew. *Still good to meet up?*

Yeah. See you there.

I pocketed my phone and headed to the meeting place. The dying embers of the day bled orange in the sky, light flickering off the glass windows I biked past on the sidewalk. The burden of humidity the day carried lessened, and a soft breeze filtered through the day.

The smell of cinnamon caught my attention when I zoomed by Michel's Donut Shop. I took a whiff and my mouth watered. I thought about stopping to grab a warm, melt-in-your-mouth glazed donut, but the weight of what I carried in my backpack beckoned me to the alleyway across from the shop. I crossed the street to my destination.

My fingers itched and my body ticked for a release. Painting could take off the edge while I waited for Drew. I pulled my bike into a safe spot in the alley, hidden from view. I took off my backpack, slipped on the mask, grabbed a can, and shook it before beginning my work. Green first. I arced it across the empty canvas, or in this case, the gray concrete behind the clothing store. Then came the black. I shadowed it across the shape of the green tree I'd chosen to paint. A reminder of my and Tim's childhood. The forest we explored and claimed as our own. A memory I clung to during desperate times when life felt like too much of a burden.

Painting was the only vice I allowed myself. Some people smoked, some drank, others got high to forget. Me? I painted. Everything else in my life I did out of necessity: being in a gang, running around with Vance, and helping his crew. Painting was all mine—the one thing I could control.

Almost an hour later, I finished and stepped back to inspect my work. I tugged off my mask and took a few heavy breaths, closing my eyes. The storm brewing inside of me, the one that threatened to blow me away, calmed.

Drew walked up the back alley a moment later. "Good one, Corey," he said, stopping next to me, dropping his cigarette on the ground and grinding out the tip.

I tossed the cans in the nearby trash and pulled on my backpack. "Thanks. You ready to talk?" I didn't feel like discussing my painting. Once I got done with one, I was ready to move on and start another. I rarely went back to look at my old work.

Drew scratched his barely there beard. "What do you want to know?"

"Everything I missed while I was away. Is X still planning on expanding to Peyson?"

Drew stared up at the painting, a nervous energy rising in the alleyway.

"What's going on, Drew? What aren't you telling me?"

He took in a breath. "Things changed while you were gone,

man. Vance has more power than ever, and it seems like X stopped caring." He shook his head. "Vance started buying up new cars." I remembered the new SUV we drove the other night. "Hired more guys to work for him. And he's paying them more than what we're bringing in."

Before I got locked up, I warned Vance that we were losing business in Branson. The cops were getting closer, and Hopper had put away one too many of our crew members. Yet Vance kept hemorrhaging money, spending it like we weren't on a sinking ship. I told him it was time to go to X but he refused, told me to keep my mouth shut. I didn't listen and went to X anyway, told him he needed to look into a different market. Vance retaliated by setting me up for the drugs.

I knew it was him right away. Not that he tried to hide it from me. I knew Vance hated the "in" I had with X, but I didn't think he would go behind my back and throw me to the wolves. Or that X would let him.

"X has some of his guys working in Peyson now, and I think Vance is gunning to take over that territory. He wants to get out of Branson. *Expand his horizons* is the wording he used."

"But where is the money coming from? How is Vance able to afford new cars and guys unless business has picked up since I left?"

Drew shook his head. "It's still down."

I crossed my arms and started pacing, trying to work out the details Drew had shared. "What about the robberies that happened last winter?" While I was away, a couple of X's shipments were stolen. No one knew who was responsible. There were rumors about a rival gang trying to send him a message.

Drew shook his head. "No leads. But I've heard that there are some new guys coming into town. No one's sure who they are or what they want. I tried to talk to Vance about it, but he said it didn't matter."

"You think it might be the people responsible for the robberies?"

"Maybe."

"Get me more information about that if you can. Maybe it'll lead us to some answers."

Drew furrowed his brows. "What are you thinking?"

I shrugged. "Not sure yet. X asked me to keep a better eye on Vance, so that's what I'm trying to do. But I can't go to him until I have more evidence of Vance's screwups."

"Be careful, Corey. Vance still has it in for you. He thinks you're the only person standing in his way of full control over Branson and Peyson. Watch your back."

Whatever calm I'd found in painting evaporated with Drew's words. It left me cold and helpless. Naked. Exposed. The shadows gathered, starting to crowd around me. I shook out my arms, trying to get rid of that feeling.

Drew left me in that alley. I stood there for a while, staring at the ground, thinking, planning. Daylight disappeared, and the dark wings of night spread across the sky. After what felt like hours, I got on my bike and started for home. I may have been on borrowed time, but I could use that time and be there for my family.

Mom had a late shift, and Tim had texted earlier to say he'd be home after dark. I had to get back to the apartment and cook for them. I needed to take care of them for as long as possible. Before I couldn't anymore.

TESSA

y eyes were glazing over as Dad's voice droned on and on about the great and fabulous Corey.

"And he put everything away like I asked without complaint." His hands were covered in dry rub for the pork ribs he was going to cook for our poker game tonight.

"I'm so glad he turned out to be everything you hoped and dreamed." I rolled my eyes and squeezed the lemons in my hand. Stepping around Dad, who stood by the kitchen island working on the ribs, I grabbed the carton of strawberries and a knife for my homemade lemonade.

"I really think this is going to turn out great, Tess. Your suggestion was spot-on. I'm proud of you for thinking outside the box. I know you said you don't want anything to do with Corey, but maybe if you spend some time with him, you'll realize he's not a bad guy."

"Dad, do you hear yourself right now?" I waved the knife. "You're seriously encouraging me to spend time with an ex-convict. Who vandalized our home."

Dad wiped at his nose with the back of his arm. He twitched his nose and kept rubbing. "Will you get it?" He stuck his face out at me. "It's itchy."

I put the knife down and scratched. "Better?"

Dad stood up straight, his eyes weary, hands up in the air so he didn't get his germ-y hands on me. I grabbed a strawberry and popped it in my mouth.

"Tessa, you've been very hostile toward Corey. Not that I blame you after what he did, but I'm wondering why you wanted to help him if you dislike him that much?"

I choked on the strawberry and started coughing, eyes watering. Dad smacked my back with his elbow. Which did very little to help.

"Better?" he asked once my fit was under control.

I wiped my eyes and nodded. "Yup. Fine." I wasn't fine at all. Not with him asking why I decided to help Corey. "I'm worried about Corey's past and your health is all," I finally answered Dad.

Liar.

Then again, I excelled at lying to my father. I found the familiar words of the confession I had rehearsed many times in the past start to bubble.

But every time the words formed in my mouth, they refused to leave the tip of my tongue. I didn't know how to be honest. I was afraid. And I resented Corey for his ability to do something that I couldn't. My phone buzzed, and I made a grab for it.

Can we meet? It's important.

Jared. I worried my lower lip and contemplated my next move.

"I do think you two could learn a lot from each other, Tess."

Flaring my nostrils, I put my phone back on the counter and went to wash my hands.

"You know, I'm going to miss having you around in the fall," Dad said, emotion lacing his words.

I dried my hands and leaned my hip against the island. Dad stood across from me, emotion glinting from his eyes. I hated the idea of leaving Dad, especially after his heart attack. I slid a socked foot back and forth across the floor, a warm sickness spreading in my belly.

"Don't get mushy on me now, Dad," I deflected. I was heading to Randall Community College in the fall and it was only an hour away, but my dad got all misty-eyed over it. I opted for community college because I slacked a lot my sophomore and junior years. Plus, I didn't want to be too far from Dad.

I hated thinking about being away from him and my uncles and Paige and Alex. We were drifting in different directions, and I wanted to grab ahold of every moment we had left together before that happened.

"Can't help it," he said with a laugh. "Listen, I wanted to run something by you really quick." Dad finished with the dry rub and washed his hands before placing the ribs in the oven.

"What?"

He walked over to me and leaned his elbows on the counter. "My schedule is more hectic than I assumed and turns out I can't be here as much I would like with Corey . . ."

I furrowed my brows. "And?"

"I thought maybe you could keep an eye on him for me on days I'm unavailable?"

I tried not to wince or grimace and failed at both.

"Listen, if you think it's too dangerous, then I can ask a uniformed officer to be here as well. But if I'm being honest, I think that might be a bit excessive."

I thought over his words. I wasn't Corey's biggest fan, but the whole reason I came up with the volunteering idea was because I thought he deserved a second chance. For doing the right thing. Maybe Dad was right, and I needed to spend some time with him.

"Can I think about it?"

"Of course. But will you let me know before the end of the night? I have him on the schedule for tomorrow afternoon, and if you can't, then I'll reschedule with him. I have a court date I can't miss."

I massaged my shoulders. "Okay."

Dad came over to me and gave me a quick hug. "I know it's a tough situation, Tessa. I've tried to shield you from that life, but I think it's time for you to see what it's like for kids on the other side."

I bit my tongue. The house felt too warm, and I needed to get out. "I'm going to get some ice cream for tonight. I think we ate the last of it the other day." I moved away from him.

"Be careful," Dad yelled when he saw me grabbing my motorcycle helmet and jacket.

"Always," I tossed over my shoulder before heading back to the garage where Black Beauty waited for me.

I hadn't gone for a ride in a few days, and it was exactly what the doctor called for. The tautness wringing my muscles instantaneously loosened, letting me breathe. I drove down our lane and onto the main road. A few cars littered the streets, people scurrying to their destinations, but for the most part I had the asphalt to myself. I rode all the way to the back road, deserted and quiet, except for the sound of Beauty's engine and the scent of rubber burning the road.

With my jacket on, the wind creating a melody with its forceful brush against my helmet, my mind quieted. Guiding my bike to the familiar back road I enjoyed cruising along the most, my skin started to stretch again. Jared waited by his car in the field, and the sight of him caused my anxiety to take flight. Before I allowed it to fly off, I seized it and forced it back down on the ground.

It was so easy to let the past dictate the present. Every move I made. All my decisions. I was the ghost of Tessa Hopper, a phantom living inside of an unoccupied body. At times I caught glimpses of my old self. When Alex and I rode our bikes. When Paige made a sarcastic comment and I smiled because for an instant I'd forgotten. The one who agreed to let Corey make up for his mistakes. That was the Tessa Hopper I knew and loved. The me I wanted to be again. Someone who tried to help others. I'd locked her away for so long, made a new identity for myself.

When I neared the field, I noticed another car parked next to Jared's pristine BMW. A white sedan with rust outlining parts of it and an Eagles bumper sticker. In contrast to Jared's, the other car appeared grungy and old. The driver poked his head out and spoke to Jared. When he caught sight of my bike, he put his window up and drove away. I could not believe Jared, after all that crap about him changing.

I parked my bike and headed to Jared, ready for a fight while the memories from our past hammered against my head. Memories of when he'd take my hand and kiss my palm, smirk like he knew a secret I didn't and wasn't willing to share. Then there were the times I said the wrong thing, and he'd send me that mocking expression right before he let out a stream of cutting words.

"Hey." He leaned against his car, arms crossed, eyes searching mine with an almost hopeful quality.

"Jared." I unzipped my jacket and took it off. Too hot for the night, too prohibiting. I slung it over my arm and stared up at the sky. Clouds hovered beneath the stars, creating a barricade over the view. The crescent moon was a thin slip of light.

"Thanks for coming," Jared spoke.

I tore my gaze away from the sky and met Jared's blue stare. "Was that your dealer?"

Jared sighed and stood up straight. The collar to his polo shirt was popped up. I held back a snicker. "No. I'm not using. I swear."

"Then who was it?"

"Just some guy asking for directions. I promise." He raised his arms up high. "You're more than welcome to pat me down," he said, his eyes sparkling.

"No thanks, I'll pass. What did you want to talk about?"

He dropped his arms, and his shoulders slumped forward. "Someone mentioned that your dad hired an ex-con to help around the house. Is that true?"

I stiffened for a millisecond then got ahold of myself and cleared my face. "What about it?"

Jared took a step forward. "Tessa, you really think that's a good idea after what happened? I'm worried about your safety."

"Wow, it's so sweet of you to care. Would have been nice to see that sort of compassion last year."

"I'm sorry about that. I swear I'm not that guy anymore. And this doesn't have anything to do with last year. I did some investigating into this guy—Corey, right?"

My heart skipped at the mention of his name. Jared had done his homework. Not that we'd tried to keep it a secret. Most people knew about our situation. Except for Corey's guilt. "Yes. What about him?"

"Did you know he's still hanging with his crew? Do you have any idea how dangerous he is? Your dad is crazy for letting him anywhere near either of you."

I scoffed at his words. Jared had left right before Dad's heart attack last year. While I spent my days with him in the hospital, a part of me kept hoping and waiting for my ex to show up. Even though I was angry and hurt, I couldn't stop myself from needing him.

"Don't you dare talk about my dad like that." I stepped close enough to him to poke him in the chest. "You have no idea what's going on in our lives. You don't know Corey. You know nothing, and it's going to stay that way. Thanks for the warning, Jared, but I can take care of myself." I stalked back to my bike and put on my jacket.

"Tessa, are you into this guy?"

I paused while zipping up. I turned back to Jared. "Why? You jealous?" That was what it came back to in the end.

Jared narrowed his eyes and even in the darkness I could make out the red of his cheeks. "Why the hell would I be jealous of a piece of trash?"

And there it was. The real Jared. The one whose memory I'd buried so deep it was almost like a faint outline of an image you weren't quite sure you'd even seen. Jared and that glint in his eyes that sent a warning through my mind and made the hairs on the back of my neck rise. It had come out now and again when we dated. That hate he held for people he thought were beneath him. The way he laughed at them; the mocking scowl he would wear. Jared claimed he'd changed, but underneath that pretty face and his nice clothes, he remained the same.

I resisted the urge to throw my helmet at his head. I gripped it tight in my hand instead and let my lips slip into a thin smile that I hoped sent him the message blaring in my head. Brittle, angry, threatening.

Jared swallowed and backed away. "Fine. Have it your way."

I slid onto Beauty and rode away with my heart pounding a beat in my ears, overpowering the song of the wind and engine. I kept replaying Jared's words. About Corey's gang. Dad said he'd discussed it with him already, but the unease had settled heavy in my limbs and I had to be sure. For myself. Suddenly Dad's suggestion of having me watch him didn't seem so bad. Then I could finally get answers to my own questions.

COREY

I stood in front of Hopper's front door, finger hovering over the doorbell, hesitation making me freeze. I dropped my hand and shook out my arms, working up the courage to finally push the damn button. I'd faced a lot of scary things in my life. I'd seen guys get beaten to within an inch of their lives, lost friends to shootings, went to jail, but the idea of being alone with Tessa Hopper scared the living shit out of me.

With one big gulp of air, I finally pushed the button.

Jiminy's muffled barking grew closer. The door swung in and there stood Tessa Hopper. Her eyes narrowed a fraction.

"You're late," she said, cocking a hip.

I checked my watch. It was exactly one o'clock. "I'm on time." I lifted my watch to show her.

"Which means you're late," she said, ignoring the watch and stepping aside to let me in.

So that was how it was going to be—pretty much exactly how I imagined.

"Sorry for inconveniencing you." I brushed past her into the air-conditioned house. The day was sweltering, the humidity a thick, suffocating layer. I was glad Stan finally fixed our own air conditioner. A day like this would have been killer without the relief of the cool air.

Jiminy barked and jumped on me with his paws, trying to lick my face.

"Whoa, boy." I patted him and set him back on the ground, his tail wagging.

"My dad made you a list." Tessa strolled into the kitchen and picked up a piece of paper. I followed after her, Jiminy racing ahead.

The kitchen smelled like lemons, and bright yellow rays of light sliced across the hardwood floors. The counters were a black granite that glinted. It was one of those open-concept houses where the kitchen and living room were connected. A long oak table sat in the middle of the room with a vase full of fresh daisies sitting in it. A large flat-screen was mounted in the living room with nice leather couches around it.

I glanced up at the vaulted ceilings and moved my gaze along the walls until it ended at an old jukebox standing by the stainless-steel fridge. I went to check it out. Nothing but Elvis. The smooth, red surface was cold when I ran a hand over the machine, and the back of my neck prickled.

"What's with the Elvis?"

Tessa remained standing by the counter, her eyes predatory. She crossed her arms. "My grandfather was really into him. My dad and uncle bought that for him before he passed away."

"Oh. Sorry for your loss." I cleared my throat.

She lifted a shoulder. "It's okay. It happened a long time ago."

Silence sank into the room.

"I guess I should start."

Crossing the space between us, I pulled the paper out of her hand, avoiding her touch. Tessa remained silent, but her eyes watched my every move.

Reading over Hopper's instructions, I started planning. Today's task included putting in the new windows he'd ordered for the house.

"I think this is the first instance of my dad *asking* a boy to go into my bedroom."

I folded the paper and put it in my pocket. "I'm honored."

Tessa's face turned red and she looked like she might punch me, but Jiminy started scratching at the back door.

"Everything you need is out in the garage." Tessa opened the door to let him out. "Don't get any ideas."

My chest squeezed at the implication of her words.

I followed her down the steps and grabbed the supplies from the dark garage, hauling the toolbox, then the windows, into the house and down the hall. Tessa remained outside while waiting for Jiminy to finish his business, playing a game on her phone. Her shoulders tensed every time I neared her and mine did the same. I had no idea how to act around her and she wasn't my biggest fan, so we continued to ignore each other.

The hallway walls were full of family pictures. I tried not to look, made myself walk faster to the end of the hall, clenching the toolbox in my hand. My family didn't have those photos. The ones that were portraits of happy families. I lowered my head, the thought ringing loud in my ears. Mom was great—she did the best she could for us—but while she worked her ass off to give me a good life, we missed out on family stuff.

Old, partially ripped-off My Little Pony stickers covered the door at the end of the hall. I let out a laugh before pushing it open and flipping the switch. Light rained down on the room. Pale yellow paint—the same I'd mopped the other day—covered the walls, along with pictures, posters of bands, anything Tessa thought looked good. I stared, fascinated by her eclectic taste. There were pictures of boy bands, indie bands, and collages of models in fancy clothes, collages of photographs, collages of animals.

A floral print covered the bed, and an old vanity sat on the same side of the room as the door. The closet was shut, and a pair of black heels lay on the ground. The tan carpet covered the sound of my feet entering the room.

A trophy blinked in my eye. I walked over to the bookshelf across from her bed, filled with books, books, and more books. The same name from the garage was etched on the side of the golden trophy. *Danielle Hopper.*

"What the hell do you think you're doing?"

I whirled around in time to catch a glimpse of Tessa as she stormed up to me. She snatched the trophy from my hand and placed it back on the shelf.

"I'm sorry. I need to fix the window." I pointed. "Remember?"

The blue of Tessa's eyes blazed darker, a storm brewing inside of them. Tension rippled in the space between us. Shit. I didn't blame her for being angry. I shouldn't have been snooping in the first place.

"Oh, I'm sorry; was fixing the window code for 'rifle through Tessa's private things'?"

"Look, I know you don't want me here, and I don't blame you, but could we please call a truce until I'm done? I promise I won't mess with any of your stuff."

Tessa walked over to her bed, putting some distance between us. We did the staring game for a bit. Her with her arms crossed, completely hostile; me gripping the toolbox, waiting for her to decide if she wanted to throw something at me.

"I guess that's fair."

I let a breath through my nose. "Okay. Great." I headed to the window.

"But first I need to ask you something."

Shit. I hung my head and held back a groan. "And what's that?" Placing the toolbox on the floor, I started shuffling through it.

"Did you lie to my father when you told him your gang isn't a threat to us?"

My hands stilled. I turned around, and the heat on her cheeks caught my attention. Her arms were down by her sides. She wore a flowery blouse and a pair of shorts that showed off her legs. My gaze drifted to her lips, a dark shade of pink that made me want to do things with her that were completely inappropriate. Our gazes clashed, and her eyes narrowed a fraction like she'd heard my thoughts. I cleared my throat.

"I didn't lie. You guys are safe. And if anything changes, then you'll never hear from me again."

The answer seemed to satisfy her, and she proceeded to plop down on the bed. "I was told to keep an eye on you." She scooted back against her headboard and took out her phone.

I started sorting the tools I needed onto the floor. Tessa glanced up every now and then, and I felt like a spotlight was on my ass.

"How was work?" I needed to get her attention away from me.

Tessa placed her phone on her lap. "I took off early after one of our best customers yelled at me for clipping her dog's nails too short, even though it was exactly the same length Dr. Ford cut them last time. I was going to give her a piece of my mind but, well, let's just say spending the rest of my life in jail for homicide, no matter how justifiable it may be, isn't on my bucket list."

"Yeah, jail sucks," I commented, leaning my head forward so I wouldn't have to look at her face and see her reaction.

"I'll take your word for it. Did you have fun going through my things?" She pointed to the trophy I'd held earlier.

Heat clouded my neck. "I thought all those were done for."

Tessa slid off the bed and strode over, taking it in her hand. "I managed to salvage that one."

"Who's Danielle?" The question slipped out before I told myself to shut the hell up and be quiet and do my job without causing more trouble.

Her eyes shot to mine and back to the trophy. She placed it onto the bookshelf. "My mom. She isn't around anymore."

My face burned red. "Sorry for your loss." Again.

"She's not dead," she said, her voice tight. A cloud of emotion put a wall between us. "She left when I was fifteen."

The uncomfortable feeling settled in my stomach. I was such an ass. I shouldn't have said anything. This time it was her who looked away. I suddenly missed the force of her stare. It made my stomach twist up in the kind of knots that didn't make it seem like I was getting kicked in the gut.

Tessa had secrets. People didn't learn to put up their walls that fast if they didn't. I knew because I got to be pretty good at it myself over the years.

"Can you help me put this thing up?" I pointed to the glass covered in brown paper.

Tessa flicked her gaze to my hand. Neither of us said anything. Her eyes roamed up to my face and I held still. She finally settled them on mine, and they widened in surprise. What did she see, I wondered? What did anyone see when I stopped pretending?

I watched her throat move as she swallowed. "If you ask politely." Her shoulders remained rigid, but she didn't watch me like she was contemplating whether to stab me in the heart anymore.

"Please. I would appreciate it. A lot."

Tessa nodded and the stiffness in her movements loosened. "Okay." She took a step forward. Her hair glimmered brown and golden down her back. She smelled good. Sweet, not floral. It made it hard to concentrate.

"Grab some gloves. Don't want you cutting your fingers off."

She silently followed instructions before joining me. We took off the plywood covering her window before getting to the glass I'd dragged into the room.

The air brushed through the hollowed opening that used to be a window. The room held a chill from the air-conditioning and the warmth from outside felt good. We placed the glass inside the windowpane and worked in silence.

I put in the shims with Tessa's help. Her hair fell forward as we worked in the points. I bent down to grab the putty and noticed her eyes on mine. They followed my movements. I averted my face to block her out, but the pressure continued to wind into my skin.

"Need me for anything else?" she asked, taking off the gloves and tossing them into the toolbox after we got done.

"No, thanks, I think I can handle the rest." The other window was smaller and more manageable. I stared at our work, satisfied with it, and bent over to start cleaning up the tools.

"It's good to see you branching out." Tessa grabbed at my shirt, fingers brushing my bicep, stilling my movements. "Gray is a nice departure from your usual black on black."

I made myself stand up straight. "You've only seen me twice."

"Yeah, but I have a feeling you like to stick to somber colors in order to keep up the whole bad-boy thing you have going on."

"Bad boy, right." I gently pried my shirt away from her hands, feeling her warm, soft skin. I dropped it quick and resumed cleaning up, needing a distraction while Tessa stood there watching.

"I noticed you riding your bike the other day," I found myself saying. "Where'd you get it?" There I went, trying to make conversation again. I sounded like my mom, and I held back a cringe at the odd choice of my question.

"My mom. The one that abandoned me."

Shit shit shit. "Uh . . ." I tried to recover but couldn't find my words after falling hard on my face after that disaster.

Tessa smiled, though it didn't quite reach her eyes. "I'm messing with you."

My shoulders loosened and dropped low from my ears. "Oh. Okay."

"What about you? You have any family?"

I nodded. "My mom. She's a nurse. She's pretty good at her job and works hard. And I have a little brother. He's a smart kid and has a really bright future ahead of him." Heat crawled up my face. "I don't know why I told you all that." Probably because I was trying to show her that there was more to me than the guy who went to jail. That I was flesh and blood and made mistakes, but that wasn't everything to me. Maybe to justify my life.

"And your dad?"

"My dad died when I was eleven."

Her eyes widened a fraction. "Sorry."

"It was about time for you to apologize for something. I was getting sick of having to do all of it."

A smile peaked at the corner of her lips. "You're not exactly what I expected." Her face burned red. "I mean, I don't know what I'm saying. Please ignore me."

"No. It's cool. What were you expecting?" I was curious about people's expectations of me. I knew what I looked like on the outside. Sullen, maybe a little angry, but what else was there to me besides those things? What did she see?

"I don't know exactly. Someone brittle, hard around the edges."

"And I'm not?" I finished cleaning up and stood up with the toolbox in hand.

Tessa messed with the bottom of her hair, pulling at the ends with her thumb and finger. "Maybe. I'm still figuring you out."

She stepped forward and the air around us got warm. Before I knew it, she was in front of me, looking up into my face, scrutinizing it. Our gazes locked, and I held in a breath.

"So far it's been unexpected. That's all."

Her words were a whispered breath on my skin. Everything in my body was telling me to stay in the locked small space between us.

"I hope I don't let you down, then." I walked past her, my shoulder grazing hers, suddenly desperate to escape the confines of her room. It felt intimate, the two of us hanging out in there.

"Hey." She grabbed my arm, and her skin on my skin shot a zap through me. "I'll go. You stay."

"Nah, I'm done." I had to get the window in the bathroom next. I should have started there but was drawn into Tessa's room by the desire to find out more about her. It itched at me like wool, and I had to leave, otherwise I'd be in trouble.

"No, I mean I'll go to the kitchen so you can work without me hovering over you like a prison guard." Her face flushed. "Bad choice of words."

Tessa twisted the bottom of her shirt. I stared at her hands for a second and noticed how uncertain her stance had become.

"You're prettier than any prison guards I came in contact with, so you have that going for you." There I went running my mouth again. My jaw twitched from clenching it so hard. Sometimes my brain didn't process my words fast enough, and I ended up saying some really stupid stuff. My ex, Taylor, called it word vomit and said I was awkwardly charming.

Tessa's hands stilled, and she let out a raspy laugh that tugged at my nerves. "Thanks. I guess?"

"You're welcome."

I needed to end it there. I forced myself not to say anything else, like how her hair looked nice because of the way the sun hit the gold of it and how her eyes reminded me of the ocean right before a storm. Not that I had ever seen the ocean so I didn't even know if that was true.

The silence swooped back in. The toolbox in my hand grew heavier, weighting me to the spot, making it impossible to move. Her eyes softened around their edges.

"Let me know if you need anything," she finally said and cleared her throat when her voice wavered.

I nodded and left the room to fix the other broken window. Having her help would make things easier, but no way was I putting myself in a position like that again. Getting that close to her was dangerous and stupid.

TESSA

The clang of a hammer touched along the walls into my room. Annoyance scourged my mind. I didn't like the way my body reacted to Corey's. At all. It was an unnecessary complication and the last thing I needed in my life. Ugh, then when he talked about his mom and brother, the pride that exuded through his voice and eyes? Completely inconvenient.

I needed to keep my guard up around Corey. The air around us had swirled with unspoken words and a pressure I didn't want to place. My stomach grumbled. Maybe eating would help distract me from the weirdness and indecision varnishing my thoughts. I made my way to the kitchen, forcing myself to stare ahead and not back to the bathroom where Corey worked. Crossing to the fridge, I went to see what we had in terms of food.

A bag of roast beef sat in the cold-cuts drawer. One thing we always had plenty of? Bread. The bread box sat by the toaster on the counter next to the sink. Sandwiches sounded good. I scoured the fridge and found tomatoes, lettuce, mayo, cheese, and mustard. One by one, I placed the ingredients on the counter then grabbed a butter knife.

Every time I looked up from my task my eyes managed to wander to the motorcycle. I wanted to explain to Corey why I rode the bike my absentee mom had left behind. Wanted to make him understand how it made me feel more like me than anything else in the world. Maybe he'd look at me like I was crazy, or perhaps he'd understand like Paige and Alex. I put away the food and placed the sandwiches I'd made on a couple of plates and somehow managed to make my way to the bathroom down the hall.

Corey's taut back was to me. He was working the shims into the window like we had done together earlier.

"Hey, I thought you might be hungry." I set down the plate and cup of juice on the sink. His hair fell over his eyes when he turned, and he pushed it away, hand gliding with more grace than one should be able to when pushing back hair.

He stared at the plate, then at me standing there, my insides writhing with heat and emotions I did not want pumping through my veins, especially for the guy in front of me.

"Thanks." He turned back to the window.

Part of me felt relieved; the knots in my stomach loosened. The other part of me slumped in disappointment because, well, I kind of wanted him to stare at me like he had earlier in my bedroom. In my very yellow, very frilly, very personal bedroom. Heat swept over me, finally forcing me to move my legs.

By the time I got back to the kitchen, my breathing had grown erratic. Again, a reaction I didn't want to have for the guy who vandalized our home and I didn't fully trust. I fell into the dining room chair and pulled out my phone to text Dad about when he'd be home tonight. I needed to focus on something. Anything else but the thought of Corey and the smell of pine he carried on his skin. Why was this happening?

The phone buzzed on the table.

Another late night. Sorry sweetie. Dad.

No worries. I'll leave a plate in the fridge for you.

"Thanks for the sandwich; it was good." Corey sauntered into the kitchen, his sneakers squeaking against the wood. His plate and cup were empty.

I pushed my hair back from my face and told myself to put my guard back up. "No problem."

The faucet creaked as he turned it on and proceeded to hand-wash the dishes and place them in the strainer.

"You don't need to do that." I jumped up and grabbed for the cup in his hand. He swiped it above his head and my balance shifted, knocking my face into his chest. His hands came down around my shoulders to help straighten me; the cup he held pressed against my shirt.

My hands somehow managed to land on his chest. His gray shirt was surprisingly soft, and I found myself grabbing the material in my fists and rubbing it in between my fingers.

"What are you doing?" One of Corey's brows sidled up.

"Uh, your shirt is really soft." My eyes couldn't move from his, even though my brain kept reminding me how stupid I was. "What kind of material is it?"

Corey half smiled, his eyes scanning my face, landing on my lips. Was it me or did he lean in closer? Was I the one leaning? We were breathing each other's air, that was all I knew.

He cleared his throat. "It's cotton." He pushed me back by the shoulders, adding more than just centimeters between us.

My face started to heat up, but for some reason I couldn't get my mouth to shut up. "Are you sure?"

"Pretty sure. I can't afford cashmere or any of that other expensive shit."

"I've never worn cashmere." Oh my gosh, I was standing remarkably close to a hot guy in my kitchen, almost kissed him, and we were discussing fabric.

He shrugged. "Guess we have something in common. Now, if you're done feeling me up, I should get home."

It wasn't until he said so that I realized my hands were still on his chest. I snatched them back and proceeded to fidget while trying to find something else to do with them, even though all they wanted was to go back on his chest. They were rather comfortable there.

"Sorry." I settled on keeping them crossed with my hands tucked beneath my pits, where the likelihood of them doing something stupid like feeling up a boy with a very hard chest wasn't possible. One thing had been confirmed after my little display—Corey worked out.

He grabbed the toolbox and headed for the back door. "It's okay. Not every day I get sexually harassed by the daughter of the man who put me in jail." He ran his hand over his hair, giving it a good shake, putting it back into its messy place. It worked for him. Red dots appeared on his cheeks.

My guard immediately shot up. That was right. My dad had prosecuted Corey and sent him to jail. Thank goodness he reminded me, because I couldn't forget. Ever. The air, the words, they stirred around me and dropped. Everything I had felt up to that moment dissipated.

"Don't flatter yourself." I stalked past him to the table and sat down in front of my half-eaten sandwich.

I felt his shadow at my back but refused to turn. When he didn't move I knew I couldn't ignore him anymore.

"What?" I turned in my chair and stared him down. I really did not need my heart to do that when I looked at him. This inconvenient crush I had on a guy that destroyed my dad's car had me questioning my sanity.

"I'm sorry about what I did. I know I really messed up. I'll do whatever I can to make up for it."

I found myself speechless.

"Oh. Okay."

He left and I stared at the space he had occupied, chastising myself for being such a jerk.

COREY

The weather outside held no welcome, with the humidity lingering even though the sun had started to set. But it was a nice change from the weird vibe in the house with Tessa. The heat of her hands on my chest lingered. Then the coldness of her tone when I mentioned my past with her dad. I shook it off. I needed to clear my head.

Drew texted to let me know he had some more information on what was going on with Vance. He said he would pick me up later to go over everything. Good. I had a plan. A weak one, but it was something. If I could show X that Vance caused more harm than good to the business, then maybe he'd finally cut him out. It wouldn't be easy—Vance was X's family after all—but I had to try.

I went home to get cleaned up after leaving Hopper's. Tessa kept surfacing in my mind, and I made myself forget everything I might have felt around her. There was no time for it.

I was sitting on my bed, tying my shoelaces after a quick shower, when the familiar squeak of Mom's bedroom door cut through the quiet. Pulling down my pant leg, I turned off the bedroom light and headed to say hi to her, but it wasn't her standing by the kitchen faucet when I entered.

"Stan."

He turned to me, almost dropping the cup in his hand and spilling water all over the front of his shirt. Which was rumpled. Along with his pants. And his eyes held that hazy quality after waking up from a nap.

"Hey, didn't hear you come in." Stan placed the cup on the counter. "How was Hopper's?"

I didn't move and tried not to look surprised. Stan hadn't stayed over since I got home from prison. I had no idea how to react to the situation. "Good. Got a lot done."

Stan scratched at his beard. "That's great. Where you heading now?" He stared down at my clean clothes and shoes.

"I'm meeting up with a friend. Won't be back 'til late."

Stan's focus cleared. "Which friend?"

I ignored the tension rising up my back. "No one you know."

"Corey, you have to get away from them at some point. It's getting too dangerous. Your mother is worried sick about you."

"Please don't bring her into this. You don't think it kills me that she worries about me? You don't think that I've thought about getting out? I have. A lot. But I can't think of one way that wouldn't end with either Mom or Tim dead. I can't take that risk, Stan."

I turned away from him.

"Corey. Please don't leave like this. Let's talk. We can figure something out together."

"Tell Mom I'll be back before she has to leave for work," I said, shutting the door behind me.

Drew drove us to our destination in his crappy car. The enclosed space smelled like stale cigarettes and vanilla. The heat of the night grew oppressive, and I was glad I'd chosen not to wear my hoodie.

"What did you find out?" I asked, resisting the urge to put down the window.

"You know how I said there's been talk of some guys bringing stuff into town? I guess they're using the old back highway. Jaimie heard that some guys saw a white van going in and out. I decided we could scout them."

I noticed the sag underneath Drew's eyes. "I'm guessing this isn't your first night?"

"No. I've seen a white van three times now. Haven't slept much because of it."

"Drew, you should have told me sooner. I would have come out with you."

He shook his head. "I had to be sure about the intel. A lot of guys have been complaining about Vance, and I think you're our best shot at taking him down."

I balled my hands into fists. "I'm not taking him down." Not yet anyway. "Don't get your hopes up. You know how unpredictable Vance can be."

Drew shifted in the driver's seat. "I know that, man. I don't want to put pressure on you. But it feels like we're running out of time, you know?"

I did know. "Anything else about this van?"

"Yeah. I followed them once to a warehouse. They were definitely making a drop. Couldn't get a good look at what it was, so I brought these along this time." Drew held up some binoculars.

We drove in silence the rest of the time. I couldn't quiet my mind of the words Drew had spoken. About me being the hope for the crew. Made me want to laugh with bitterness. If I was their hope, then they were screwed. My plan wasn't even solid. But I held on to it because it was better than nothing.

Drew turned on the radio, and a soft song began to play. I leaned back against my seat but couldn't relax. Driving around with Drew on a scouting mission almost felt like old times. Except everything had changed. Most of all me. Running a job, tracking threats, it never used to bother me. It came with the territory. Now I held on to the door handle, knuckles whitening in order to resist the urge to jump out of the moving vehicle. Danger waited around every corner.

It used to be easy to ignore all the red flags in my life. Now it took more effort, constant diligence. Sometimes I wished I could go back to being that idiot who didn't think before he put himself in those situations.

Drew turned off into the tall brush and grass, the car bumping along the road, until we were hidden behind the first outline of trees. My hands grew clammy, and I wiped them on my pants.

"Mind if I smoke?" Drew asked after he parked the car and turned off the headlights.

My head got woozy, and the view outside tilted to the side with my heart gaining speed. I blinked a couple of times.

"I'll get out." I pushed open the car door and stepped into the night. The fresh air would help clear my head. I hoped.

One of the aftereffects since my release from jail was the physical reaction I now got when I went out on a job. Since I got out, Vance had me go on a couple before the night at Hopper's. That was when it started. I never knew when it would show up or how strong it would be. It took a couple of minutes of pacing and forcing myself to breathe evenly for my grip on reality to return.

I took out my phone and checked the time. Almost ten o'clock.

"What time do they usually come around?" I leaned over to ask Drew.

He checked his watch. "Shouldn't be much longer."

Good, that meant the panic had less time to grind against my brain.

I closed my eyes and started to form a picture. My fingers itched for a pencil or a can. Painting usually helped with meltdowns. But I was shit out of luck at that moment, out in the middle of nowhere with none of my supplies. Instead, Tessa's face took shape. The arch of her brow. The tilt to her mouth. The fire in her eyes.

My heart calmed and I opened my eyes. She was just a girl. Yeah, it had been a while since I was with someone, but that didn't mean I should stop being careful. Feeling jumpy, I started pacing the length of the car again. It wasn't even ten minutes of me failing not to think about Tessa that a van came into view. A white one.

"Corey," Drew called.

I jumped into the car, and we started tailing it from a safe distance. We followed it for fifteen miles before the driver took a detour and pulled into a Chinese restaurant off the side of the road.

"This is what they did last time, too," Drew explained. "Looks like it's their thing before making the drop-off."

The guy in the passenger side got out of the van and walked into the building, tucking what appeared to be a menu into his back pocket, while the driver stayed behind.

"Are you sure?" I asked. "Could be a craving."

Drew pointed a finger in their direction. "They do this every time."

"Do we know anything about the people responsible for stealing from X?"

"One of the guys mentioned that Vance gets real quiet whenever they bring it up. Usually changes the subject."

That was interesting. My theory about Vance and the stolen goods became more solidified. Almost fifteen minutes later, the guy in the restaurant came out with a couple of bags of food. He got in, and they were off again. We followed them all the way back to a deserted warehouse. Drew turned off his headlights and parked in a shadowed area.

I pulled out the binoculars and watched. The driver went to the front entrance of the warehouse and knocked. I finally got a good look at his face, and he didn't seem familiar. His dark hair was buzzed short, and his chin jutted out. The door opened, and I moved to see the new guard.

The hairs on my neck shot up.

"Hey, look at this." I handed the binoculars over to Drew. "Isn't that Suthers?"

Drew took them and stared at the guard "Shit. Yeah. He said Vance came to him to see if he wanted to join the crew but he said no."

"Apparently he changed his mind." I took back the binoculars.

Drew leaned forward over the steering wheel, eyes sharp. "Or maybe someone else made him a better offer."

The passenger-side door pushed open, and the third guard walked back. The other two guards followed him. Two more guards streamed out of the building. So not as deserted as I thought when we first arrived. None of the new ones were familiar.

They started lifting out duffel bags and taking them inside, five in total, one for each guard. Suthers was the last one in and shut the door behind him.

"What the hell is in those bags?" I asked out loud.

A few minutes later, the driver and passenger from the van rolled up the side doors and I caught a glimpse of what was inside the warehouse.

Crates.

Crates that looked an awful like the kind X used for his shipments.

"Damn it." I put down the binoculars. "That's X's stuff in there. Those are definitely the guys who stole from him."

We waited until the men finished filling up the back of the van and drove off. My heart pounded inside my skull, and I rubbed my eyes. This was more than I bargained for, but it was better than nothing. My initial theory about Vance being the one who stole the goods was on shaky ground. He wasn't organized enough to hire new men and move around the money. Then again, Vance was full of surprises.

"What are you thinking?" Drew asked, driving us back. "You going to X?"

I sighed and cracked my knuckles. "I still think Vance might be the one behind the robberies, but I don't have enough evidence to share that with X. Not yet." Not to mention X wanted to keep his distance from me because of Hopper. "You think you can get the guys on the crew to talk?"

Drew turned back onto the main highway. "Yeah, I can be careful."

"Good. Once we know for sure, then I'll go to him."

I needed to know whether Vance was screwing over X. Maybe I

could use that against him. Leverage to get out of the crew. Or at least get away from Vance. If X found out his nephew stole from him, he wouldn't protect Vance anymore. My future was uncertain and that scared me, but I did know one thing: I had to get out and paint. I needed to get rid of the restlessness that wouldn't let me go.

TESSA

I ran the kitchen faucet and washed off the broccoli. Being the child of a single parent who worked long hours, I taught myself to cook out of survival. Mom did most of the cooking before she left. She used to let me help when she had the patience for it. A little furl of resentment pricked my ribs, and I shook off the droplets of water clinging to the florets.

Jiminy's whining caught ahold of me, and I dropped the broccoli on the cutting board. Jiminy hadn't eaten much earlier and seemed sluggish. I thought he was tired, but maybe I was wrong. Worry hastened my steps. Jiminy lay on the living room floor when I went to check on him. His eyes were wide, and he didn't move as I walked over and knelt in front of him.

"What's wrong, buddy?" I asked, rubbing his ears.

His answer came in a form of another whine.

"Can you try and get up?" I nudged Jiminy, and he rolled from his side to his belly and gave up. Lifting his head, I placed it in my lap and tried to keep calm despite my heart picking up its pace and my belly turning with queasy rolls. "Okay. I'm going to call Dr. Ford. Stay right here." I kept my voice cheerful despite heavy dread weighing my legs.

I dialed Dr. Ford's number, and she told me to bring in Jiminy right away when I explained his symptoms. Rushing around the house, I grabbed my car keys and slipped on my flip-flops.

"Okay, buddy, let's get you out. Think you can walk?" I urged him to stand, but he turned his head away from me and closed his eyes.

My breath quickened and came out in hefty bursts while I assessed my options. Jiminy weighed close to eighty pounds, and when I tried to lift him it became abundantly clear that I wasn't strong enough to carry him into the car. Frustrated tears welled from my eyes, and I wiped them away. I had to get a grip and keep Jiminy calm. If I started freaking out, he would, too.

Grabbing my phone from the couch, I called Paige.

"Please pick up," I said, pacing the floor.

"Hey, what's up?"

"Where are you?" My voice shook.

"What's wrong?" Her voice went on alert, sending me reminders of the night of the accident.

"Jiminy's sick, and I need help lifting him to the car."

Paige let out a breath. "Give me ten."

Relief flooded my senses, but the dread hung low in my belly when I hung up. At times like these, I missed having an adult in close proximity. I never resented Dad's job. He did the best he could to provide for us, and he loved what he did so much I could never begrudge him his passions.

But sometimes it really sucked being left on my own. After Mom bailed, Dad threw himself into his work. It was nearly impossible for him to give it his full attention when Mom was around because of her erratic behavior. Her absence almost seemed like a relief for him, like a thick curtain lifting and spilling light into the house. One less stress in his life. No more worrying about what she would do to herself, or me, when he wasn't around.

The anger remained steady inside of me; I held it off as much as possible. Pushed it down until I could only feel little flickers of heat from it. I never knew when it would be too much and explode into every crevice of my being. It hadn't happened in some time, that inexplicable rage rising to the surface in a sudden burst that left everyone around me charred.

It happened so frequently after Mom ran off, I thought I was turning into her. Becoming unhinged and erratic. Then two things happened: I started riding and racing. Whenever I neared that edge, I would get on Beauty and ride it out. And I met Jared and I learned to lock up those emotions in a box. Until the box grew too big and I'd lose my grip. We would get into these fights. Screaming matches that left plenty of emotional marks along both of us. I stared down at Jiminy, tears pricking my eyes, the helplessness clinging to me.

I thought that the anger had retreated, that maybe I finally conquered it. Then on the night of the vandalism, it returned with a quiet force. A soft brush against my skin. A simmer that turned to a full boil.

I couldn't lose Jiminy.

All those nights of being alone, I hadn't truly been by myself. I'd had him. My constant companion. The idea of not having him there for me, waiting, made me want to throw something against a wall.

When Paige arrived, I was sitting on the floor rubbing Jiminy's belly.

"Okay, let's do this," she said, rolling up her sleeves.

We worked together and got Jiminy into the car. I texted Dad to let him know what was going on while Paige drove. At the office, we carried Jiminy back to the observation room and Dr. Ford proceeded to check him out.

"What are his symptoms?" Dr. Ford asked, pressing the stethoscope to Jiminy's belly.

I listed the ones I had noticed, and she nodded along.

"Okay. Let me run a couple of tests. Why don't you hang out in the waiting room?"

Paige touched my elbow. "Come on, Tess."

I pressed a kiss to Jiminy's head and followed Paige out to the waiting area, taking a seat by the entrance. A chill sank into my bones from the air-conditioning vent above my head. I thought about moving, but it helped quiet the rage.

"You okay?" Paige took the seat next to mine, grabbing my hand.

I ran a thumb over my lip, picking at the dry skin. I shook my head. "I feel like this is my fault somehow."

Paige let out a long breath and leaned back against her seat. The silence stretched thinner and thinner until it was ready to snap in half.

"Is this about the accident?" she asked, and I nodded. "Tess, what happened that night wasn't your fault. Jared was the one driving. He was the one that was high. He was the one who walked away. Not you."

I sank a little in my seat. "Yeah, but what about all the things I did before then? Dad and I fought all the time. I pushed you and Alex away. I knew Jared was bad news, but I kept seeing him."

"You're eighteen, Tessa. I don't know if you know this, but people our age tend to make a lot of questionable decisions. And you're not that person anymore."

Then why did I feel like I still was? Or at least caught in murky waters that made it hard to find my direction.

My throat grew tighter, and swallowing caused the pain to ring out. "I hate it. I think about how easy it is for people like Jared, people like me, to get away with so much while everyone else suffers for the smallest crimes. Guilty or not." Please, I begged, don't take Jiminy away from me. I may have deserved the pain, but he didn't. He was innocent.

"I know. But you can't punish yourself forever. You'll only end up hurting yourself." Paige's voice grew soft, and I leaned my head on her shoulder.

I squeezed my eyes shut and silently begged that Jiminy would be okay. I needed him.

"Tessa?" Dr. Ford walked out of the patient area.

I stood up too fast and stumbled, and Paige reached out to steady me.

"What is it? What's wrong with him?" Panic etched my words.

"Jiminy has an ear infection. Nothing major, but I'll keep him overnight to make sure he's okay."

My body sagged with relief, and I leaned into Paige. "An ear infection?" I frowned. "How did I not see the signs?" I was around animals all the time. I knew what to look for, but as soon as Jiminy started showing symptoms of being sick, all that knowledge evaporated.

Dr. Ford offered me a kind smile. "Don't blame yourself. It's fairly common to go into panic mode when someone close to us exhibits signs of a sickness. It's been known to happen to me with my own pets. Why don't you head out and get some rest? Jiminy will be ready for you in the morning."

I nodded and mumbled a thank-you before following Paige out to the car. The night air dropped with its weighty humidity, and my mind wouldn't stop whirring. Sleep didn't seem likely. Even though Jiminy was okay and it made me happy, I couldn't shake the guilt. I'd spend the rest of the night fighting my demons.

Paige drove me home, but I didn't stick around for long. I didn't want to go for a ride, either; the reminder of my mom wasn't welcome. Instead I got in my car, unsure of my destination. I needed to be away from the house and agonize over the hollowness the cowardice left in my chest. I had to figure out a way to get rid of the nagging questions: Who next? And when? Dad with his heart attack, Jiminy with his sickness. Who else would pay for my mistakes?

It was only a coincidence, I thought, pressing my foot harder on the pedal. Bad things happened to people all the time. The road was quiet, and it didn't help calm the storm raging inside of me. I took in a shaky breath because my train of thought refused to ease my mind. Nausea made my skin clammy, and tears touched the tip of my lashes. Something else was going to happen. Someone else would pay for my mistakes. The walls were closing in around me, and I didn't know how much longer I could hold on to the secret because I wasn't willing to risk anyone else I loved.

COREY

Drew dropped me off at the apartment. Mom was asleep on the couch when I got home. The TV was still on and ran colored pictures across her face. I put a blanket over her and turned it off.

I checked in on Tim. He was out cold underneath his covers, snoring.

There was no sign of Stan, and that helped me breathe easier.

An ache branched out from my shoulders, down to my lower back, and I stretched to loosen the muscles. The soreness in my arms settled after a day of helping fix up the windows at Hopper's. And just as I thought I had forgotten Tessa, the pain brought it all back.

I filled my backpack with supplies and grabbed my bicycle. I rode down the street and took in a breath, getting used to the feeling of the pedals. When I got to the corner of Milwaukee and Charleston, I made a right toward downtown. I knew the streets better than the back of my hand. Behind Shutter Bug Photography was where I had my first tag because the lighting from the street was perfect enough to give me room to see but dark enough to hide me in the shadows from the cops.

I slipped around the back alleys I'd grown up with. The restaurants that always smelled like too much grease and not enough substance. Then there were the ones that had enough garlic streaming out to leave the smell on your skin for days. Luigi's was my favorite, though, because it actually smelled like pizza back there.

No one knew that the alley in between Cecelia's Dog Grooming service and Sherrie's Nails eventually led to the tail end of Wheaton Street. The path was too narrow for cars but perfect for biking.

I knew exactly which cameras worked and which ones were fakes. Knew when the cops checked up on things. The shifts rotated between the rookies. Being a graffiti artist helped me gain the knowledge. I knew the streets better than most and knew escape routes no one thought to use because they hadn't bothered to learn them. A smile worked its way up my face when I thought about Tessa flying free, feeling alive as she rode along the streets on her motorcycle.

Biking in the darkness while the rest of the town slept reminded me what it was like to be alive. Not living, but really alive, feeling everything around you, finding yourself smiling about something stupid without even realizing it.

Smoky clouds covered the moon, and the stars were barely visible through them. It looked like snow. The night was cooler than the day had been; it wrapped its arms around me. I hitched up the backpack I wore when it started to slide.

The wind felt good. I felt alive despite the death of my neighborhood surrounding me. It was funny how towns were split up. There was always a rich side and a poor side.

Only a few blocks of concrete and boxed-out wooden homes separated a class of people. One block covered in broken sidewalk, rickety houses, chain-link fences with barking dogs. The next, clean pathways lined with dead trees that sprang to life during the spring and summer, shining new cars and full grass lawns.

Even the air smelled fresher, cleaner, less toxic with the scent of bad choices and dead-end lives behind me. I usually stuck to my side of town. Biking to the other side was a slap to the face. Most nights, I only made it to the outskirts of the nicer neighborhoods, and that was more than enough of a reminder of my designated place in life. But this time I decided to screw it.

Train tracks split Branson in half, tracing the lines of the city from beginning to end.

Prospect Park zoomed by. Whispering, full trees stretched shadows onto the sidewalk. A swing squeaked in the distance. I stopped to catch my breath. I'd made it several miles and my body felt warm, but my legs were cramping.

The squeaking swing got louder, the movements more rapid, echoing in the night. I took in deep breaths and shook my head. From the peripheral line of sight, a shadow kicked its legs.

The person swung higher and higher, and when reaching the desired height, stopped moving their legs, until the swing slowed down and they jumped off. I paused to watch. Mom used to push me on the swings until I was around eight. It took me forever to learn how to pump. It was embarrassing seeing kids a couple of years younger than me conquer such an easy milestone, while I struggled to work out the rhythm.

Some kids called me slow. I think I was a perfectionist.

The lone figure on the hillside began the descent back. The closer it got, I realized it was a girl, from the way her ponytail swished and her hips swayed.

I couldn't take my gaze off her. Her eyes were downcast and her hands were in the pockets of her sweatshirt. Her shoulders were slumped, her steps heavy, and she was headed straight for me. I jumped out of the way but wasn't quite fast enough. Her shoulder collided against mine. It barely budged me, but she lost her balance and started falling back and let out a yelp of surprise. I grabbed her elbow to keep her from breaking her tailbone.

She pushed me and threw a punch my way. I ducked in time for her to catch the side of my shoulder and let go of her.

"Hey, hey, sorry for trying to help," I said, rubbing my shoulder. She was surprisingly strong.

She hissed, straight up hissed, at me and held a pair of keys that I hadn't seen before in front of her like a knife. Her hair came loose in front of her eyes. "It's you," she breathed out, loosening her defensive stance.

I was trying to forget this girl, and she was standing right in front of me. I held myself still with my bike while my heart took off like a rocket.

"My name is Corey," I found myself saying. The streetlamp we stood under showed the blush working its way onto her face. "Thought you'd at least remember the guy you felt up a few hours ago."

Rage colored her eyes. "What. The. Hell. You don't do that to a person!" she yelled at me. "It's the middle of the night and I'm walking alone and some guy appears out of nowhere. Did you really think touching me was a good idea? Do you have a death wish?"

"I'm sorry. Really, I am." I tried to smother the laugh, but I couldn't stop the smile.

"It's not funny," she said, pushing my shoulder.

"No. Not at all." I cleared my throat and wiped my face clean.

The silence dropped like a bomb, and the only sounds were the crickets and the whistling of the train. I took a closer look at her and noticed the bit of red lining her eyes.

"Rough night?" What a stupid thing to ask. What a stupid thing to do, engaging her in a conversation.

She peeked up at me. "Something like that."

"Want to talk about it?" I found myself asking. The exact opposite of following X's orders. I squeezed the strap of my backpack, tension running along my shoulders.

Tessa pulled the tie out of her hair before pulling it up into one of those buns I could never figure out. "Jiminy had a health issue." Her voice wobbled, and she cleared it before dropping her arms.

I didn't know much about Tessa Hopper, but from what little interaction we'd had, I knew how much she loved her dad and her dog.

"Is he okay?" I started to step forward but stopped myself when I realized what I was doing.

Tessa noticed my hesitation and frowned. "Why do you care?" she asked, not in a cruel way, almost like she was genuinely curious.

"Am I not allowed to?" I wanted her to say no. To turn me away, lash out at me. It would be easier that way.

"I don't get you at all, Corey. If I were in your place, I would be so angry," she whispered.

"Who said I'm not angry?"

She jerked her stare to mine, and I saw a glimpse of the truth. I wasn't the only one pissed off. Tessa Hopper had secrets hidden beneath the layers of cool indifference, and I wanted to know what they were.

She nodded to my backpack. The strap slid down, and I shouldered it back up. The cans of spray paint dug into my back, getting heavier. "What's in there?"

"Nothing."

She narrowed her eyes. "You're heading to the skate park, aren't you?"

I eyed her up and down. "You continue to surprise me, Tessa Hopper. I didn't know you hung out at the skate park."

It wasn't far from Prospect, but the differences were like night and day. The ramps and rails were worn down and rusted, and the concrete in the bowl was chipped everywhere. Most people avoided it because of the hazards, but sometimes I came across a kid or two hanging out or a homeless person taking shelter from the weather.

"There's a lot you don't know about me." Her face closed off; her voice changed. It was deeper, hushed. She crossed her arms.

I tightened my grip around the handlebars, feeling the ridged rubber mold against my skin. My gut curled uncomfortably, and I knew I'd said the wrong thing.

"Yeah, you're right. There are a lot of things I don't know about you. But I do know you're a thrill seeker who likes to ride a motorcycle, who loves her dog and her dad, whose mother abandoned her."

Tessa angled her head to the side. "Okay. Maybe you know me a little bit. But that doesn't mean we're, like, friends or whatever. I still don't trust you."

"I don't expect you to."

She let out a slow breath and nodded. "Good."

I waited for her to say something else. Anything. Because the longer we stood out there in the silence, the longer I started to notice the way she bit her lip or how the breeze caught her hair. Things I shouldn't be noticing.

I swallowed when her eyes caught mine and she looked away quick.

"You want to come with?"

Suspicion pulled at her brows. She stood there for a minute, quiet, lost in thought. I figured a no was coming my way when she finally spoke.

"Really?"

I shifted on my bike, staring at the way the light caught her lips. "Hop on." I nodded to the pegs on the back.

She peeked over my shoulder and laughed. "I haven't ridden on a bicycle like that since I was a kid."

"You making fun of my ride?" I feigned insult.

"Yes. But I'm bored and I want to see what you'll paint, so I'll go." She walked past me and lifted herself up onto the pegs.

Sliding onto the seat, I kicked off the ground and pedaled fast. It was a quick ride, less than five minutes, but enough time to cool down some of the heat I felt around Tessa. Until her hands slipped under my arms, squeezing into my chest, her face behind my neck, her breath going down my back.

She gripped me tighter when I took a corner. Passing shadows came to life as we neared, flying past and revealing themselves to be everyday normal things like water fountains and slides, not the boogeyman.

I let out a breath when we arrived and Tessa finally let go of me. I parked the bike and led the way to the graffiti tunnel, flexing my fingers. Touching Tessa was sure to lead to something explosive. I was a charged wire and she was water—someone was bound to get electrocuted.

Darkness confined the skate park, but I had brought along a flashlight. Sliding off my backpack, I unzipped it and got out my supplies.

"Here, hold this." I handed Tessa the flashlight. She flipped it on, shedding light around the blackened tunnel.

Paintings of monsters and lolling tongues covered the walls, so many colors it was hard to focus on only one of the pictures.

"It's way spookier in here at night. And quieter."

"You scared?"

Tessa turned the light toward me, and I shielded my face with my hands. "With you around as my only protection? Yes."

"Ouch. Don't hold back," I said, continuing to unpack my bag.

Tessa moved the light around the tunnel. "I almost kicked your ass just a few minutes ago after you decided to sneak attack me."

"First of all, I wasn't sneaking. Second of all, I don't remember any ass kicking taking place. Although I will give you props for the one hit you managed to land."

Tessa snorted. "Whatever. I totally had you."

"You keep telling yourself that." I couldn't hide the smile from my voice. I liked this version of Tessa. The one who didn't have her shield up. It was a nice change.

"Wow, it's been forever since I was down here. A lot has been added." Tessa turned around, lighting the different works of art. "Which ones are yours?"

I lined the cans up against the concrete, the sound echoing around the tunnel. Brushing my hands on my shirt, I turned to her.

"That one." I pointed to the black crow that inspired my tattoo. "And that one." The next was bubbled, multicolored letters that read *Dead End*.

"Dead end? What does that mean?"

I grabbed a can of spray. It felt light, accessible. Something I could count on. I stared down at it, turning over her question.

"That's how I felt at that point in my life. Like I was stuck at a dead end and couldn't get out."

"And now?"

I sighed. "The same."

She scrutinized me through her lashes. "It must be hard. Feeling trapped," she whispered. In her eyes, I found something unexpected: understanding. Maybe she did get it.

"Point that here, will you?" I turned to the small piece of blank space left in the otherwise covered tunnel, swallowing the need I kept pushing away.

Light splayed against the faded gray wall, growing brighter as Tessa took a step forward.

I shook the can, letting the feel of it gloss over my limbs as it became an extension of me. I trusted the can to do my will, and I knew it was exactly what I needed to not think about Tessa and her lips.

The first hiss of paint was always the best. It filled the silence with the euphoria of what was to come, a clean slate to create a worthwhile piece. It might not last forever, but it was something only I could do.

I didn't know exactly what I was going to paint, but I needed to get the itch to do so out of me. It was a nagging that settled in my fingers, making them twitch.

The smell of the fumes puffed like a cloud of smoke, filling the tunnel. I grabbed my bag and pulled out a couple of masks.

"Here," I said, handing one to Tessa. She put it on.

I turned back to the wall and pulled on the mask, breathing in the heat. Most of the time I didn't know what I was doing until it was finished. With the raven, there wasn't a significant reason I chose it; maybe I wanted something dark and eerie. When I finished and saw its wings spread out and ready to take flight, I knew I had to do more with it. That's when the idea for my tattoo hit me.

Same with Dead End. When the words came out, it was the first time I faced the truth in my own life.

That was why I drew, painted, because it brought everything out of me I didn't know I had.

Tessa shuffled behind me, the light shifting along the wall. I didn't turn to see what she was doing, but the angle of the light let on that she sat down on the ground.

When I was in the zone, time wasn't a part of the equation. It ceased to exist, an idea ground into us until we believed it to be true. But time wasn't real. Not in my head, not when I painted.

The first ache lanced along my shoulder as the picture began to take a shape. I stepped back to take a closer look and smirked. Of course. I wasn't surprised by what I saw. The dying hiss of the can let me know it was time for another. I tossed the empty one aside and took off my hoodie before picking up another black.

Altogether, there were about fifteen of them. I bought a few at a time. Store clerks gave you certain looks only reserved for meth heads and junkies when you bought too many at one time.

By the time I got done, the picture branched out and came to life. Pain sweltered down my arm, to my shoulders and back. I never felt it until I stopped, when I wasn't focused on the task at hand.

"Wow." Tessa stood up, light bouncing as she walked to stand next to me. "It looks just like Beauty."

My arms hung limp by my side, the ache weighing my right side down heavier than the other. I'd brought Tessa's motorcycle to life in the tunnel. A headlight sliced across the front, a bright beacon in the otherwise midnight-black bike that shaped across the wall. I pulled my mask off and took a breath of the paint-filled air. I snuck a glance at Tessa when she remained silent.

"That was incredible." Tessa turned the light on my face, and I held my hand up to block the brightness burning my eyes.

"Point that thing somewhere else, will you?" I asked, ducking.

Tessa laughed. "Sorry, didn't mean to blind you. I just can't believe you did that." She gestured to the wall before sliding her phone out of her back pocket. "It's been over two hours," she said before snapping a picture of my work.

I rolled my shoulders back and dropped the empty can by the others. "Really? That's one of the faster ones I've made."

I massaged my shoulders to help loosen the knots that had gripped tight while I worked, hardening over the muscle.

"You're so blasé about the whole thing. You just made something so beautiful. I would be so incredibly full of myself if I was as talented as you are." She showed me the picture she'd taken, emphasizing her point.

If only she knew how many hours I'd agonized over my drawing of her, which I had yet to perfect. I thought I sucked. And no one was going to convince me otherwise. That didn't mean I didn't appreciate compliments; it meant I'd always strive for a nonexistent point of perfection.

I'd made countless murals around town. I started at eleven and hadn't stopped since. It took years to make something I was half proud of. On my side of town, you could still find my earlier messy works, the ones created by a lost little boy hoping to find a piece of himself.

The skate park was one of the easiest places to create. Cops rarely bothered to patrol the area, and when they did, there was enough cover to hide out until they were done. Which was why I had at least several of my pieces around, although a few had been painted over since. The best place I liked to paint, though, wasn't a secret I wanted to share. I kept my eyes trained on Tessa. She couldn't stop staring at the motorcycle.

"Can I ask you something?" Her voice echoed in the tunnel.

I stared at the dark wall, turning over the question. I already knew I'd say yes, but my gut told me that I might not be able to offer an answer to whatever she asked.

"Sure."

I heard her take in a breath, like she was preparing herself. "Do you think when we mess up, other people end up paying the price for us?"

My heartbeat got faster, startled by her question. It was like she could finally see me. "I used to," I answered.

"What changed?" Her question held a sense of urgency, and I hesitated because I didn't know what kind of solace she was seeking and I didn't know if I could provide it.

"Jail," I answered. "I had a lot of time to think, and I realized that sometimes bad shit happens no matter how we live our lives. I talked to enough guys in there to recognize that life isn't always fair even when you're doing the right thing."

"That's bleak."

I picked up the empty cans and started putting them back in my bag. "Maybe, but it's reality. We can't control the way people treat us, or the bad stuff that comes our way, but that doesn't mean you should give up. It means you shouldn't take anything for granted. No matter what."

Give up. Wasn't that what I was doing? Giving up by accepting my fate in the crew? Letting X and Vance dictate my life? I wanted to rip off the shackles around my wrists, keeping me tethered to a life I didn't fit into anymore. But I couldn't. Not yet. Maybe not ever. Maybe I was giving up.

Tessa dropped her arms, and I felt her stare on my back. I resisted turning around and returning it, instead choosing to focus on the cleanup. *Danger*, screamed a voice in the back of my head. If I gave in and looked at her, I wasn't sure where it would lead. If I ignored the way my heart started picking up, then I could pretend like it didn't mean anything.

"Thanks," she said, her voice fading into the dark.

I stood up and noticed how close we were standing to each other. Shoulder to shoulder, we both hesitated.

"You're welcome."

I didn't know if my answer helped her at all. In fact, she seemed more agitated than earlier, like she was working up the courage to speak. I found myself reaching out a hand and wrapping it around hers. It was exactly like I thought it would be. The shock of it nearly made me jump back. Instead I squeezed, feeling the softness of her skin.

Tessa turned her body to mine. The edge I skirted narrowed. One more minuscule move and I'd be over the cliff.

I remained tense, hoping not to fall over. I wanted to kiss her, touch her lips, feel the pulse beating on her neck. She tipped her head up, and we were breathing each other's air. She closed her eyes as I inched forward.

I wanted to close the gap. Really wanted it, wanted Tessa. Instead, I stepped away and let go of her hand.

Before I could stop myself, my hand was on her cheek, my thumb brushing her skin. Her bun had come loose, and a tendril of hair fell across her eyes. I swept it back and pulled my hand away. I needed to stop touching her.

Her eyes flew open. "Are we really going to do this?" she asked, her stare unflinching.

"What?"

"Bad boy from the wrong side of the tracks and the lawyer's daughter? Sort of cliché, don't you think?" Her words were rough.

"We're from the same side."

"What?"

"Technically, we're from the same side of the tracks."

She crossed her arms and leaned back, one leg forward, one back, a stance that meant business. "You may be right. That doesn't explain why you didn't kiss me." And there it was. I pulled at my ear. "Seriously. I gave you all the signals. You had an open invitation."

"And what makes you think I'm interested?" I stepped away from her.

"You tucked my hair behind my ear. In every single romance novel I've ever read, a guy always pulls that lame-ass move when he's interested in a girl."

"Romance novels, huh? Are they the kind with half-naked dudes and women with flowing hair?"

"I—I don't read those."

Her hand on one hip while the other fiddled with her falling-apart bun, she looked vulnerable without that shield she liked to carry all the time.

"If you like me, you should ask me out already," she said. Yup, definitely confident. Maybe it was me who felt her effects brushing against my skin even with the dark space between us.

"I thought you said it was cliché." My skin prickled.

"Clichés exist for a reason. Because they're fun."

"Look, if you're one of those girls desperate for Daddy's attention so she dates the bad boy, then you have the wrong guy. I'm not interested." Her eyes shut down. Not closed, but the spark blew out. "It's not that you're not attractive. You're hot. I mean, I can't—Hopper would kill me."

She held up her hand. "Okay, stop. I get it. A lot of guys are afraid of the big bad wolf-dad at home."

"I'm not afraid of him." I respected him. I couldn't say that out loud. It tasted strange on my tongue because there were very few people in the world I respected. And one of them being the guy who put you away was disconcerting.

"Prove it," she challenged.

I let out a breath. "I have nothing to prove."

"You say that, but I think you do."

I narrowed my eyes at her. "And you know me so well?"

"The guy who shows up at my dad's garage after vandalizing it has something to prove. Most definitely."

I wondered if I had the guts to do what it took to make myself believe I was the guy she thought I was.

"How do I? Prove it?" I asked because I had to find the answer.

The half smile on the side of Tessa's mouth slipped off. "You really want to?"

I paused at her question. Did I? Yes. I wanted her to look at me like the way she had earlier. Like she wasn't seeing through me. I wanted to show that I was more than who people thought I was.

I looked back down the path we'd taken earlier from Prospect. It would be easy to ride away right now. Not answer her question. Not think about anything that happened tonight. But I couldn't make myself move. I didn't want to run away.

"Yes, I do." Her brows shot up. "What do I have to do?"

She opened her mouth but then closed it. "Oh. Well. Um." She fumbled with her words. "You're just full of surprises, aren't you?" she said with a huff, shaking her head.

Her expression left me marked. I couldn't tell if she was angry or not. What kind of surprises did she mean? Good or bad? "What can I do to make you stop staring at me like that?" I pointed to her face.

"How am I looking at you?"

"Like you can't decide if you want to hit me or not."

She let out a slow breath. "You mean it? You really want to prove yourself?" I nodded. She bit down on her lip. "Then come help me at the vet clinic I work at."

"Why there?"

She lifted a shoulder. "We could always use more volunteers. And because animals are very good at picking up on people's BS, and I want to see how they react to you."

"Jiminy likes me," I pointed out.

She rolled her eyes. "He likes everyone. He's a terrible guard dog. Are you in or not?"

"I'm in."

"Then I guess I'll talk to you soon." She took a step back toward Prospect. "By the way." She turned enough so that her breath brushed my cheek. "Thanks for letting me watch; it was amazing." The warmth of her lips made contact with my cheek. Before I could register the kiss, she was gone.

I stared after her. Why the hell hadn't I kissed her? My heart pounded a rhythm in my skull thinking about the next time I'd see her. I was doing exactly what I'd set out not to do, getting pulled in by Tessa Hopper. I stood no chance.

TESSA

Beauty and I drove along the streets over to Alex's family's restaurant. Paige, Alex, and I had spent the day in Peyson doing some shopping. Alex and I both needed to stock up for dorm rooms. Paige would grab her supplies in Colorado once she flew out for orientation in a couple of months. The thought of her leaving and being so far away held fast, and I couldn't shake away the sadness.

After our little shopping spree, we went and watched a couple of motorcycle races. The wind lashed out at me while I zoomed down the road, thinking about racing. How free I felt. How my body felt anything and everything flying down the road. I fought the nostalgia and remembered the night of my last race.

I sped up.

The highway remained empty, the only sound the engine I revved. Paige and Alex opted to drive home in Alex's car. It was nice. I needed the quiet. My thoughts felt like they were filled with cotton, fuzzy and stuffed. Being on Beauty helped to untangle all my messy emotions. My heart only raced at the beginning of a ride, when I was busy getting used to the movement of Black Beauty, of maneuvering her around the streets. Then it was all smooth sailing.

By the time I pulled up to the restaurant, Alex and Paige had already arrived, and it was getting late. I parked my bike and noticed that the white van that had driven behind me most of the way into town also pulled into the restaurant. I took off my helmet and glanced at the other vehicles in the lot. Alex's Honda, a blue hatchback, a white truck.

But one caught my attention right away. Tucked at the farthest corner of the lot, like it was trying to hide itself in the shadows, was the car I had seen with Jared the other night.

I stared at the white exterior with rusted parts, the dark making it difficult to decipher the bodies occupying the inside. You wouldn't even notice it if you weren't looking. My skin prickled with the sensation of watchfulness, like invisible eyes staring at me. The hairs on my arms rose, and I darted my eyes away from the car. Hopping off the bike, I hurried into the restaurant without a backward glance.

My heart had jumped into my throat, and with every step it settled back down, the racing beat in my veins regaining control. Despite the logical part of my brain working out a pretty likely story for the car, I couldn't get rid of that sense of dread in the pit of my belly.

"Kung pao chicken?" Paige asked when I approached the booth where she and Alex had taken a seat.

"You know me so well." I kept a hint of a laugh in my voice. I took off my riding jacket and placed it on the seat by the wall along with my helmet.

Paige scrutinized the menu, a little line forming between her brows, like she wasn't going to order the exact same thing she always did. As I slid into the booth, Alex and I exchanged a look. We both ordered the same thing every time we ate here. Alex, the sesame chicken, me, the kung pao chicken. Paige always liked to pretend she wasn't going to order her favorite, the beef and broccoli, and usually stared at the menu for a good fifteen minutes before choosing it.

"Ugh, that guy's here again," Alex mumbled, his eyes trained on a man sitting by the front entrance waiting for his order. The guy from the van. He wore a uniform and a hat.

"Who is he?" I asked, hoping the change in topic would finally put to rest the fear making my stomach queasy.

Alex shrugged. "Not sure, but he always comes in right before closing and orders a feast. Never says anything to anyone and sits and stares at the wall until the food's ready. I don't know . . . he gives me a weird vibe."

I gave the guy a once-over again but didn't find anything particularly creepy or off-putting about him.

"Oh my gosh, look at that, isn't that so sad?" Paige pointed to the television behind our booth playing the local news.

"The body of nineteen-year-old Jaimie Camden was pulled from Branson Lake earlier this morning," reported the newscaster.

The screen switched to the view of the police cars and coroner's van sitting by the lake.

"It is believed that his death was the result of a dispute between rival gangs. Camden was found with tattoos depicting his own gang affiliation."

I turned away from the screen and stared at the table. My body heated at the thought of that being Corey someday. He was in a gang. It could easily be his future. How could he live like that? With that hanging over his head? I didn't know if I would ever be able to function if I were in his situation.

Danger surrounded him, and I had invited him into our home. I was crazy, stupid, reckless. Then I thought about what we shared in that tunnel, and I couldn't find it in my heart to muster the anger and hate needed to push him away.

The memory of Corey's warm cheek lingering against my lips invaded my thoughts. I had kissed plenty of boys on the lips before, but the innocence of the action, and that I was the one who initiated it, caused goose bumps of pleasure to burst onto my skin. A little trill of excitement danced in my chest cavity.

"I think I'm going to get the beef and broccoli," Paige announced, the news story an afterthought. Alex stood up to put our orders in.

It hit me then how easy it was for people to move on when horrible things happened to other people. If it didn't directly affect their lives, it was easy to pretend like it could never happen to them. Was it selfish when they did that? Maybe, but it was also a survival instinct. I had done it on more than one occasion.

Pushing Corey away, getting him out of my life as quickly as possible, would be what most people would encourage me to do. Out of sight, out of mind. And yet I knew what it was like to be the one forgotten. After my mom left, people moved on. Then with my dad's heart attack, my phone flooded with messages, but that lasted all of one week.

I didn't want to be one of those people. I didn't want to take the easy way out.

A few minutes later, Alex arrived with our dishes. "That poor guy." Alex shook his head, scooting back into his seat. "I can't believe stuff like that happens around here."

Paige dished up her food, leaned back against her seat, and took a quick bite before turning her attention to me, a little lift to her brow.

"I don't know; why don't we ask Tessa since she's an expert in that department now. She seems to have a soft spot for criminals."

I narrowed my eyes and put down my fork. "Excuse you." I tried not to lock my jaw.

"How did it go the other day?" Paige asked, taking a bite of broccoli. She knew I had watched Corey by myself.

"I can't get a good read on him," I lied. She had no idea we shared a moment at the skate park. I didn't want to imagine the freak-out that awaited me if she ever did.

"Because he's playing you." Paige pointed her fork at me.

"He's not playing me. Give me some credit here." I honestly didn't think Corey had some master plan up his sleeve. I bit my lip, thinking about the other night. The way his hand brushed against my cheek. My heart stuttered and my body heated.

"Why are you smiling like that? Oh my gosh, do you like him?" Paige's incredulous tone gave me pause.

Did I like him? I didn't know. He definitely interested me.

Paige opened her mouth, probably to tell me how stupid I was being, but Alex covered her mouth with his hand. He gave her a glare, and she shut her mouth.

"What kinds of things is this guy into?"

"Besides selling drugs and burglarizing homes?" Paige bit out.

I took my straw out of its cup and threw it at her. She shrieked and covered her face with her hands.

"He paints. And is very talented, might I add." I glared at Paige.

She ignored me and went back to eating.

"What about biking?" Alex asked. Poor guy desperately wanted another male in our little trio. He'd tried for years to introduce us to new guys who might fit with us, but it never worked out.

I laughed. "Yeah. He's into biking." Alex's eyes brightened. "In fact, I have yet to see him without his adorable ten speeder."

Alex's shoulders slackened, and I felt a little bad for teasing him.

"Maybe he needs try it out first?" Alex said, hopeful.

I almost scoffed at the suggestion, but an idea formed in my head.

"That's actually not a bad idea, Alex."

Alex and Paige started coordinating their work schedules to plan out a date night, and I started making a plan, too. One that involved me, Corey, and my bike.

COREY

Drew sat on the couch in my living room. The apartment was quiet, his sniffles filling it in places. I sat in the chair next to him, hands clasped in front of me.

Jaimie was dead. I was still trying to make sense of it.

I called Drew right after the news broke, asked him to come over. I didn't know what else to do. I figured he needed to get out of the house. A break from the hefty emotions. After my dad died, it felt like our lives were covered in darkness and all I wanted was to escape it. Being home was difficult, choking and repressive, so I found excuses to leave. Dragging Tim from one adventure to the next, trying to avoid the bleak texture that started to consume us.

"Is there anything I can do?" I asked. "Does your family need any money for the funeral?"

Drew shook his head. "They started one of those online donation things. Thanks for the offer."

A few more minutes of silence. "I don't know what to say, Drew. I'm sorry. I know that's not enough." It never would be.

Death was almost a given when it came to the job. Sometimes we forgot that and then something like this happened—Drew losing his cousin—and it started to eat away at you.

Drew shook his head. "I don't know what's going on anymore, man. With Vance. With X."

"What happened?"

"I told Jaimie about what we saw at the warehouse. I said that Vance might be responsible but didn't have hard enough evidence and to keep his mouth shut about it. Except he didn't. He went to Vance and accused him of stealing from X. Shit, Corey. I'm sorry."

I tensed but kept quiet. Damn Jaimie. It confirmed my theory about Vance. If only it hadn't cost Jaimie his life.

Drew shook his head, tears dripping down his nose. He wiped them away with the back of his arm. "He didn't deserve to go out like that. He deserved more dignity."

My stomach knotted. "How did it happen?"

"Gunshot wound to the back of the head," Drew said, his voice hollow.

Neither of us spoke for a few minutes.

"Jaimie wasn't even gone that long," Drew said. "Barely a couple of days. None of us thought anything of it. I didn't even know until after they found his body."

"Who told you he went to Vance?"

Drew rubbed his nose. "A couple of guys on the crew who saw it go down. The ones who haven't forgotten how to be loyal." He clenched his jaw, his anger rising. His leg started to shake and he rubbed his palms together before standing up.

"You should know, that girl, Hopper's daughter? I saw her the other night while I was staking those guys out at that restaurant."

My heart jumped. "Tessa?"

Drew nodded. "I don't think she's connected, looked like she was there meeting some friends, but be careful."

"Yeah, I will. I appreciate it, man." I walked him to the door. "Anything else I should know?"

Drew stood in the dimly lit hall, a shadow in the light. "I don't know if Jaimie said anything about your involvement to Vance. He probably won't come after you because he knows X has your back, but he might retaliate some other way. You thinking about talking to X about what's going on?"

"Yeah. It sounds like things with Vance are getting out of hand." There was no way in hell Vance wasn't responsible for what happened to Jaimie. I should have spoken up sooner—maybe then he would still be alive.

"Don't put yourself in the same position as Jaimie," Drew warned.

Right. The same position. The one that we all eventually had to put ourselves in because we didn't have another choice. It was an infection that spread across the neighborhood and none of us had a cure.

"Good luck, man," I said, offering him my hand.

Drew shook it before walking down the hall, a slump to his back, a weight I knew too well.

I shut the door behind him and walked back to my bedroom. My phone sat on my desk. I tapped it with my finger before making a grab for the sketch pad that sat next to it. My eyes burned as I stared down at pages filled with my failed attempts at drawing Tessa. I couldn't get her eyes. They were too hollow, devoid of emotion.

Brightness fizzled into a gray fog within the irises of her blue eyes, sad and lonely, when she talked about her mother. Hidden beneath was a Tessa I wanted to know.

I didn't have time for that, though, didn't have time to pull every single part of her that she hid behind her hard exterior.

Jaimie was dead, and I had a phone call to make. I picked up the phone and kept my fingers from shaking. Scrolling through my contacts, I found the one I needed and pressed the call button.

It rang. And rang. And rang.

X wasn't going to pick up.

I ended the call and let out a deep breath. I hated how scared I still was of him. That X had that kind of power over me. I felt like a fish caught on the line, squirming to get out while being reeled in.

For a long time, I took the bait. I allowed myself to be a part of that world. Told myself I liked it. That the money was good because it helped my family.

Now I knew I was getting hooked, and I wanted to fight back, resist the temptation of my past life. Being around Hopper and Tessa showed me another world—another way—and I was starting to think there might be a way out.

My phone buzzed in my hand, making me jump. I read the message that came through.

Meet me tonight at 11 at the back highway by the broken part of the fence.

I scrutinized the text, not recognizing the number.

Wear pants-Tessa

How did she get my number? I shook my head and pocketed my phone. Tonight. Her and me. Maybe it would be the perfect time to tell her to back off. To warn her about me and the danger I posed to her life. Yeah, that was what I would do. So then why was there a smile on my face when I texted back that I'd see her then?

TESSA

I got Corey's number from Dad, making an excuse about needing to confirm his volunteer time at the vet's office. Dad was thrilled. He thought it was an excellent idea and told me he was proud of me for thinking outside the box. He did not need to know about my ulterior motives. Or how those motives came about in the first place.

I found myself inexplicably excited about seeing Corey work with the animals at the office. I had a feeling he was going to be a natural. Even though he tended to be quiet and stay in the background, there was something gentle about Corey that I hadn't noticed until the night at the skate park. I wanted to see more of that from him.

I waited in the field, worrying that he might not come, suddenly realizing that I had only ever seen him on his bicycle and it was quite possible that he didn't have access to a car. I kicked myself for being so presumptuous, but he never texted back that he couldn't make it, so I assumed he'd found a way to get here.

He showed up fourteen minutes after eleven. Driving up in an old, gray four-door sedan, he pulled into the field, the car bouncing along the uneven ground.

"Sorry I'm late," he said, getting out of the car. "I had to wait until my mom got back from work to take the car."

"I'm sorry. You should have told me. I could have waited until tomorrow."

He shook out his pant leg where it had gotten caught around his ankle. "Not a problem. You want to tell me what we're doing out here?" He straightened and his eyes pierced mine.

I swallowed at his stare. He wore a loose-fitting, dark, sleeveless shirt, the kind guys usually wore to gyms, and jeans along with some beat-up sneakers. My eyes flitted to his bare arms and the tattoo I had spotted the other night at the park. Dark feathers sleeked across the skin of his biceps before slipping under his clothes, hiding the full view. I desperately wanted to see the whole thing.

I forced my gaze up to his, where one of his brows hitched up in anticipation of an answer.

I pointed to my motorcycle. "I'm going to teach you how to ride my bike."

Corey let out a short, uncertain laugh. "Wait, you're serious?" he asked when I crossed my arms.

I nodded.

"Why would you want me near your motorcycle? You saw what I did to your dad's car."

I walked over to my bike and knew he followed me by the sound of his steps crunching along the half-dead grass.

"Are you planning on crashing it?" I asked, turning back to him.

"Not on purpose. But I might accidently. I've never ridden one of those things." Concern flooded his eyes.

I smirked. "Don't worry. I'm an excellent teacher; you won't crash." He didn't appear convinced. "Are you scared?"

"Of getting on that death machine? Yeah, kind of. I like being alive."

I found his nervousness cute, which was problematic. I couldn't think he was cute. I pushed out a breath.

"You'll be fine. I promise. Here, let me show you how it all works. We can practice in the field before you take it on the road, if that makes you feel any better."

Corey crossed his arms and walked around the bike, assessing it. "A little. Now I'm only ninety-eight percent sure I'm going to die tonight."

"Come on, don't be such a wuss. Trust me, once you're on this thing, you're not going to want to get off it. Besides, you're the one who wanted to prove himself."

"Kissing and riding a motorcycle are on two very different scopes when it comes to dangerous activities."

"Some might disagree with you," I said, leveling a look at him.

His cheeks burned a little, and he rubbed the back of his neck. Oh my gosh, I was flirting with him. I needed to stop doing that.

"I thought I was proving myself by helping at the vet's office?" he said, switching gears to a much safer topic. Which was good for both of us.

"I know. This is just an added bonus." I smirked up at him. "It'll be fun. I can give you a ride around first so you can get a feel for it, if that makes any difference." I held out the helmet I'd brought for him.

Corey grabbed the helmet and turned it over in his hand. "Okay. Yeah. Let's do that."

I lifted my leg over Beauty and put on my own helmet while on my tiptoes. Corey did the same, the bike bouncing a little under his weight.

"I'm guessing I need to put my arms around you like we're in one of those cheesy music videos?"

I let out a laugh. "*Exactly* like that. Only you need to keep your shirt on. Or you can take it off, whatever you're more comfortable with." Again with the flirting. *Get it together, Tessa Marie*, I chastised myself. I put the keys in the ignition to distract myself.

Corey's chuckle rumbled against my back, and he wrapped his arms around my middle. I let out a short gasp of surprise and quickly coughed to cover it up.

"You okay?" Corey asked.

"I'm good." I kicked back the stand, turned the key, and pulled on the clutch before turning on the engine. Corey's grasp on me tightened.

"Promise you won't get me killed?" Corey asked, his voice near my ear. I suddenly wished I wasn't wearing the helmet so I could feel his breath near my skin. I remembered the scent of his soap when I rode on the back of his bicycle the other night, sharp and clean.

I nodded. "Promise." I lifted a foot off the ground. "Hold on tight. And follow my movements." I engaged the clutch, a burst of vibration moving up the bike, applied the throttle, and we were off.

I started out slow, not wanting to freak out Corey too much. His body tensed against mine. When I felt him relax into me, I drove out of the field onto the road, still in first gear because I didn't think he was quite ready for me to go faster. The hum of calm rose through the motorcycle and settled in me.

Corey stiffened a bit when I started picking up speed, but eased a bit after a minute. We only hit about forty miles per hour, not enough to really get my adrenaline going, but enough to give Corey an idea of what to expect, to show him that it wasn't really that scary and actually pretty awesome. I turned the bike around and drove back to the field, parking next to his car.

"How was that?" I asked after we got off the bike and took off our helmets.

Corey held an easiness around him that I'd yet to experience. His smile, wide enough to show off the dimple on his right cheek, his eyes bright and alive, his stance laid-back. It caught me off guard, and my stare lingered a little too long while I took in all of him.

"Fun. Really fun. Show me how to ride this thing." His energy bounced all around him.

I pointed out all the important parts of the bike to Corey: the foot peg, the shifter, the clutch, the throttle, and, of course, the brakes. Corey paid attention to every single detail, soaking it in. I could almost see the gears in his head working as he followed me around the bike.

"First, you need to get on and get comfortable," I instructed Corey after going over the basics.

He lifted his leg over the bike and sat down, helmet on his head. Alex let me borrow his riding gloves and jacket for Corey. The two of them were about the same size so the fit didn't end up being an issue. I tried not to be transfixed by Corey in the riding outfit. It looked so natural on him, from the tight fit of the jacket across his chest to the gloves. I found myself reaching out and trying to touch him, but I stopped myself before he noticed.

"You're in neutral right now, which is perfect." I pointed to the green light. "That's where you want to be. Pull on the clutch before you start."

Corey followed my instructions and squeezed back the clutch.

"Okay, start the bike." Corey pushed the button and Beauty burst to life, idling. "From there it's pretty simple. Move into first gear with your foot, slowly release the clutch because if you engage it too fast it'll die. It won't hurt the bike, so don't worry if that happens."

Corey did what I said and the bike started moving, his feet sliding along the ground while he got used to the feel of it.

"Engage the throttle to make it go faster. And if you start to freak out, pull on the clutch and apply the brakes, got it?"

Corey nodded.

"I think you're good to go."

Corey lifted his feet and applied the throttle, moving faster down the field. He ended up stopping after a minute the first time, stalling the bike.

"It takes a while to get used to all the gears and shifts, so expect to do that a couple more times," I explained.

Corey took a deep breath and started going again. Twenty minutes later, he looked like he knew what he was doing. I stood by and watched him start to get more comfortable, offering up encouragement.

"I think I want to try it out on the road for a smoother ride," he said.

I nodded. "Go for it." I didn't worry about it too much, because Corey was a cautious rider, and I thought he was more than ready to move on to the next phase.

Sure enough, he glided along the road in a smooth, straight line, body loosening with each mile he racked up. I clapped on the side of the road and jumped up and down like his own personal cheering section when he started to go faster. After a few minutes, he pulled up beside me and turned off the bike.

"I might have to get me one of these someday," he said with a laugh after taking off his helmet.

"Told you so," I said, smug, but unable to move my gaze from his face.

Corey's hair was mussed to the side from the helmet. He shook it out and placed the helmet on the bike seat. I crossed my arms, the two of us inches from each other, like the other night at the skate park.

I pushed my own hair away from my face when a breeze shifted between the strands, pushing it up in small tufts.

"Have you ever been to those races in Peyson?" he asked. I paused to give him time to continue and to make sure I kept my composure. "I went a couple of times back in the day, and they're pretty amazing."

"Uh. No. I haven't. Tell me about them." I ran a hand through my hair.

"There's this track on the east side of town that they use for the races. I've seen cars and motorcycles race down it. It's pretty straightforward drag racing, but the crowd can be pretty electric. And you can win some big money from it, too."

Boy, did I know. Too bad my winnings went to fixing what Jared broke.

"That sounds pretty cool. I'll have to check it out sometime." Lying made my throat close up.

"Why did you start riding?"

I hid my surprise by glancing to the side and staring at the stretch of empty highway. This I could answer. Anything to move away from talk of racing.

"My mom. She left me this note before taking off. She said that riding was the only thing that ever made her truly happy and she hoped it would bring me happiness as well."

"Does it?"

"I refused to get on it for the first year. I was really angry at her for leaving. I spent so much time taking care of her, trying to be the best daughter I could be, to make her happy. And it never worked, but she wasn't healthy. Not mentally anyway. She'd run off sometimes.

Disappear for a day or a week here or there. She was so restless." I couldn't stop the memories from colliding with the present, like a movie reel in my head. They came one after another, image after image.

Corey reached out a hand and held on to my wrist, running a thumb over my pulse. I sucked in a breath.

"What did you do when that happened?"

"You're awfully chatty tonight," I said, trying to deflect, but his eyes were serious and steadfast.

"I'm curious about the girl who saved me from wasting another year or more of my life in jail. Trying to figure out why she did what she did."

I held my breath for a beat too long, and it came out in uneven huffs. I would answer every question he asked, but not the one he truly wanted.

"I didn't really save you, Corey. It was my dad's idea. Remember?"

He shook his head. "I'm pretty sure you could have convinced your dad to toss me in jail if you really wanted him to."

"Dad used to take me to the arcade before breaking the news. It kind of became this tradition for us. Every time she had an episode or left, we went to the arcade and spent way too much money on tokens and played air hockey until our arms wore out. I haven't been in years."

"So why did you start riding?" he asked me again.

"Because she was right. It does make me feel better. Closer to her. I might be angry at her, but I can't bring myself to hate her. She still sends me postcards every now and then." They were like a flare gun going off in the dead of night, letting me know she was safe.

"Thank you," Corey said.

I frowned up at him. "For what?"

He put his hands in his pockets. "For trusting me with your bike. After everything." His voice held a smooth fluctuation of gratitude.

I bit my lip. "You're welcome."

My fingers began to tremble and I slowed my breathing, unsure of what I should do next. I stood still and waited.

Corey tentatively placed his hands on my hips, as if he were asking with his motions for my permission. I granted it and placed mine on his chest, sighing. I stared at the zipper up by his throat, afraid to look in his eyes. One of his hands slid up my side, and he cupped my neck, thumbing my fluttering pulse.

"What do you want from me, Tessa Hopper?" The question came with a yearning I felt deep in my core. I thought it was yearning. I hoped for it.

I finally dared to look into Corey's dark eyes. His hair fell over his brow, his mouth parted slightly, and I took my hand and ran a thumb over the bottom of his lip.

"A kiss. The one you never gave me the other night."

He moved my hand away from his face and held it. "Why?"

I swallowed. "Because. I do. Isn't that enough?"

He frowned down at me, and I waited with bated breath for an answer.

"Okay."

Corey lowered his face, and I raised myself up to my toes. Our lips brushed in the middle, timid at first, like we were memorizing each other's features, reading cues. Finally, I pushed myself up and crashed my mouth against his. The kiss started out reckless, both of us unable to hold back. He pulled me closer until I felt him and only him surrounding me. He was the air, the night, the ground. Everything.

His hands moved from one part of my body to another, and I

wrapped my arms around his neck, needing more. All too fast it ended and I kept my eyes closed. Corey pressed his forehead against mine, and my breathing became steady again. I opened my eyes and found Corey's trained on me.

"There's no going back, is there?" he asked.

I moved away from him. "No, there isn't."

COREY

I didn't want to go back. That night with Tessa, the way she patiently taught me how to ride her bike, the passion burning in her eyes anytime she neared it, the same one that shone through when she looked at me, sent a jolt of electricity through my body.

Sick and tired of never allowing myself one good thing, I finally gave in and kissed her like I'd wanted to since the day she saved me. But a warning bell sounded in my head and I knew it probably couldn't last, like everything else good in my life. It was an impossible dream.

"I should probably go home before my dad notices I'm gone," Tessa said, taking a reluctant step away from me.

She kept her hand on my chest and I took it in mine, giving it a good squeeze before letting it go.

"Here, don't forget your gear." I unzipped the jacket she'd borrowed from her friend and pulled off the gloves. Her eyes traveled along my movements, that burning igniting again. I liked being the one who brought it out and smiled to myself when she took the gear, moving her eyes away from mine.

She stuffed everything into a backpack and shouldered it.

"You want to go on a date?" I found myself asking, mesmerized by this unpredictable girl that made me lose sight of all the reasons why me asking her out was the dumbest thing I could do.

Her cheeks flamed red. Her mouth parted. I stared at her lips, the perfect tint of pink.

"Yeah. I'd like that." She wouldn't meet my eye.

I took her chin in my hand and tilted it up. She was so damn adorable when she was uncertain and embarrassed.

"You sure about that?" I wanted to be one hundred percent certain before moving forward.

Tessa raised herself up onto her toes and placed a soft kiss on my lips. "Yes. Definitely."

I cleared my throat. "Okay. I'll pick you up?"

She nodded. "I'll see you at the clinic." She lifted a leg over her bike and drove away into the night, the bright light of her bike guiding the way.

I stared until she was a dot in the darkness, calling to me. Walking back to my car, I continued to ignore the sirens in my head. I had no idea what I was getting myself into. But I would hate myself if I didn't at least try.

I jumped off the bicycle as I approached my destination, the dark apartment building with its cracked sidewalk, faded and chipped paint, where dirt bled along the siding. It wasn't much, but it was home. Cool air greeted me when I entered the dim apartment. Mom must have turned on the air-conditioning earlier, and Tim had yet to turn it off.

I loosened the tie around my neck and pulled off the suit coat. It was a size too small and tight around my arms. I slung it into the coat closet. I went to Jaimie's funeral, paid my respects to his family, hung out with Drew until I couldn't take the haunted look in everyone's eyes anymore. A few other guys from the crew had shown up. Vance hadn't.

I leaned my bike against the hallway wall and walked into the living room. Tim sat on the couch, holding a book in his hands. I stared at him for a minute, taking in his concentration over the words on his lap.

"Hey."

Tim glanced up briefly.

"Hungry?"

He nodded, this time keeping his eyes on the book.

A pang of pride whittled away at the host of disappointments I safeguarded inside myself. Knowing Tim wasn't anything like me, that he was better, kept me going on the worst of days. Even though dark, liquid, black paint spilled across what potential I used to hold, Tim still had a chance at something extraordinary.

"Not much for talking?" Tim refused to meet my eye. Usually he had some kind of crack about me being a loser who couldn't cook mac and cheese to save his life. When I moved closer, his hands trembled and his gaze became uneven. "What's wrong, Tim?"

His eyes shifted to the side, down the hallway.

The light from my bedroom leaked into the hall. I thought I turned it off this morning. If I hadn't, Mom would have gotten to it before she left for work. I squeezed my brother's shoulder before taking a few slow steps toward it. As soon as I entered, the stale smell of cigarettes and aftershave clogged the entrance. Vance lay across my bed, staring up at the ceiling.

My legs stopped functioning, and I stood there like a gaping idiot while he sat up. This was the first time Vance had ever entered my home. Him staying away was part of whatever messed-up silent pact we'd made years ago when I started helping him.

"I was wondering when you'd show." He cracked a sharp smile.

I loosened my grip on the doorknob. Unease prickled against my brain.

Vance wasn't necessarily that intimidating. He was only a few years older than me and a couple of inches taller, kind of on the skinny side, with tattoos lining up and down his arm. He kept his dark hair in a buzz cut and grew a goatee. His eyes were the scariest part of him: beady, washed-out brown, watching like a hawk preparing to take down an unsuspecting mouse.

"How'd you get in?"

"Little Bro was quite accommodating."

I forced myself to stay put. "Didn't see you at Jaimie's funeral."

Vance snickered. "You've been to one, you've been to them all."

I decided standing around my room, with its video-game posters and dirty laundry, wasn't doing anything for my street cred, so I walked out into the living room and kitchen.

"Tim, go to your room," I ordered when his eyes flickered over Vance and me. He didn't hesitate, grabbing his stuff and running to his room. The door slammed behind him.

"When are you working at the lawyer's house?"

I stiffened for a second before grabbing a cup out of the cupboard and walked to the sink. "Not until tomorrow. Why are you here, Vance?"

I was yanked backward before my hand could grab ahold of the faucet. Vance threw me on the ground. Sharp pain zapped up my back and the cup in my hand shattered after falling out of my grip, breaking into a thousand shards.

Vance stood over me, the smile on his face twisted and sinister. "I'm here to tell you to stay out of my business. Get up."

He stepped away and took a seat at the small table and chair Mom got a few years back from a garage sale. Having meals together was the closest thing to tradition we had. Seeing Vance sit there, where Mom usually would, blurred that image and turned it into some dark warped thing I only imagined in my nightmares.

"You've been a pain in my ass for years. Tattling to X whenever you didn't think I could handle a situation. Or when I was getting *out of control*," he said, using air quotes. "I'm sick of it. I thought maybe prison would smarten you up, but nothing's changed. You need to back off, Fowler."

"You think I wanted this any more than you? I can't say no when X asks me to do something like keep an eye on you."

It didn't used to be this way. Back when I first went to work for X, Vance and I were friends. He took me under his wing, showed me the ropes. Then a few years back, X realized that Vance needed someone to keep him out of trouble. He got out of control, using too much of his own product, stealing cars that belonged to some higher-ups in the community—including a judge—threatening and beating too many of his guys.

Things changed between us after that. He grew resentful, angry; he thought I was trying to push him out. His paranoia destroyed anything resembling a friendship we had left.

Vance leaned forward. "You answer to me. Not X. Not anymore. Things are changing, and trust me when I say you want to be on my side when it happens. Just look at what happened to Jaimie when he decided to open his big mouth. Do you understand?"

I held back a growl. Vance's threats used to mean nothing to me, but since the stunt he pulled last year I knew he wasn't bluffing. He admitted to taking out Jaimie and my fists were clenched, begging to hit him square in the jaw.

"I understand. Doesn't mean I can keep things from X."

Vance laughed. "Has he called you back recently, Fowler? X may say he needs you, but actions speak louder than words. He's leaving you behind, and I'm going to take your place. Got that?"

Vance voiced my fears. The ones that said X was trying to push me out. "Got it." I fought the nausea squirming in my stomach.

"That's not good enough. Come on. We're going for a ride." He pushed away from the table and stood up, heading down the hall.

I stared after him for a minute before forcing my legs to move. I knocked on Tim's door. He sat on his bed, still staring at the book.

"I'm going out. Be home later."

I didn't give him time to respond before leaving. I didn't want to see that look in his eyes any longer, the one that read of fear. I was pissed at myself for putting Tim in a situation like that. I needed to figure out what was going on with Vance.

I followed Vance into his car and slammed the door shut. The night had bled into the sky, stars dotting it. I checked the time. Almost ten. I had spent almost all day with Drew, and exhaustion threatened to pull me under.

My mind wandered to the other night. To Tessa. To what we had shared.

The memory of her still clung to me. Vance may haunt my life, but a girl with silken brown hair and blue eyes haunted my dreams.

Vance drove us to his place in the woods. Neither of us said a word. We got out of the car after he parked behind a dozen others. Looked like he was having a party.

The smell of melting tires waned in the air. A fire burned inside.

We entered the building and were greeted by thumping bass and a room clouded with smoke. The air reeked with the smell of stale beer, sweat, and drugs. I cracked my neck and tried to keep my shit together. I hated the smell. It was all too familiar to a past I didn't want to remember. Like cologne, the scent drudged up memories of my dad. I would have preferred cheap cologne to the drugs. At least it would have meant that my dad had bad taste in smell, not that he wasted part of his life on the hard stuff.

Flames of orange hues danced along with the people surrounding the fire in the middle of the building. Vance headed over to his usual crew members. I stood waiting. He whispered something to a few guys, a snakelike smile splitting his face when he looked back at me.

Sweat beaded on my skin and my chest got tight. Vance approached me with a few of his guys following behind.

"Let's go, Fowler."

Fear coursed through my veins, heavy and sludgelike, but I wasn't running. I never had before, wasn't going to start now.

The night managed to turn chilly in that brief amount of time. The building had been hot, humid, the kind of air that suffocated from within. Outside the air was less choking, but it still pressed against my lungs.

Junk cars and abandoned appliances filled the empty lot at the back of the building. Vance had no idea how to keep a place neat and tidy, which was the opposite of our boss. X required a level of organization from all those around him. Vance was the exception, though.

"You ready?" Vance asked, his guys circling me.

This wouldn't be my first time being beaten by the crew; it came with the territory. I didn't regret my decision. I did regret what would happen once Tessa got a look at me after. I clenched my fists by my side, misery streaming into my veins. She and I were going to end before we ever even began.

The air shifted, drops of rain falling on the ground. Perfect. The chill of the rain penetrated my shirt and slacks, leaving an anxious residue on my skin. The crew advanced and I prepared myself for the first hit.

A deafening punch hit the side of my face and I fell to the ground, hands and knees scraping against the hard dirt. I grunted when a kick met my stomach. Then another sharp jab in my ribs. I couldn't hold myself up and dropped to my side and squeezed my eyes shut. I tried to pull myself away and go to a different place. I pictured the night with Tessa. The two of us on her bike, riding away into the darkness, leaving behind a burning city full of ash and desolation. Escaping to a future I'd only ever dreamed about. The world blurred. I couldn't see straight through the hurt spiking inside of me.

By the time they were done, I barely felt anything at all. I lay on my back. Couldn't remember how I got there. At some point, my mind lost track of the hits. Vance's blurred image stood over me. He knelt down next to my ear, cigarette hanging out the side of his mouth.

"Don't cross the line with me, Fowler. You keep your mouth shut with X about my business." He took the cigarette out and blew smoke in my face, laughing. "Or your mom and little brother will pay the price. Got it?"

I couldn't answer; the pain made it hard to even breathe.

I choked on my own blood and spat out the phlegm in my mouth. "Got it," I managed to answer before blacking out.

TESSA

Thoughts of Corey raced through my head. I sat in front of the computer screen in the back of the waiting area inputting patient information for our new online database. Dr. Ford had finally decided to join the twenty-first century and do away with the paper filing system, and it was up to me and Paige to finish it up.

Paige sat up front with Linda, the forty-year-old receptionist who had worked at the office for a dozen or so years. I read and reread files, pretending like the mix of words actually made any sort of sense with my mind jumbled.

I checked the clock for the umpteenth time. Corey had another hour before it was time for his community-service day at the vet's. I ran a finger over my lips and leaned back against my chair. I hadn't seen Corey in several days. Not since the night he rode my motorcycle. Or kissed me. My lips tingled.

"Linda sent me back here to relieve you of your duties. It's my turn to sit in front of the computer in a daze," Paige said, appearing by my side.

I blinked at the screen and stared up at her. "Oh."

Paige quirked a brow. "What's up?"

I shook my head and stood up. "Nothing." I rubbed my eyes to clear the blur caused from staring at the bright screen for too long.

"Liar," she said, cocking her hip to the side. Her hair was up in an intricate braid, and she wore slacks and a button-up, our usual work attire. "You're totally worrying about that criminal headed this way."

I glared at her. "No, I'm not." Okay, I totally was, but she didn't need to know that. I made my way up to the front desk.

"I need to let Dr. Ford know about some updates on a patient. You okay up here by yourself?" Linda asked. Her blond bangs hung over her eyes and made her already heart-shaped face that much smaller. I wanted to sweep them out of the way.

"Yeah. I'm good."

"I'm curious to finally meet the ever-elusive Corey," Paige picked up as soon as Linda walked away. I held back a sigh and tapped a finger on the counter. "Maybe I'll lock him in one of the dog crates and finally question his motives."

"Paige. No. You're not even going to be here." I distracted myself by picking up a random file and scanning the words.

"Who says?"

"Dr. Ford. Your shift ends in a half hour." I pointed to the clock on the wall and dropped the file.

Paige waved a hand. "That means nothing. Dr. Ford doesn't care if I hang out a little longer. You're not getting off so easy, Tess. I want to meet this guy and see what the big deal is. He can't vandalize your home and then put his lips all over you and expect not to deal with me."

I severely regretted telling her about the kiss. I hadn't told her that Corey was the one who vandalized our home, that was all Dad. Paige had not been thrilled about that part, either. Especially when she found out it was me who came up with the idea to help Corey instead of turning him over to the police.

"Don't you have some computer filing to do?"

Paige shook her head. "Fine. But you can't avoid this forever," she said, sashaying back to the computer.

The doorbell rang, and I turned my attention back up front. My heart stopped momentarily. Or maybe it jumped into my throat. Either way, the surprise hit me square in the chest. I stumbled a little on my own feet as Jared's grandfather entered. I caught myself before falling flat on my face.

"Mr. Wilson, haven't seen you in a while." I offered him a smile.

"Good to see you, Tessa." Mr. Wilson nodded at me. His face held a warmth despite the sunglasses covering his eyes.

Mr. Wilson was the epitome of the kindly grandfather. He wore a tweed hat over his white hair, khakis, and a short-sleeved button-up. He removed his glasses and that twinkle in his familiar blue eyes sparkled.

"It's nice to see you," I said, swallowing.

Chloe, Jared's cousin, stood beside her grandfather and blushed. She kept her eyes cast downward. She and I kind of got to know each other while Jared and I dated, although he wasn't all that close to her. She was sweet, shy, and a little awkward, but mostly harmless. We barely spoke to each other at school during my senior year. I didn't know if she was aware of the reason Jared and I broke up, and I had no desire to ask.

"What brings you in this afternoon?" I asked, keeping a polite ring to my voice.

"Tweety has an appointment." Chloe held up her black-and-white Boston terrier.

"Great, let me get the paperwork ready." I needed to do something with my hands to keep myself from thinking too much about my ex and his family.

"Hey, Mr. Wilson, you work a lot with criminals—can I ask you a few questions about your experience?" Paige was suddenly by my side.

I shot her a look that clearly said *don't you dare*, but she ignored me. I gathered the papers and placed them on a clipboard before handing them over to Mr. Wilson.

Years ago, at the ripe old age of twenty, Mr. Wilson opened up a local drugstore called Wilson's. His parents had passed away and left some money to him and his sister, and he convinced her to invest it in his business scheme. It ended up paying off, and now Wilson's was a staple all across the state of Pennsylvania. Mr. Wilson had a string of other businesses and investments and was a pillar of our community.

In the last ten years, he came out less frequently and had become a bit of a recluse. He emerged every now and again for various events, but mostly kept to himself. Mr. Wilson also started a program to help rehabilitate ex-cons once they were released from prison, and he did know a thing or two about working with them.

I got to know a lot about Jared's family over the course of the two years we were together.

Two years wasted on a person who never really cared in the first place.

"Of course, what is it?" Mr. Wilson frowned.

Paige gave me a sly smile. "Do you think that it's smart to hire an ex-con for some, say, home-renovation projects fairly soon after his or her release?"

I folded my arms. It was becoming more difficult by the minute not to hurt my cousin. Chloe frowned at me and got out her phone before taking a seat in the waiting area. I really hoped she wasn't texting Jared.

Mr. Wilson gave a thoughtful nod. "Well, I think it depends on why the young man was put away and your friend's own gut instincts about him. I do think people deserve a second chance. If it were his first offense, I wouldn't think much of it, but if he has a record, then I would definitely be wary."

"I agree, Mr. Wilson."

Paige rolled her eyes. "But what if this guy has a personal vendetta against a family member of this friend?"

That was enough. "Paige, don't you have some filing to do?" I said through gritted teeth.

Paige got the hint. "See you later, Mr. Wilson."

I turned my attention back to Mr. Wilson and apologized for Paige's behavior and asked him to return the papers to me once he was done.

"Tessa, this doesn't have anything to do with Jared, does it?" Mr. Wilson asked when he handed me back the clipboard.

I paused briefly, taken aback. I glanced down at the clipboard and shook my head, trying to keep a nonchalant stance. "No. Not at all."

Mr. Wilson let out a breath. "Good. I am very sorry for Jared's behavior, by the way. It was shameful. I hope you can forgive him someday. I do miss seeing your face around the house. You were a very good influence on him."

I held back a laugh. Right. I honestly wasn't much of an influence at all. All I did was help him hide his issues or pretend like they weren't there in the first place. When he and I got together, I was in a dark place, and he kept me in the dark longer than necessary.

"It's okay. It's all in the past," I answered.

Mr. Wilson's face softened. "I'm glad to hear that." He started to turn, hand pulling away from the counter, and thought better of it, facing me again. "I was sorry to hear about what happened at your home, Tessa." I swallowed. "I'm glad both you and your father are safe."

"Thank you." I waited for him to walk away, but instead he tapped a finger on the counter.

"If Paige is referring to the events of that night, I think it's kind of you two to hire someone in need of a second chance. So many of the young men and women I come across never get that." He shook his head. "But remember to keep your guard up. It's not up to you to fix them. The choice is ultimately theirs."

"Thank you, Mr. Wilson, for your candor." I swallowed and forced my breathing to remain calm.

Was I trying to fix Corey like I tried to fix my mom and Jared? No. I didn't think so. Because the truth was, I knew I couldn't fix or save anyone. Not Mom, not Jared, and in the end not even myself. And that haunted me every day.

With a short nod, Mr. Wilson headed to the seats.

I went back to staring at the clock. Everyone kept telling me to keep my guard up around Corey. I had done a good job of it at first, but now doubts lingered. We shared a moment in that field, and I didn't regret it. That didn't mean it wasn't a good idea to keep some distance between us. Depending on how today went, I needed to finally decide what to do: Cut him out or let him in.

COREY

"You really should go to the doctor." Mom gently wrapped more tape around my broken rib.

"I can deal with a few cuts and bruises, Ma." I sucked in a breath when she touched a tender spot.

Mom's hands stilled. I stood in front of her with my shirt lifted as she sat on a dining room chair. Her face, though blank, contained glistening tears.

My gut felt like it had taken another hit. How many times had I told her things were different? How many times had I promised myself to keep her out of this world? But here we were again.

"You said you were done with them," Mom said.

Anger didn't mar her words. Instead it was the disappointment that left me squirming and feeling like a loser.

"You know that's not possible." Who was I kidding? It never would be.

Tim walked into the kitchen and wordlessly stood there watching us.

"Hey, baby boy, how's your day going?" Fake happiness filled Mom's voice, shaking. She discreetly wiped her eyes and went back to fixing me up.

"I'm heading out. Gonna go hang at Natalie's." He left without another word.

After a few more minutes of silence, Mom finally finished.

I gave her a quick hug and kiss on the cheek, but Mom only stood there still, unwilling to return the affection. I fled after that, desperate to get out of the thick air that made it harder to breathe.

Even though my whole body ached and I felt like shit, I headed to the vet's office, if nothing else to escape the misery I'd brought back with me since my return from jail. I figured it had been enough time to sort of heal. I was wrong. Pain shot straight across my torso and deep into my muscles, stabbing me from the inside while I rode my bicycle. Mom was used to fixing up the men in her life after a beatdown. She'd done the same for my dad.

Dad. I clenched my jaw at the thought of him. X's lackey. Look how well that turned out. He always told me he wanted more for us, wanted to build a better life, but he could never follow through with his dreams and ambitions. He was too high half the time, and the other half he was too busy trying to make money to keep up the habit.

There were times when he was lucid. Either on a job for X or very rarely when he was around home. I don't know how Mom put up with it. Then I thought of the flowers he'd bring her, the way he whispered poems in her ear when he didn't think we were paying attention. Or how he'd take Tim and me to the fair and try to help us with our homework. How he'd pretend to hurt himself in the exact same spot as us when we fell or hurt our heads to make us smile. Then there were those promises for a better future he made, the dreams he said we could achieve.

I had to fight the burst of anger as those memories rushed at me, because that meant at one point he had actually cared. And that was worse than not caring at all.

Dr. Ford's Animal Clinic came into view. I rode my bike to the back and parked it there. I didn't think any of the customers needed to see my face. I shot Tessa a text letting her know I was at the back door and waited for her to open it for me. The side of the building had an open, fenced-off grassy area, and I stared at the clicking sprinklers while they watered it.

The door hinges squeaked, and I pulled my hoodie up higher to hide my face. Tessa's head popped out. "Hey, you made it." She opened the door wider to let me in.

"You say that like I had a choice," I joked.

Tessa shrugged. "You kind of do. You don't have to be here, you know. But I'm glad you are."

I ignored the way my body relaxed around her.

"You talking to yourself again?" Some girl walked up behind her. She grabbed ahold of Tessa's braid and flipped it over her shoulder.

My guard immediately went up. An ingrained reaction. Never trust anyone because they hardly ever trusted me. They took one look and made up their minds. You only ever had one chance to make an impression, and mine always left people nervous.

The girl with some kind of blond, red hair took her sweet time checking me out. Her eyes narrowed, and her stance mimicked mine. I wasn't the only one with trust issues.

"You must be the help." The glimmer in her eyes led me to believe this was supposed to be an insult. But it barely grazed the armor I wore on a daily basis. She'd have to try harder.

Tessa, on the other hand, looked downright pissed and elbowed her friend.

"What happened to your face?" Tessa took a step forward.

I almost forgot about the bruises. I pulled the hoodie tighter around my head to help me disappear into oblivion. It was too hot outside for it, but the air-conditioned building made it bearable.

"Nothing. Should we get started?" Tessa maneuvered in front of me, blocking my path when I tried to step around her.

"Tess." Her friend's tone sent a warning.

"Paige, why don't you go check on some of our overnight pets?"

"Don't do anything I would," Paige whispered before walking down the hall.

I wondered why the hell Tessa did anything with me the other night. Why she'd let me kiss her.

I clenched my fists. She was nothing to me. We barely even knew each other. No matter how hard I tried to push away my growing feelings for her, they kept swinging away at me like the bat I'd used the night I ruined the Porsche. But I could handle it. After the beating I'd taken from Vance's guys, I knew my place. And it didn't belong by her side.

Tessa's hand jolted me back. She rested it on my shoulder, gently pressing her fingertips into my sweatshirt. Damn, now I wished I wasn't wearing the stupid thing.

"Corey, what happened?" she asked, quiet, insistent, worry revealing itself in her eyes.

I grabbed her hand in mine, because I needed to touch her. They were soft and made my calloused hands feel pathetic. I didn't want her to see the real me. The one who got into trouble because of the stubbornness he couldn't let go, the one controlled by his demons, but if I ever had a chance to push her away, it was now and I had to take it.

"You know, the usual bad-boy brawl you read about in romance novels."

Unsmiling, she didn't take the bait, the grooves in her forehead only deepening. "Does this have something to do with your community service?"

Her eyes were unflinching, and it unnerved me how much my cuts and bruises didn't bother her. Most people turned the other way or avoided eye contact, pretending I didn't even exist.

"Doesn't matter."

"It does to me."

"Shouldn't you show me around so your friend doesn't think I'm here to rob the place?" I slicked a hand over my hair.

"Paige is my cousin and best friend, which is why I let her get away with being an ass to you earlier. Doesn't excuse it by any means, but I don't agree with her."

"Hey, I can hear you out here!" A yell bounced down the back room. "And I'm not that much of an ass."

"Don't believe her," Tessa yelled back. "She is most definitely the assiest of asses."

"I'll take that as a compliment! My behind is fine!"

Tessa laughed, her shoulders shaking, eyes brightening. She nudged me lightly with her hand, landing right on a bruise.

I grimaced and pulled away.

"I'm so sorry. Did I hurt you?" She kept her hand on my shoulder.

Shame rose and fell, a wave of reality. How was she capable of caring for me after everything I'd done? I'd brought darkness into her home, destroyed parts of it, and she didn't hate me. Not from lack of trying on her part. Oh, Tessa definitely wanted to hate me. From our earlier interactions it couldn't be missed. But she couldn't seem to help herself, like she was physically incapable of holding on to that anger that burned in her eyes at times. Tessa Hopper was an enigma I wanted to solve.

I placed my hand over hers and pried it away from my body. "I'm fine."

She flinched at my curt answer and hurt slapped over her face, making me feel like a jackass. But I deserved to be looked at that way.

"Okay. Let's get started, then." Her voice remained cool, her shoulders straight.

I followed after her into the hall, dim fluorescent lights brightening the pale blue walls filled with pictures of animals.

The room we'd left looked like the break room, with a kitchen sink, fridge, and tables squeezing around. We walked past a few exam rooms, and around the corner sat the receptionist area. Tessa walked down to the other end of the hall, and I kept my head down so no one could see my face while we walked past the waiting room.

Barking, meowing, and maybe even a bird call grew louder. One of the exam rooms on the other side opened and a tall woman exited.

"Tessa, is this your friend?"

Tessa stopped, and I held back.

"Yes. This is Corey." She stepped aside to let me stand next to her. "Corey, this is Dr. Ford."

Dr. Ford eyed me up and down with her dark eyes, and a warm smile spread across her mouth. "Welcome, Corey. We're happy to have some extra hands to help out today."

We shook hands, and I almost let out a relieved breath. I loosened my stance and mumbled a thank-you.

Dr. Ford went back up front to check on some more of her patients, and Tessa opened the door straight ahead of us. The animal calls hit a peak.

"Wow." I took a look around. The room had been set up with large kennels for dogs and other animal crates. The floors were clean, and it smelled like a mix of air freshener and wet dog. Not the most pleasant mixture.

"Dr. Ford has an overnight service for her patients, and today you're going to take some of our visitors out to play."

Tessa grabbed a few leashes and giggled a hello to a large white dog with so much fur I couldn't see its face. It was about half her size and tried to jump up on her when she entered the kennel. I stayed behind her as she shut the door.

"This is Winston," she said, patting the dog. "He is here while his owner, Mrs. Carter, is on vacation." She clipped the leash around Winston's collar. He sat patiently while she finished.

"That doesn't look too bad," I commented when they walked out of the kennel together.

She sent me a devious smile. "Oh, that's because Winston has been to doggie school and passed with flying colors. The rest of them are not so well behaved."

"Which ones?" I eyed her nervously. The glimmer of mischief in her eyes made me think I was in trouble.

She led me to the end of the room where a pair of puppies slept together. "Corey, meet Jasper and Minx; they're brother and sister and only six months old. You will be in charge of them."

I stared at the cute tan puppies.

"What are they?"

Tessa grabbed two more leashes. "They're yellow Labs."

The two dogs had perked up as soon as we started talking and were barking up a storm. Their tails wagged, and they jumped up so their paws caught the kennel door.

"They seem sweet."

"*Seem* being the operative word," Tessa said with an ominous note. "Here, hold Winston; I'll wrangle these two for you."

I took Winston's leash and watched Jasper and Minx jump all over Tessa. She used calming tones and commands but nothing worked. It took her about ten minutes longer to get the leashes on their collars than it had with Winston, who sat watching the entire exchange with a twitching ear.

"I have no idea what I've gotten myself into, do I, buddy?"

Winston tilted his head up at me and his mouth opened and he let out a bark.

Yup, no idea.

⁓

Jasper and Minx had it in for me. It was the only explanation for their behavior. I ran around the fenced-off grassy area at the back of the building, chasing after them while they roughhoused each other, then me, then Winston. Not Tessa, though. They left her alone.

Our eyes met every now and then, and the laughter in hers nearly knocked me down. She was having a really great time at my expense. We spent thirty minutes out there while I played fetch. Or threw the ball and watched the dogs attack each other. After that, we moved on to the next dogs. That time I only had to worry about an older bulldog that would rather lie on the ground than chase after a ball.

Tessa had a way with the animals. It seemed to come to her naturally, the way she played with them, petted them, calmed them. I watched her in awe, unable to keep the direction of my gaze from finding her.

What was it? The driving force? It was a rope, a gravitational pull. Tessa was the sun and I was the Earth, rotating around her. The way she drew me in, without even trying, scared me in a way that made me want to jump off the cliff.

After we got done with the last rotation of dogs, Tessa told me to take the Pomeranian named Dessa that she had put me in charge of inside. I walked into the back room and opened up the crate for Dessa. She gave me a few happy barks before settling into the back corner where her pillow waited for her.

I locked the door and bent low. "Thanks for letting me play with you today, Dessa. You're a good girl." Dessa stood up and walked up to me, and I ruffled her hair before standing back up.

It was a good day after all. My body still hurt, but the ache hadn't bothered me at all while I played with the dogs and watched Tessa in her element.

Footsteps echoed behind me and I waited in anticipation for Tessa to enter, but it wasn't her.

"Have fun?" Paige leaned against the door.

I turned back to the dogs. "Yeah. It was good."

Silence settled and I forced myself to look at Paige. Her eyes held a familiar expression: suspicion.

"Be careful with Tessa; she's more fragile than she appears." Paige's words held an edge, but her eyes softened at the mention of her cousin.

"You don't need to give me that whole *if you hurt her I'll kill you* speech. She can handle herself."

Paige laughed and shook her head. "I appreciate your honesty. And you're right, she *can* handle herself. It doesn't mean I don't worry."

Maybe Paige and I had more in common than I thought. Paige headed back out front, leaving me to my thoughts. Worrying happened when you cared about someone. It was a part of that messy thing called emotions. I slowly realized Tessa now took a place in that picture. I hated the hurt I'd caused by pushing her away earlier. I needed to fix it, even if it was dangerous, because even if I was a royal screwup and would never be good enough for her, I wanted to try. She made me want to try.

X told me to keep my distance and I had to push her away, but whenever I did I ended up hurting her. I hurt everyone around me. But if I pushed her away, would she be any safer? I warred with my intentions.

I was used to giving up the things that I wanted, to putting myself second for the people I cared about, and this once I wanted to give in to my needs. I wanted to do something happy. Before it was too late.

TESSA

Bruises and black eyes didn't scare me. I grew up with a cop for an uncle and had witnessed plenty of fights during our back-road races. But seeing them on Corey felt wrong. Having him push me away for caring felt even worse.

"I'm finally heading out." Paige met me in the hall while I walked Sparkles back in from her exercise time. A white Chihuahua, Sparkles was tiny but had a bite to her, and her owner loved to dress her up in cute little dog outfits. Currently she wore a glittered, purple tulle skirt.

I stared down the hall to the room where Corey had taken Dessa. I couldn't see him but also couldn't help looking. I caught myself doing it more than a few times since he'd dismissed me earlier. How could I not? A hot guy playing with dogs? That was like my kryptonite. It didn't help that he was so good with them. Gentle and patient with a smile I'd never once seen before.

"So that's him," Paige said thoughtfully, jerking me back to reality.

I glanced at her and regretted it instantly when the knowing smile unfurled on her face.

"Yup." I blew out a sigh.

"Are you sure?"

I met her gaze and without blinking said, "Yes. Why?"

"Because he looks like he just walked out of a UFC fight while working part-time as Avan Jogia's twin."

"Hey, he is way better looking than Avan Jogia." I made sure to say my words quietly. I didn't want Corey to hear.

Paige gasped. "You take that back!"

I held up a hand. "Okay, I didn't think that one through."

Paige smirked, but her eyes still held that glint of worry. "I know I can't talk you out of doing something—no one can because you're stubborn as all hell—but please think this through. I don't want you to get hurt." She gave me a hug goodbye.

"I promise I will," I said before she walked out the door.

"Your cousin gone?" Corey asked when Sparkles and I walked into the room. He'd taken off his hoodie while playing outside, and without it hiding him he appeared vulnerable. I edged off the need I suddenly felt to reach over and touch his face, to comfort him. He didn't want it.

I really didn't know Corey well enough to understand why he did the things he did, and that was a problem I wanted to remedy. Badly. Possibly with some more kissing.

I turned away and put Sparkles back in her kennel.

"You hungry?" I asked.

He gave me a short nod.

"Come on." We walked down the hall and into the break room to wash our hands. After we got done, I went to the fridge and grabbed my lunch box. "Here." I handed him a sandwich I'd made for him. Just in case.

My dad once told me that if you ever upset a guy, make sure to feed him and he'd forget all about why he'd gotten pissed in the first place. I hoped the strategy worked with guys who were denying their feelings by pushing you away. I knew that was what Corey had done earlier. He couldn't fool me, though. I hadn't imagined what happened between us the other night.

Corey took the sandwich with a hint of amusement glinting in his eyes. "You're going to spoil me with all your sandwiches."

I studied him for a second. His demeanor had changed since our earlier exchange. The stiffness that clung to his body was gone. "You don't have to eat them."

He took a bite, never breaking eye contact. "But they're so good."

I tried to hold back a smile, but it was useless. I got a better look at the smudges of deep purple on his face. Mostly on his left side. His eye was still a little swollen, but for the most part it had healed. I flinched looking at it.

What other injuries had he sustained? From the way he winced earlier, there had to be several.

"I'm way better looking than Avan Jogia?"

Heat scorched my skin, rushing to cover me from head to toe. I brushed off the rising irritation and went back to feeling embarrassed. "Only slightly."

"That's not what you said." Corey took a deliberate step forward, and my heart raced faster.

He placed the sandwich on the Ziploc bag next to where I stood. I leaned back, the edge of the counter pinching at me.

"I only said that because I wanted Paige to get off my case about—" I stopped short.

"About what?" he insisted with a smug smile.

"About you." I swallowed.

His hands went on either side of the counter, caging me in. I leaned away and the counter bit back. I didn't want to distance myself from him; in fact, I wanted to close the very little space between us.

Uncrossing my arms, I found myself in a position that left me exposed in a way I didn't normally like. If it were anyone else but Corey, my heart would be beating with the rhythm of my erratic breathing, but not the way I wanted it to. Not like when a boy you were attracted to drew closer. Instead, it was in a way that made the room blur into a blob of mess and emotions.

With Corey, it was the way it was supposed to be.

His fingers brushed mine, zapping through my core. Instead of taking my hand in his, he kept brushing them. When I thought it was going to drive me crazy, he traced a finger over my hand. From my thumb to my pinkie. He took my hand, finally, and held it palm up.

"You ever heard of palm readings?" he asked. I nodded. "This is supposed to be your life line. Then there's your career line over here." His finger roamed my palm. I wasn't paying attention to any of the places he pointed. My stare remained firmly on his face, where a smile peaked the edges of his mouth and where his eyes held the full smile he refused to show. "Here's your love line."

I laughed. "There's a love line?"

He nodded. "There are lines that predict how many children you'll have. But your lines change constantly so they're not etched in permanently like people think. Every decision you make alters the course of your life."

I kept breathing, rapidly, softly. "That sounds very profound and adult."

"That's because it is." He grinned.

"You make it up yourself?"

"Nah, picked it up from some Indian kid in jail." I gave him an incredulous gaze. "I'm kidding. I can be profound and adult all on my own."

I repressed the thick expectation in my throat. Our eyes were glued to each other. I didn't want it to end. The feeling washing over my skin, tingling through my body, the anticipation for the next move. I licked my lips. His stare shifted to them. I wasn't the only one feeling the moment. Like at the skate park, it stirred all around us, and I didn't know how much longer I could hold out.

"Honestly, that's not true. My nani, my mom's mom, taught me when I was a kid."

I held back the surprise that jumped in my chest. "That's sweet."

He smirked. "Yeah. That's me. Sweet." His gaze finally moved on from my lips and he stared into my eyes. "What time should I pick you up for the date?" He dropped my hand and stepped away, amusement etching along the lines of his mouth.

I let out a breath, unable to control the uneasy rhythm of my heart. Damn him. "What?"

He shrugged. "Date? Friday night?"

"Oh. Right?"

"Sorry, should have given you another minute to stop swooning before I asked."

My face flushed. "Cocky much?" I lifted my hand to shove his shoulder but remembered his injury and quickly shifted gears and instead pinched his arm.

"Did you just pinch me?"

"I don't know what part of you is hurt, and I figured it was a safer bet than knocking your ass down, which apparently happens a lot to you."

His mouth opened, brows drew up, and hand crossed over his heart. "I'm hurt you think so little of me."

"I wouldn't if you told me what happened to you."

The smile on his face faded, and I regretted asking him the question. "If I did, would you walk away?"

I knew the answer to that. I wasn't exactly known for walking away from those I cared about; it was usually the opposite. I shook my head. "No. Tell me the truth, Corey."

"It's not something you should worry yourself about."

But I do. Lifting my hand, I skimmed the contusions on his face, feeling the small swell beneath my fingers. The skin was still soft, frail yet durable.

The surprise of my own actions stopped me short of touching his lips. That would have been really embarrassing.

"Why?" he asked.

My eyes grew big when I realized I'd spoken the words out loud. I reminded myself of those girls in romance novels who fell in love in an instant. But I wasn't in love, I was in over my head. I was in attraction. That was a partial lie, because it was more than that. A connection, a sense of knowing I couldn't describe.

Unable to form the words, I pulled back my hand instead. Corey leaned in closer, his breath on my face, slipping next to my ear as my heartbeat roared and rushed. The inhalation and exhalation skimmed against my neck. My body tensed, expecting, hoping.

"I'll pick you up at eight," he whispered before pushing away.

I flushed red, more angry than embarrassed. He smirked and left me standing there, all hot and bothered and unsatisfied.

Dad had another late night, and I couldn't sleep. Jiminy snored by my side and I gently lifted my leg over the side of the bed, trying not to wake him up. Tiptoeing out of the room, I let out a breath. I closed the door behind me and started pacing the living room, running a thumb along the bottom of my lip.

Lights lit up the front of the house, blazing through the window. Dad pulled the car up to the garage and I stood still, waiting. It was almost midnight. He had thrown himself into his work even more than usual. The thing with Corey, his gang, and the recently discovered body of that kid weighed on him.

"What are you doing up?" Dad asked when he entered. He flicked on the kitchen light and blinked a few times, adjusting to the brightness.

"Do you know what happened to Corey's face?" I asked.

Dad paused by the kitchen counter, placing his briefcase on top of it. "I believe that's called genetics, sweetie."

I crossed my arms and tapped my foot. "Dad."

He looked right at me. "No. I haven't seen him since last week." I walked into the kitchen and stood across the counter from Dad, thinking over the exchange Corey and I had earlier. "Why?" Dad asked.

My heart jumped a little at his question. The answer stood at the tip of my tongue. The need to come clean about everything. I warred with myself over it almost every day. Dad had so much on his plate right now that I didn't want to add more to it, I rationalized. I also knew that wasn't the whole truth. The fact was I didn't want him to ever look at me like I had let him down. I didn't want him to blame himself for the bad choices I had made.

It kept me up at night. Stalked me in my dreams. Tugged at my heart whenever my dad made a comment about how proud he was of me for getting my life back together after Mom left. The lies stacked up on top of one another, and sooner or later they would crash down around me.

"He was in pretty bad shape when he came into the office."

Dad leaned back and crossed his arms. "How bad is bad?"

"Like his face was covered in bruises, and he flinched every time he moved his arms too quickly."

"I should give him a call. Make sure this won't end up causing more problems here."

"I don't think it had anything to do with us," I protested.

Dad furrowed his brows. "Tessa, I don't need to remind you how dangerous it is for you to involve yourself further with Corey Fowler."

"I thought you wanted me to give him a chance? Wasn't that the whole point of not turning him over? And weren't you the one singing his praises just last week?"

"Yes. But that doesn't mean I want you dating the guy."

A nervous giggle worked up my chest. "Oh please. Like that would ever happen." I waved my hand. Play it cool, I told myself, even though I was doing exactly the opposite.

Dad glared at me. "Tessa Marie, is there anything you need to tell me?"

I shook my head. "Nope. Nothing. Except that Corey is really good with animals, so I trust him."

Dad rolled his eyes. "Of course."

I bit down on my lip, contemplating whether I should tell my dad about the date I had planned with Corey. The one I really didn't want to cancel.

"Okay, I'm going to bed." I gave him a quick hug and forced myself to walk back to my bedroom.

It wasn't time. Not yet. Who even knew if anything would come of me going on the date with Corey? Despite the words I used to justify lying to my dad again, it didn't work, and I lay awake for hours. What would happen, I wondered, if I did speak the truth and finally laid it out there for everyone? Would they all see the marks that ran across my skin, marking all my mistakes? I didn't know if I was strong enough to withstand the fallout. Corey was braver than me in pretty much every way. I was drawn to that side of him, the one willing to admit his wrongs and face the shame that followed.

I wanted that—to be brave enough to finally tell the truth.

COREY

opper asked me to come over a couple of days later, which I expected after Tessa saw me in my current condition. The bruises didn't hurt as much and were fading a bit, and my ribs were only a little sore.

I walked up the driveway. Hopper waited by his garage. The day was bright, and the sun caused a glare in my eyes that I had to blink away. I decided to leave my sweatshirt at home. There was no use trying to hide my injuries from him. I had to accept them for what they were—a part of my life.

"Corey," he said, unfolding his arms. "What happened?"

I swallowed. "My boss didn't like the way I was handling a situation."

Hopper sighed and rubbed his hands together. "Does this have anything to do with you being here?"

I shook my head. "No, sir. You don't need to worry about your or Tessa's safety."

"I don't know, Corey. I'm beginning to think this might not have been such a great idea."

I let his words sink in and didn't react, keeping my expression neutral. A lawn mower started running somewhere in the neighborhood, and it cut through the silence.

"Whatever you think is best."

Hopper walked back to his porch steps and sat down. He hung his head and I stayed put, afraid to move. I took in a breath, and it smelled humid and like hot asphalt.

"You know I can help you. If you want to get out, we'll find a way."

His offer sounded tempting. More than he knew. But I kept my mouth shut.

"You have your whole life ahead of you, Corey. You're talented and smart. Have you thought about what you would do if circumstances were different?"

I had. Plenty of times. I thought about art school, even considered applying at one point. It was a distant dream, an impossible one at that. Thinking about it too much made me want to tear out my hair so I tried to avoid it as much as possible. But lately it had started to pop back up. He didn't need to know that.

"I appreciate what you're trying to do for me, Mr. Hopper, but it's not that easy. I understand if you don't want me to come around here anymore. I can make up for my mistakes in another way." I stared down at my feet.

Hopper stood up and placed his hand on the railing, his grip tight. "No. I don't think so. I'm not going to let what happened scare me into turning my back on you." I jerked my eyes up to his. I didn't expect him to say that. "But you definitely need time to rest up. We'll start painting in a couple of weeks. Sound good?"

I swallowed even though my mouth had gotten dry. "Why are you doing this?" I asked. "Why are you still trying to help me?"

Hopper raised a brow. "Because I don't know how to give up on people. Which is both good and bad."

How willing would he be to help me if he knew I was taking his daughter out on a date? I opened my mouth to tell him. Instead the words that came out were different. "Yes, sir. That sounds great. Thank you."

Hopper nodded. "Okay, then. And, Corey, if you ever change your mind, please reach out. I know you don't think there's a way out, but you're wrong. You don't have to resign yourself to this life anymore."

I didn't know what to say to him. Instead I nodded and got back on my bike with my heart running on overdrive. A way out. The possibility of it knocked inside my head. X hadn't contacted me since our last call even though I had tried to reach out to him.

Vance wanted to kill me. What the hell was I waiting for? Could Hopper help me find a way out? I didn't know. My thoughts turned to Tessa and our date. I should have told him. I would tell him. I wanted that one date with Tessa. Then I'd tell Hopper, and he would put an end to it. Just one date. That was all I needed.

I showered and tried to find something to wear before picking up Tessa. Mom had come home earlier so the car was free tonight. I shouldn't be excited. Or nervous. Scared? Maybe.

Because of Vance, X, Drew.

The silence that echoed from X threatened to ruin my mood. Vance was right—things had changed. I had no idea where I stood in the world that used to be familiar. I pushed away those thoughts and tried to focus on tonight.

"Where are you going?" Mom asked when I grabbed for the keys hanging by the front door. She looked me up and down, hands on her hips. "Does this have to do with a girl?"

Tim's laughter filtered in from the kitchen.

"Shut up, Tim!"

A slight smile tipped along Mom's mouth. "The one from the picture?"

I lifted a shoulder. My face got hot, and I pulled at the collar of my shirt. "Maybe."

"Well, I'm happy for you. It's nice to see you get all dressed up for a date."

"I'm not dressed up." I looked down at the clothes I'd picked for the night. A dark blue T-shirt with a checkered button-up over it, the sleeves rolled up to my elbows. I had on a pair of jeans and sneakers.

Tim poked his head around the corner. "Dude, you wearing any sort of color or patterns is considered fancy. You usually dress like a homeless person. Wait, is that my shirt?" He stared at me, disbelief coating his expression.

"Yeah. Like you said, I usually dress like a homeless person. I needed something nice." I tried not to think too hard on the fact that Tim and I were now the same size.

"Okay. Just make sure to wash it using the gentle cycle and dry it on low," he said, pointing the spoon he held in his hand at me. It smelled like peanut butter. The kid was obsessed with that stuff.

I gave him a mock salute. "Yes, sir."

Mom stared at me with that raised brow that felt like she was in on some secret I wasn't.

I cleared my throat. "I'm going to be late. I should head out."

"Have a good time. I'm glad you're getting out and doing something fun." She paused and smiled. "Oh, and before I forget, I turned in the application for that position at the hospital."

"Mom, that's amazing." I walked over and squeezed her into a hug.

Tim walked into the living room carrying a cup. "What are you talking about?"

Mom stepped away from me and waved a hand. "It's nothing big. Probably a long shot. But they did ask me to come in for an interview."

Pride beamed through every pore on my body, I was sure of it. "I knew it. I knew you'd get it."

Mom folded her arms. "Don't get ahead of yourself. I don't have it yet. Anyway, you need to get going or you'll be late." Mom started shooing me to the door.

"Okay, but we're going to celebrate sometime this weekend."

Mom shook her head, smiling. "That sounds wonderful. I'll let Stan know."

I gave her another quick hug and ran down to the car, lightness spreading along my bones. For the first time in a long time, my family's future didn't hold a tint of muted grays. Things were looking up for them. And maybe they would survive if anything happened to me.

Right then I needed to shift focus, though. Onto my date.

Tessa.

Her name pinged around my head and left me wanting more. I hadn't seen her all week. Her work schedule had been busy, and I decided to take up Stan on his offer and work a couple of shifts at the auto shop. It had taken a lot to reach out to him. He told me he had forgiven me, but I was still ashamed for using him back in the day. We were working things out.

When I pulled up to the house, Tessa waited on the front porch, sitting on the steps, head bent over her phone. I honked to get her attention and parked on the street. She shot up when she saw me and skipped down the driveway to my car. I got out and slid across the hood to open her door for her.

Tessa's eyebrows shot up. "Sweet move, Corey. What other tricks do you have up your sleeve?"

Red inched up my neck and I held the door for her. "You'll see."

Her hand gripped the top of the car door, checking me out. I did the same. She wore white shorts, a pair of white sandals, and a red, loose tank top that flowed around her stomach. Tessa kept her hair down and it cascaded around her face, curled in places, the tips reaching her elbows. I resisted the urge to reach out and touch it.

"Like what you see?" she asked.

I leaned in, slow, testing her reaction. She closed her eyes and leaned in, too. I pressed my lips to hers, slow but quick, still getting used to the feel of her. We'd only done this once before.

"Yeah. Definitely."

She ducked into the car, and I got situated behind the driver's seat, fighting the nerves kicking at my stomach.

"Are you going to tell me where we're going?" she asked, foot tapping impatiently.

"It's a surprise."

Tessa made a face. "Have I told you how much I hate surprises?"

I laughed. "You'll love this one."

I reached over and fidgeted with the radio to keep my mind busy. I kept sneaking looks at Tessa and it was distracting. The night darkened into a map of stars, and streetlamps lit up the side of the road. The focus I needed escaped me when she touched my hand.

I glanced over to her and those lips were calling to me. Tessa Hopper was most definitely a siren.

"I like this song." Tessa placed her hand on top of mine to stop me on an oldies station.

Her hands went back to her lap. They were graceful, slender, soft, but more than able to take care of business.

I found the courage to reach over and grasp one of her hands in mine. She didn't turn me away, but squeezed instead. And I found myself squeezing back, daring to hope for something impossible. It'd been a long time since I'd really hoped for much of anything besides not being sent back to jail or disappointing my family. This hope was completely selfish.

The windows to the car were rolled down halfway and the wind brushed our skin, whipping Tessa's hair. A strand of hair flew across Tessa's face. She swiped it away and closed her eyes.

We drove along the back hills of Branson, riding along the edge of our designated stations in life. I tapped the wheel of the car with my thumb, drumming with the song playing on the radio.

Tap-tap tap-tap. It didn't distract me from the thoughts pulling at me from every direction imaginable. Mom, Tim, Vance, Tessa, my sorry ass. How I wasn't good enough for her. The wind picked up speed, trying to match the race of my thoughts. I tried to ignore the invisible line still laid in Branson. A darkened, taunting thing, laughing at me, reminding me of my place.

I told my brain to shut the hell up for a minute. I wanted one night to enjoy being around Tessa. To kiss her, taste her mouth, feel her hair, her skin, to give her the attention she deserved without my head taking away from the experience. This may be the last time I got the chance to just be. To not have the worries of consequences knocking at my head, a constant reminder of a past I couldn't escape.

Before those thoughts could consume all of me, we arrived at our destination. I pulled into the parking lot and Tessa's eyes widened.

"What is this?" she asked.

"You said you hadn't been to one of these in years. Thought it might be time to make a comeback."

Tessa tilted her head and let out a laugh. "This is perfect." She jumped out of the car and ran to the entrance of the arcade.

The bright lights slanted patterns along the sidewalk, and the smell of stale popcorn and weathered metal greeted us when we entered. I paid for the tokens while Tessa bounced on her toes.

"What first?" I asked.

"Definitely air hockey. Then Skee-Ball. A basketball shoot-out . . ." Tessa started planning out our night.

Relief washed over me, loosening the hold tension had strung along my muscles. I worried that it might be too much for Tessa, considering the reason she used to come here in the first place. But the way she talked about it, her memories of it, the love woven in the words she'd spoken the other night, I knew she missed it.

Tessa took the lead, and I followed her along on the journey. Air hockey was first. Tessa proceeded to kick my ass and did so again at Skee-Ball. But I got the best of her at the basketball shoot-out, restoring some of my dignity.

"It's nice to see you have *some* other skills," Tessa teased. "Painting and kissing can only get you so far."

I laughed. "I know there was an insult hidden in there somewhere but all I heard was that you think I'm a good kisser." I tugged her closer to me, her palm landing on my chest, before pressing my lips to hers. She smiled into the kiss.

"We should probably stop before I drag you out of this building to test out your other skills." Tessa pulled me down the aisle, and I couldn't wipe the stupid grin off my face.

An hour later, our tokens were all but spent while we weighed our options; the sound of laughter and pinging music from all the games trying to tempt us swarmed over every inch of the building.

Tessa stopped in front of a couple of motorcycles, screens set up in front, a digital race rounding the course over and over. She patted the seat.

"You think you're up for it?" She hitched a brow.

I straightened my shoulders and put on my best game face. "Let's do this."

Tessa pushed in the tokens, and we chose the two-player option. It took a few seconds for me to get the feel for the fake bike. Tessa had no problem adjusting to the difference and proceeded to beat me in no time.

"I'm calling it," I said, sliding my leg off the bike. "You're definitely Queen of the Arcade."

Tessa did a little curtsy. "Thank you. I reign supreme. Where's my crown?" she teased, leaning into me, grabbing ahold of my shirt and staring up at me through her lashes.

My heart stuttered beats. "Let's take our tickets up front and see if we can get you one."

Turns out they did have a crown, and we ended up using almost all our tickets for it.

"What next?" Tessa asked, placing the plastic crown covered in bling on her head.

Our hands twined together while we walked back to the car, swinging back and forth between us.

"Dinner. Then another surprise."

"I think I can handle the surprise part as long as you get me a milkshake."

She leaned against the car when we reached it, and I pressed myself against her. She smelled sweet and the scent tempted me, along with the gloss that made her lips shimmer. "As you wish," I whispered, placing a soft kiss on her lips.

"Or maybe we should skip all of it and do that for the rest of the night," she said, her eyes sparkling.

I laughed. "As tempting as that is, I think you're going to like what I have planned."

Tessa scowled. "I'm trusting you, Corey Fowler. Don't let me down."

I stiffened for a second and swallowed hard. "I won't."

TESSA

We rounded the corners up to Madman's Hill. I hitched a brow at my date.

"I thought we weren't going to take my suggestion and make out all night."

Corey laughed. "It's not what you think."

Or maybe it would be. Everyone in town knew Madman's was the ultimate make-out spot. Although I didn't know if I wanted to kiss Corey after we'd grabbed some burgers from The Onion. Unzipping my purse, I fished out a couple of pieces of gum and handed one to Corey.

He took it and popped it in his mouth.

"You're really not doing a good job of convincing me that we aren't about to kiss until we're both dizzy."

Corey's thumbs tapped the wheel of the car. "Were you testing me with the gum?"

I shrugged. "Maybe."

"Did I fail?"

"It depends on what we end up doing here."

His skin flushed a deep red. I really liked making Corey blush. It made him appear younger, less burdened, more human. At times he appeared to carry the weight of the world on his shoulders, and perhaps he did in a way, but these moments when it was the two of us and he got shy and acted like a boy on his first date, I lived for it.

The wind from the open windows whispered in my ears as Corey slowed the car and parked on the side of the road. A view of the town hung to our right. Lights dotted the peaking rooftops and hidden shadows.

Corey pushed open his door. "Come on," he encouraged me to get out before shutting it.

His nervousness punctuated the air around us, and I wondered what he was up to. Corey moved to the trunk of the car and pulled out a blanket. I followed him back up front where he lay it on the ground. Beneath his arm he'd tucked away a pad and pen. I walked to the edge of the cliffside and stared at the view.

"I love this place." I took in a deep breath, letting in the cool summer air. I tilted my head up and stared at the stars. "There's the Big Dipper." I pointed, tracing the shape of the constellation with my finger.

"You like astronomy?" Corey asked. He gestured me over. I didn't need another invitation and joined him on the ground.

The air shifted when memories began to push at me, fighting for first place. "My mom taught me a little bit when I was a kid. She loved astronomy. She kept a telescope by the window in her room. It was one of the few things she took with her when she left."

She left the bike and took the telescope. I never understood why. I felt Corey's eyes on me while I warred with myself over my mom. I never knew where to go next when I talked about Mom. Was I supposed to pretend like it wasn't a big deal? Did I allow myself to feel the sadness squeezing at my heart? More often than not, other people decided for me by simply ignoring my words, masking their discomfort by moving on.

"You miss her," Corey said, a statement instead of a question.

I pulled my knees up against my chest. "Yes. But I don't know if I'm allowed to."

"You are."

The way he said it, like he knew exactly the way I felt, made my insides soft and I relaxed. I didn't even realize how much tension had clamped down on my bones.

"Your staring is giving me a complex." I rolled my head to the side to look at Corey. "I keep thinking I have a booger hanging from my nose."

He bent forward. "None that I can see."

"I can't believe you checked my nose." I covered my face with my hand. "That's so gross." After a second, I leaned across and kissed him. "I'm sorry for being weird about my mom," I whispered against his shoulder, the heat of my breath seeping through his shirt.

"Don't be. I'm glad you told me."

He meant it. I knew from the way he listened to my words, inching closer as I spoke, eyes trained on mine.

"Sometimes it takes me by surprise. How much I miss her. How much I hate her. How much I wonder about her. I'm pretty good at shoving it all back and compartmentalizing my emotions." I sighed. "But every now and then, all the boxes get knocked over and I forget how to put it all back together again and it makes me feel like I might break apart. Have you ever felt like that?" I asked. "Like one single moment might leave you in pieces?"

Corey nodded. "In jail, I had bad days and some really bad days. On the bad ones, I'd close my eyes and pretend like I was anywhere but there. At home, sitting on my bed while my brother played his Xbox obnoxiously loud and I tried to work on my art. Or at the beach, because I've never been there and figured it was the only way I'd ever see it. Anything to help me deal."

"And on the really bad days?"

He cracked his knuckles. "I tried not to think at all."

I let out a slow breath. "Thank you. For sharing that with me. For allowing yourself to be vulnerable."

Corey picked up a rock off the ground and threw it over the edge of the cliff. "You make it easy for me."

I trusted Corey. The thought jolted through my veins and sank low into my belly. The confession was there again. It nipped at my toes, urged me forward. Be honest with him. Take that leap. Tell him everything. The way Corey looked at me, with such trust and hope, it made me want to be more, better. It was a lot of pressure—it built and built until I finally slammed the door shut on all of it. Not yet. The coward won.

A whisper of a moment passed before I took his chin in my hand and tilted it to me, kissing the edge of his mouth. Corey deepened the kiss, and I lost my breath. He put his hand around my waist and pulled me on top of him, gently pulling me down on the ground.

I wrapped a leg around his waist, and he moved his mouth down to my neck, making me gasp. I moved my hands to his hair, running fingers through the soft strands.

With one last kiss to my neck, Corey drew away and looked down at my face. I ran a thumb over his lips. He took my hand in his and kissed my palm before getting up to retrieve the sketch pad he'd dropped next to him earlier.

I laid my head on his lap while Corey started to draw, and I stared at the way his face contorted in a reverent sort of way while he worked. I closed my eyes for a few minutes, Corey's presence calming my erratic thoughts from earlier. I didn't feel the need to talk—the silence between us said plenty, filling up spaces inside my head and mouth, keeping my tongue quiet.

"Can I look?" I sat up and pointed to the sketch pad when Corey dropped the pencil in his hand.

He turned the pad over so I could get a better angle. Clearing his throat, he straightened his shoulders and flexed his arms, and flicked his eyes around the open space, looking anywhere but at me. His fingers shook a little. I bit back a smile and resisted the urge to tell him not to worry.

I crinkled my brows, turning page after page, taking in every detail of the pictures he'd created, like I was seeing another part of his soul. I slipped back the hair gently flying around my face when the breeze picked up.

The pages of the sketch pad lifted, lapping together. I put them back in place, fingers light and careful.

"This is amazing, Corey. Really amazing." I ran a hand over the picture he'd drawn of the city. "You're amazing." My face flushed.

He placed a hand on mine, stilling my movements. "So are you."

I touched the side of his face and ran a finger along his jaw, making a detour to his nose, brows, then lips.

"I like you," I admitted, my heart hurrying its beats when I said the words out loud.

"I'm . . . sorry?" He'd stiffened when I said it, and I knew he'd taken it the wrong way.

I shook my head and pressed a kiss to his cheek. "I'm not," I whispered, "but it does make things difficult. I mean, with whatever's going on in your life and my crap, we have enough baggage to fill an entire airplane."

His eyes drank in mine. "I know. Should we stop?"

My mouth tilted up, unable to hide the smile. "Hell no."

COREY

I was a glutton for punishment. It was the only explanation for why I fell into Tessa's trap. Or maybe I followed her willingly because I needed to know what it was about her that drew me in.

My ribs and shoulders ached when I got home from a shift at Stan's. One of the conditions of his job offer was I had to start out at base level. No working on cars yet. In other words, I was a janitor of sorts for the shop until I regained his trust.

I walked into the kitchen and popped a few painkillers before dropping the bag of groceries I'd bought on the kitchen counter. The apartment, warm and dark, sat empty. The fake-vanilla-scented candles Mom used mingled in the stale air. This was what she and Tim came home to all those months I sat in jail.

The anger grew like an expanding balloon in my chest when I pictured them sitting in the dark, Mom falling asleep while watching the TV, Tim having to be the one who put a blanket over her when she finally gave in to the heavy curtain of exhaustion she carried with herself everywhere.

My phone beeped with a new text. Heart speeding up and stomach twisting because I didn't know what waited for me: orders from

Vance or a message from Tessa asking if she could see my tattoo already.

I pulled out my phone and took a couple of breaths before checking the screen.

How big is your tattoo?

Tessa. I let out a relieved laugh. Since our date, things between us had gotten more comfortable. She teased and I teased back. This was new territory for me. I'd never let myself get that close to someone before, allowed myself to put down my guard and reveal the parts of myself I didn't even know I had. I spent most of high school trying to stay alive; having friends or girlfriends were small luxuries. Taylor and I had a good thing but it never felt permanent, and we never talked about what went on in my life outside of school and my family.

The night of our date, both Tessa and I allowed ourselves to be real, and now we were bonded in a way I never expected.

The last time I had something all to myself, a normal relationship, was back in sixth grade. At twelve, I had a group of friends I hung out with. We did the usual: rode bikes around the neighborhood, hung outside of fast-food joints, played video games. It was all so normal, I thought nothing of it. Then I went to work for X, and I dropped them all. That normal became the unusual, the unimaginable.

I pushed away those memories, tried to forget at some point I had a childhood filled with lazy days sipping soda on the curb. Pulling that out of me caused pain to shoot through my bones. I closed my eyes and stared at the text from Tessa, and that melancholy dissipated.

You're never going to let this go, are you? I typed back.

If you finally showed it to me it wouldn't be such a big issue. Just let me see you shirtless already!

This time I let out a loud laugh. Tessa had gotten even bolder with her advances, not that I was complaining.

BTW Alex is throwing a party on Friday and I wondered if you wanted to come.

I frowned at her message. A party. At her friend's place. The friend that was also her cousin's boyfriend. Sounded like a bad idea. A really bad idea. So why the hell was I even contemplating going? Because I couldn't get Tessa's lips out of my head.

Instead of texting her back, I went to my bedroom and called her.

"Why, hello there." The teasing in her voice made my heart speed up.

"What kind of party?" I asked.

Tessa let out a soft laugh. "The regular kind. Why? What were you imagining?"

"So, not an orgy?"

"Excuse you, what kind of girl do you think I am? I save those for after we've had our third date."

Her laugh, the ease in her tone, helped calm me down. *No* was on the tip of my tongue. All I had to do was say it out loud.

"Nothing fancy?"

"Who said it was going to be fancy?"

"You're kidding, right? You have any idea what a girl like Paige looks like to someone like me? The girl is fancy. I bet she drives some prissy hybrid."

"I didn't know guys referred to anyone as fancy," she said after a beat. Which meant only one thing—Paige definitely drove a hybrid.

"It was better than calling your cousin a spoiled brat."

"Hey! Okay, look, it won't be fancy. It's a pool party."

I paused at that. "You think you're pretty slick, don't you?"

I could almost feel her smiling on the other end of the line. "I don't know what you mean," she said, feigning innocence. "Please? Come on, it'll be fun."

Say no, I kept thinking. End it now. Walk away. "Okay. What time you going to pick me up?"

Tessa squealed on the other end of the line, and I let out a laugh. Not yet, I thought. I couldn't say goodbye yet.

After Tessa and I ironed out the details for the party, my stomach started telling me it was time to eat. I made my way into the kitchen and finally put away the groceries I'd bought in preparation for tonight. A home-cooked meal sounded good. Mom would be home at a decent hour tonight, and I wanted to do something nice for my family.

Back in the day, when Mom didn't work all hours trying to make ends meet, she would cook up some homemade Indian food. I missed the smell of the spices in the air, the taste of the tender butter chicken and roti. Nana and Mom taught me how to cook before he passed away. I relished those memories. Of watching my grandfather's wrinkled hands work to marinade the meat, knead the dough, and wash the rice.

I placed all the ingredients I'd purchased on the counter next to the stove and scoured the cupboards for the spices Mom continued to replenish even though she rarely used them. After Mom started working, I started helping out with the cooking. Before I went to jail anyway. Everything changed after I came back. Mom looked at me differently, with sadness, but not because of me, but as if she was disappointed in herself.

Tim withdrew altogether. I used to be someone he looked up to; now I was a tolerated part of his life. Mom did everything for us. I pictured what life would be like if Dad hadn't let drugs ruin his life, if I never went to jail. Would Tessa and I have met if circumstances had been different? I pushed away the image forming in my head. The one where Tessa and I had a future, one where I wasn't burdened by my mistakes.

The smell of garam masala permeated our small apartment while I mixed the chicken in with the curry I had made, coaxing me out of my spiraling thoughts. I had already kneaded the flour for the dough for homemade roti.

"What are you doing?"

Tim stood on the edge of the linoleum and carpet separating the living room from the kitchen. His backpack hung from one of his shoulders and he slid it off, throwing it onto the couch.

"Cooking." I held up the bowl of dough.

Tim's sneakers squeaked as he walked over to me. "Smells all right."

His approval was something I hadn't even known I'd needed until he'd spoken. I did something right this once. I held back a smile and instead rolled a ball and flattened it with a rolling pin. I already had a pan heating on the burner to cook the roti. Adjusting the flame, I tossed the dough onto the pan and waited until it bubbled up before turning it over.

"You got skills, bro." Tim's eyes were wide.

"Want me to show you how?" I asked.

He shrugged, hanging back against the counter by the fridge, arms crossed over his chest like he didn't care. It was hard to get used to the confidence suddenly hanging around him. He wore new clothes, nicer jeans, a clean button-up shirt, new shoes. Suspicion pinched at my brows.

"You go shopping?" I nodded at his getup.

He looked down at his clothes. "Yeah. I had to after you stole my shirt the other day."

Little brat. "How did you pay for it?"

"I got a part-time job over at the grocery store. My friend Deke works there."

I let out a breath and relaxed. I couldn't believe I'd thought my brother was heading down the same road as me. Tim was better, smarter.

"Come here." I waved him over. "Let me teach you something." He took a step, uncertainty passing over his face before finally walking up to me. "The key is making the perfect dough—otherwise you're screwed—then wait for it to puff before turning it over."

Tim pulled out a small piece of dough and rolled it out like I had done and then flattened it into a circle using the rolling pin before putting it in the pan.

He waited for the bubble but grabbed it too hard with the tongs and it deflated.

"Well, that was an epic failure." He smirked.

"You're not going to get it right the first time, Tim. And I promise if you had, the next time you tried it wouldn't have worked. This takes practice, just like everything else. And even with practice nothing is guaranteed to be perfect. Now try one more time."

He let out a sigh and tried again. This time he was a bit more gentle while turning the roti, and it turned out fully cooked even with its malformed shape.

"See, told you."

Tim rolled his eyes. "You should be a life coach with all this crap about practice you keep going on about."

Damn, I was spending too much time with Hopper. I flicked his ear and he flinched away, trying to get to mine, but I ducked.

For the first time in a long time, it felt like we were a real family.

It used to be that way before I went away, but now it was something that felt foreign. Since I came home, everything had been in a fog, swarming the memories in the haze of regrets.

"It's been a while since we cooked together," Tim muttered, hiding his face from mine, staring at the pan with the same look he had when we went to the carnival with Dad and watched the tightrope performers—one of the few good memories we had with the man who'd made us both.

There were words on the tip of my tongue, thick, sticking to the roof of my mouth like peanut butter.

I used to think I had a brain. But after getting caught thanks to Vance and going to jail, I reevaluated the way I lived my life and found I'd trod the same path as my dad, even though I thought I'd steered clear of it. The funny thing was, that path, the one I tried to avoid, was the easiest one of all to get lost on. The road was wide and clear. The other narrow and hidden.

Even though my dad died of an overdose, it didn't mean I was better than him for staying away from the stuff. It only meant I had found a different vice to deal with my issues.

"You doing anything this Friday?" I asked. Dwelling on the past caused a lump to form in my back.

Tim snatched a look at me, surprised. "Other than Bentley? No."

I rolled my eyes and smacked the back of his head. "Don't talk about girls that way. And if you're interested, there's a party I'm going to." His eyes narrowed. "It's going to be in Langley."

"With the rich kids?" I nodded. "Who do you know around there to get an invite like that?"

"Doesn't matter. Are you interested or not?"

"In hanging out with a bunch of spoiled, prissy kids? No thanks."
He sounded like he didn't care, but the straightness of his shoulders
and the way he tapped his fingers on the table told another story.

"You afraid?"

That got him. He swerved around with narrowed eyes.

"How am I supposed to act around those people?"

I thought for a second. How were we supposed to act? I had no
clue, but I didn't really care what they thought of me. Tim, on the
other hand, cared what everyone thought of him.

"Like you belong. It's all a game, isn't it, Tim? You already play it
with the girls you bring by. It's just a different field, but the rules are
the same."

He looked at me thoughtfully. "Okay. I can do that."

Relief loosened the tight knot in my back. I hadn't known I
wanted him to go with me until that moment. I hated admitting my
brother was growing up. He could almost look me straight in the eye,
and if that wasn't enough, it was in the broadening of his shoulders
and the way he quieted whenever my work with X was mentioned.

I didn't want him caught in a world of Xs and Vances. To feel
trapped like I did. But I also didn't want him to dream about the
other life. The rich kids weren't all that better off, and maybe he'd
finally see it for himself and wouldn't get caught up in the dreams
Dad and I used to hold.

"Hey, what's this?" Mom asked, the happiness in her voice easing
my discomfort from earlier. She walked up and gave me a quick hug.
"Garam masala chicken and roti? What a nice treat, Corey."

Mom started setting the table, and Tim went over to help her.

When everything was ready, Mom sat down and I served her
dinner. "How was your day?" she asked, before taking a bite.

Tim shrugged his answer.

"Fine. Worked at Stan's today," I answered.

Mom smiled, pride beaming from her eyes. It happened every time I did anything that didn't require me working for X.

"Anything planned for the weekend?"

I considered telling her about the party, but I didn't feel like adding more confusion to her already full plate.

I shook my head. When I glanced up at her across the table, the dim lights in the kitchen outlined every detail of her aging face. Dark circles, bruises of exhaustion, hung below her eyes. The laugh lines around her mouth were etching deeper into her skin, and her frown line was only getting worse since the whole mess with Hopper took place. Who was I kidding? She'd been frowning long before then.

I reached over and squeezed her hand. "Mom, I'm sorry. I wish things were different. I wish I was better. I hate putting you through all this shit."

"Language, Corey." Her stern tone brought a smile to my face. Tim chuckled over his plate. "And you don't need to be better. You're the best I could have ever imagined, you and Tim." She reached over and squeezed Tim's hand. "I love you both. I only wish I could have given you more. I'm the mom, remember. I'm supposed to take care of you." Her voice broke and she looked down at her plate, but not before I spotted the veil of tears waiting to fall from her eyes.

"You did the best you could. You still do. And we love you for it."

"That's right, Mom," Tim said, eyes bewildered.

She brought my hands to her lips and gave them a quick squeeze and kiss. "I love you, too."

We went back to eating. This time talking about much happier things in our lives, even though the thoughts none of us said loomed over like a shadow of doubt to the truth. My dad. His shadow. His truth and lies. I wondered what he'd make of his kids and wife. Would he be proud of my record or ashamed? It didn't matter anymore. My life, the decisions I'd made, the record I had, were permanent.

That now included Tessa. I'd decided to give in to the call she sang whenever I neared her. Maybe this time, this once, the path I chose would lead to something better.

TESSA

I was going to tell Corey the truth about the accident. It was a conclusion I came to the night of our first date but took time for me to make peace with. The idea terrified me and I spent a couple of nights tossing and turning with indecision, but I knew I had to be up-front with him, like he had been with me. My stomach twisted up in knots and the memories of the past threatened to crash down on me, but I was determined to stay standing.

Corey wasn't alone when I picked him up from his place for the party. A miniature version of him hung back, hands in pockets, shoulders bunching up by his ears. He glared at me when I said hi. Tim, Corey's little brother. He had the whole "I hate the world and everything in it" vibe going for him, but the baby fat still hung on his cheeks, and the innocence in his eyes called out.

My nerves sparked along my insides and set me on edge, more so than usual, while Corey and Tim buckled up.

"You guys got your swimming trunks?" I asked as I started driving, swallowing the lump forming in my throat. I kept my breathing even and hands steady on the wheel.

Corey held up a bag. "We're ready." A hint of a smile held on his lips.

I resisted clapping gleefully and started driving instead, but it turned out I couldn't concentrate on anything other than Corey in the passenger seat, elbow leaning on the door, hand resting on his thigh. He wore fitted jeans and a blue V-neck, short-sleeved shirt that showed off the contours of his body. Super distracting.

Tim chattered in the back seat, taking care of the silence between me and Corey. Surprising given how much he first appeared to want nothing more than to go back home when he got in the car.

"Then this girl, Kate, was all up in my business, and I told her, yo, we hooked up once, it doesn't mean I'm your boyfriend. Get it through your skull. What do you think I should do, Tessa? I need a woman's perspective."

I rolled my eyes. "I don't know. I'm not fluent in jerk."

Tim had to be kidding with this stuff. He looked so sweet and innocent, and I knew half the crap coming out of his mouth was just that. Corey warned me before Tim came down from their apartment. He was a ladies' man. Or so he claimed.

"I'm not a jerk. I love girls. I want to appreciate them, just without commitment."

"Maybe you should make sure the girl you're seducing isn't interested in a serious relationship. Makes you seem more like a gentleman and less like a douche if you're up-front about it. And not in that Neanderthal 'I'm a man and I need to sow my oats' kind of way, either. Stop stringing girls along."

Corey laughed and glanced back at Tim with a shake to his head. "He won't listen, Tessa. I've been telling him the same thing. He doesn't know how to think with the brain up top when there's a pretty girl around."

"I'm not the only one hanging out with pretty girls." Tim shoved Corey's shoulder from behind.

I glanced at the rearview mirror, and Tim stared right at me. A blush wove under my skin, but it was too dark to make out in the car. Thankfully. In times like these, when my skin buzzed and my body heated with uncontrollable beats of my heart, I missed biking. The need was strong. Instead, I gripped the steering wheel and concentrated on the road.

"How do you know my big brother anyway?"

I glanced over at Corey for a moment, stopping at a stop sign.

He stared back with a smile. "Her dad is Hopper," he answered, never moving his eyes from mine, a challenge burning behind them.

"What?" Tim's surprise was drowned out by the bass thumping through the car as we approached Alex's mansion.

His house stood on the outskirts of Branson, away from the Merry Hills subdivision, where most of the kids from my school lived, and where neighbors weren't likely to call the police to file a noise complaint.

Kids were scattered along the front lawn, some in bathing suits, others fully dressed, drinks in hands. The warm night put everyone in a mellow mood. I parked across the street and stared at the smiling, drunk faces of my friends and former classmates.

Tim escaped the confines of the car, slamming the door shut. I followed his lead and got out of the car. Corey's hand went to mine and a shiver ran up my arm.

"We ready to get this thing started?" Tim asked, voice wavering.

Corey went over and patted his little brother on the shoulder. "Don't worry too much, baby brother. Remember what I said."

We started across the street, the music getting louder, pounding through the soles of my feet.

"Rich kids know how to party," Tim said, cracking a smile.

I relaxed a little. Corey, on the other hand, frowned at his little brother, a crease of worry between his brows. I wanted to run my thumb over the space and smooth it out.

"Stay out of trouble, Tim. Please."

"How much trouble can I get into? It's not like I know anybody here."

"Plenty," Corey said under his breath.

We passed the front of the house and walked around to the fence, heading into the backyard. The floodlights illuminated the yard, and the dark forest loomed over the party. A few kids waved at me, their glances filled with curiosity when they noticed Corey and Tim. Very few of them were actually in the pool, I observed.

Corey walked stiffly, his hand like a vise around mine. I pulled him up to the deck where twinkling white lights encircled the space. The sliding door stood open, and I spotted Alex and Paige hanging out at the kitchen table.

Tim followed us into the house, grabbing a can of soda sitting in one of the large coolers set around the perimeter. Paige's brow lifted a little, eyes sharpening, when she spotted us. Alex jumped up and wrapped me in a bear hug almost on immediate entrance.

"Whoa, Al, put me down." Alex complied and released me from the hug.

"You must be Corey. I'm Alex." Alex held out his hand, unable to hide his excitement.

He reminded me of a puppy, eager to make friends with anyone who would pat him on the head. Corey shook it and sent a nod to Paige.

"Yeah. Nice to meet you. This is Tim, my brother."

Tim nodded at the group around the table.

"How old are you, Tim?" Alex asked, eyes narrowed.

Tim exchanged a look with Corey before answering. "I'm sixteen."

Alex placed his hands around his mouth. "Libby! I found you a friend!"

I stood on my toes and looked around. "Libby's here? I thought you said she wasn't allowed to go to parties until you left for college?"

Alex shrugged. "I figured it would be better to let her come with me where I can monitor her instead of waiting until I was gone."

Libby, Alex's little sister, walked into the house from the back-yard. "What?" Libby asked.

"Libby, this is Tim. Tim, this is Libby. You are now each other's designated party friend. Watch out for each other, make sure you drink responsibly—"

"He doesn't drink," Corey interjected.

Tim made a face, but Alex continued on. "Just look out for each other. Got it?"

Libby eyed Tim for a few seconds. When he didn't crumple under her stare, she shrugged and said, "Okay, cool." Tim's shoulders slack-ened. "Come on, I'll introduce you to people." Libby grabbed Tim by the elbow with her free hand and pulled him outside.

Corey pointed a thumb over his shoulder at the retreating bodies of Libby and Tim. "Your sister actually listens to you?"

Alex took the seat next to Paige and grabbed her hand. "Yeah. We're cool for the most part. As long as I don't get too overprotective on her."

I adored Alex and Libby's relationship. As an only child, I found siblings fascinating. Paige and I were practically sisters, but it wasn't the same. We didn't live together or share a room or have the same upbringing.

"You'll have to teach me some tricks for my brother," Corey said, pulling out a chair and taking a seat around the table. Even though his movements made him appear at ease, his shoulders remained rigid and his eyes roamed the room like he was taking count of how many people were around us.

"Tessa said your ride went well the other night," Alex said, taking a sip from his red Solo cup. Paige leaned over and placed her head on his shoulder. "You're going to be addicted in no time."

Corey laughed. "It was pretty fun. Maybe someday I'll get myself a bike."

Alex nodded enthusiastically. "That would be awesome. Then we could go on a ride together." Eager-beaver Alex came rearing back. Corey indulged him by agreeing to go on one as soon as he got a bike.

"Yeah, that's great. You two can totally plan out this hypothetical ride later," I cut in. "But right now we need to change." I patted Corey's back.

"Wow, Tess, be a little less obvious." Paige's eyes glittered over the red cup she tipped against her mouth.

I glowered at her. "I wasn't trying to be subtle, for your information. Corey is more than aware of the fact that I want to see him half-naked."

Corey let out a bark of laughter. "Wow, okay, I see how this is going to play out."

"Dude," Alex said. "Going to let you in on a little secret right now. The Hopper girls get what they want one way or another. It's probably for the best if you go along and change before one of them resorts to more aggressive measures."

Corey pursed his lips for a moment. "I don't know. I'm curious to see what those measures are exactly. Might be fun."

I cocked my hip to the side. "Oh, really? You want me to rip all your clothes off in front of a bunch of strangers?"

Corey's eyes grew large. "Damn, Alex wasn't kidding. You're kind of scary right now, you know that?"

"I know. Now, let's get changed."

I led Corey to the changing rooms attached to the side of the house, right by the pool.

"Can I say that I think you're also kind of hot when you're scary?" Corey whispered in my ear. We walked hand in hand to the rooms.

"You are definitely allowed to say that." I gave him a quick peck on the lips.

I stepped into the changing room and stripped off my shorts and tank top. I had opted to wear my red-and-white polka-dot two-piece under my clothes. I checked myself in the mirror to make sure I looked fine. I took in a breath and released it, staring at my reflection.

"You can do it," I said out loud. "You're brave and strong." Even as I spoke the words, doubt clouded my eyes. I blinked and pushed it away, rearranging my face so it appeared more resolute than I felt on the inside. I stuffed my clothes into my bag and stepped out. Corey hadn't come out yet so I decided to walk around after dropping my bag in Alex's guest room. If nothing else, maybe it would help my nerves.

Somehow Tim had already managed to change and was in the pool with Libby when I got out there. I bypassed people, waving hi, and made my way to the shallow end of the pool.

"Corey not out yet?" Alex stepped into the water at the same time as me.

I looked back at the corner of the house where the changing rooms were located. "Apparently not."

"He better get his butt out soon. I want to see this tattoo you keep going on and on about." Paige came to my other side.

Alex did a quick lap to the deep end and back. His hair, slicked back when he popped out next to us, grew even darker and shimmered. "Same. If it's good I'm going to ask him where he got it."

"You're thinking about getting a tattoo?" I asked, running my fingers over the top of the water.

"Maybe."

I glanced at Paige to gauge her reaction. She floated in the water on her back, staring up at the darkened sky.

"As long as it's a giant heart with my name inside of it, I'm totally cool with Alex getting one," Paige said.

"I thought you wanted it to say 'Property of Paige Hopper' so girls at college would know who I belonged to." Alex shook out his hair, droplets flying in every direction, including my face. I lifted my hands to protect it.

"Who belongs to what?" Corey's voice drifted between our conversation.

Heavy ripples of water rose up my waist as Corey made his way in. I did a slow turn to where he stood behind me. One of his brows cocked high, and the side of his mouth lifted.

I moved my eyes down to his chest, skimming over the tattoo, breath catching in my throat. The crow's head cocked to one side. The feathers in flight took up the left side of his chest. And boy, was it a nice chest. His six-pack wasn't etched in like those guys on the cover of romance novels, but it was there. His swim trunks hung nicely around his waist.

"Damn," Paige said by my side.

I resisted the urge to cover her eyes.

Corey cleared his throat and moved his hands to stuff them in his pockets before he realized he didn't have any pockets. He awkwardly crossed his arms before dropping them a second later and finally settled on scratching the back of his head. Red dotted his cheeks, and my own body grew warm. His embarrassment shattered little bits of the remaining wall that surrounded him.

I had seen many parts of Corey. The hard-edged gang member, the quiet boy who gathered solitude around himself like a shield, the boy who took me on a date and allowed himself to be something other than what the world tried to force him to be, and now this, a new side. Shy, nervous, and maybe a little lost.

Corey eyed me up and down, and I felt the heat rush to my face. I glanced down at the water and ran my fingertips over it, creating miniature waves. Paige pushed her hip against mine, and I lost balance. My hands landed on Corey's chest and his went around my waist.

"Sorry." I straightened and I glanced over my shoulder and gave Paige a glare, but she only mouthed, *I love you.*

"You gotta stop finding excuses to feel me up," Corey joked.

His hands remained steady around me.

"I can't help myself," I said, regaining my train of thought. "You're just so irresistible." I trailed a finger up his chest, running an outline around the crow, and wrapped my arms around his neck.

"Had your fill?" His smiling brown eyes stared down at me, and my heart lifted higher.

"I don't think I ever will." I pulled him down and kissed him.

"I think I'm going to puke." Gagging sounds invaded our moment as Paige went into annoying-best-friend mode.

I turned around and splashed water at Paige. She dove underneath and jumped back up, spraying us.

We spent a few minutes splashing around, and then Paige talked us into a chicken fight. A crowd gathered to cheer us on. We ended up tying at 3–3 before I called it quits. Corey and I got out and grabbed a couple of towels to dry off. Paige and Alex followed us back into the house. The air-conditioning caused goose bumps to line along my flesh, and Corey wrapped his arms around me, rubbing his hands up and down to warm me up.

"Thanks." I leaned in closer, my back resting against his chest. We grabbed a couple of drinks and pizza slices that Alex had ordered. My stomach growled at me while I munched on pizza and leaned against the kitchen counter.

Corey managed to find his shirt and put it back on, much to my disappointment. Even though I was hungry, my appetite took a slight dive when I thought about the conversation I planned on having with Corey later. It wasn't time yet. I wanted to wait until things were calmer. Or so I tried to convince myself. I was afraid, and I couldn't stop imagining the worst. Corey deserved the truth from me, and that kept me from running off into the darkened woods to hide.

There were a few kids hanging around the kitchen. The party wasn't a rager by any means, maybe thirty or forty people at most, but it still felt too crowded. I wanted to sneak away with Corey and find a quiet space. I hadn't seen him all week, and I missed being able to talk to him face-to-face. We spent nights texting and even talking over the phone, but it wasn't the same when we weren't actually physically together.

Corey took a seat at the table across from Alex, pulling me along with him. I pushed away the little sting of disappointment. It was fine. We had all night to do nefarious things in dark corners.

"Where's the food?" Tim came crashing through the sliding door with Libby at his tail.

Libby dragged along a familiar face. I startled at the sight of Chloe, and my heart jumped high, taking a moment to drop back into place. I shouldn't have been surprised to see her there. Libby and Chloe had an on-again off-again thing going for a while now. But if Chloe was here, then that meant . . . I scanned the crowd for Jared.

Chloe turned red when she noticed me and ducked farther

behind Libby as if the miniature version of Alex could protect her. What was with her? I had no idea why Chloe was so afraid of me. It wasn't like we interacted much, if at all.

The air in the room stirred, tense and suffocating. The hairs on the back of my neck lifted. Jared was nearby.

I grabbed Corey's hand and pulled us up. We needed to get out of there. "We're going to go for a walk." I swallowed.

Paige frowned at whatever caught her attention over my shoulder, lips sealing in disapproval.

"Tessa." Jared's familiar sly voice broke the barrier around us.

I froze for a moment and forced myself to keep my breathing even before turning around. "What are you doing here?"

Jared narrowed his gaze on my hand around Corey's. "Chloe invited me." That explained why she looked so worried. "Hey, I'm Jared, and you are?"

Corey let go of my hand and shook my ex's. "Corey."

Jared's jaw clenched, and his eyes fixed on mine. "Can we talk?"

I shook my head. "No." I wrapped a hand around Corey's elbow and tried to escape, but Jared was faster. He blocked our path to the exit, and I knew he wasn't going to let it go until we had it out.

"This will only take a minute." Jared grabbed my upper arm and dragged me outside.

Paige and Alex stood, ready to intervene, but I put my hand up to stop them.

"I'll see you in a minute," I called to Corey over my shoulder.

Corey's face was tense and it radiated all over his body, but he didn't come after me. The night air offered little reprieve to the heat spreading along my skin, closing in too tightly. I followed Jared down the stairs and around the corner of the house, where the back lights didn't breach the area. The dark made my heart skitter inside my chest, nervous and afraid. I didn't want to be alone with Jared. Now or ever.

Jared had never hit me. Angry, he got plenty, but never physical. But there were times I did wonder if he was capable of that kind of violence. Fear ran a hand down my spine, and I fought against his grip on my arm. He let me go, and I rubbed the spot where he had held me.

"What the hell are you thinking, bringing that trash here?"

The venom in his words squeezed at my throat. I reared back from him while he practically frothed at the mouth. I clenched my hands, resisting the urge to reach out and slap him.

"Don't you dare talk about him like that." Anxiety built along the ridges of my muscles.

Jared ran his hands over his face and clasped them around the back of his neck so his elbows stuck out from his shoulders. "You're being stupid, Tessa. Bringing him here was a big mistake."

I shook my head, holding back tears. "Are you threatening me?"

Jared let out a short laugh. "I don't need to threaten you. I'm warning you. He's trouble. He just got out of jail, Tessa!"

"We've already had this discussion, Jared. Or have you forgotten? Besides, Corey paid for his mistakes, which is more than I can say for you." I leveled him a stare. Fear still huddled deep within my rib cage, but I refused to let him turn me into the girl I used to be when we were together. I wasn't that person anymore.

He scoffed at that. "You act like you're so much better than me, Tessa. But I remember how you treated your family when we were together. How you fed off the anger when we'd fight. The truth is, you're not better than me. We're the same, Tessa. You may not have done any drugs, but you definitely got high off that shit."

His words pounded in my head.

"No. That's not the same. At all. We are not the same, Jared." I stuck my finger into his chest. He flipped it away.

"Oh really? Because it definitely wasn't me who paid off a cop to stay out of jail. I may have crashed that car, but you were drinking that night and you were the one who used her connections to keep it quiet. I may not have faced the consequences of my actions, but neither have you."

My heart pounded. Jared was completely right, but I was going to come clean. Tonight, with Corey. Jared and I were not the same. I opened my mouth to tell him to leave me alone when the sound of Corey's quiet voice made my heart ricochet in my chest.

"Tessa?"

I let out a soft gasp. Corey stood behind me, in the shadows, but I saw the pained expression on his face. He'd heard everything.

"Corey," I whispered.

He took a step back when I made a move toward him.

"I think I'm going to get Tim and head out."

"Corey, no, please let me explain." Panic seized at my limbs, and I crossed the distance between us before he could turn away from me.

"Tessa!" Jared called after me.

I ignored him and grabbed Corey's hand.

"You don't owe me an explanation." Corey's words were hard and hollow. "You don't owe me anything."

I shook my head. "Yes, I do." I jumped in front of him. "Please. Just for a minute?"

The familiar peaks appeared in between his brows. I waited for a heart-wrenching moment, unable to breathe or think. He pulled his hands away from mine, and I pinched my lips together to keep from crying.

"Okay."

COREY

I went after Tessa as soon as she was out of my sight. I knew that Jared guy was a snake the second I laid eyes on him. But the way he grabbed Tessa like she was his property and not an actual human being sealed the deal—it brought back memories. Not just of my dad and how erratic and insane he got whenever he was high and my mom tried to get us away from him, but of the gang members who surrounded me.

Jared had that same gleam Vance wore, of recklessness and danger.

It only took a couple of minutes of walking around the property to find them. It took a few seconds to make sense of the conversation I overheard. When I did, I stood there with my hands starting to shake, waiting for Tessa to say it wasn't true. That Jared was lying. I never imagined that the tough-as-nails girl I'd gotten to know would use her connections to stay out of trouble.

The betrayal had stung, but when I saw the fear and pain in Tessa's eyes, I couldn't not let her explain. I clenched my fists and followed her into the thick of trees. The woods were quiet. I thought I wanted quiet, but it only made the sound of my beating heart that much louder in my ears. I took a deep breath and told myself to get it together.

The woods reminded me of Vance. Of his hideout. Of my brother and our days riding our bikes until the sun set and the hot afternoon turned into a cooler evening, back when we were kids. When Dad was alive and Mom wanted us out of that apartment for as long as possible because of the trouble he brought with him. The trouble I brought back when I went to work for X.

I would be a hypocrite to be mad at Tessa. Maybe with this I could finally cut her loose. It was my fault when it came down to it. Disappointment covered my movements, made my face hard and unreadable, forced me to keep my distance from Tessa. I didn't want to get too close because then I might forget that we couldn't keep it up anymore.

After a couple of minutes of stomping around the woods, we ended up by a stream. Tessa turned to me, her body restless while she fidgeted with her hands. I stopped myself from reaching out to comfort her.

I wanted answers from Tessa. I meant what I said—she owed me nothing. If anything, I was the one who owed her. But I couldn't stop feeling like she'd cut me open when I overheard what she'd done. Not because she wasn't allowed to screw up, but because she hadn't trusted me enough to tell me the truth. Then there was Jared. He'd called me trash.

I almost laughed at that. Guys like Jared weren't better than people like me. If you placed us side by side, you could point out all the differences between us. From his nice clothes to my ratty ones. The way our faces told our stories, from the broken bones and the bruises on mine to his clean-shaven one. People took all those points stacked against me and came to a conclusion based on appearance. But I wasn't who people thought I was, and neither was Jared.

Tessa finally stopped in front of a log placed strategically by the creek. The water trickled downstream. I forced myself to stop thinking about Jared, about his hands on Tessa. Of the fact that she used to date a guy like that.

"I'm sorry, Corey, that you found out the way you did. I should have been honest with you from the beginning, like you were."

She was wrong. I hadn't been honest with her. "What happened?"

Tessa fiddled with her hands, and I held myself still.

"I did a lot of stupid things after my mom left. I was really awful to my dad, and I acted out. I was selfish and mean. I was an adrenaline junkie, riding my bike, chasing that high, trying to forget by getting myself into dangerous situations." Tears gathered in her eyes. "But dating Jared was the worst decision I made. People warned me about him, but I didn't listen. Or maybe I didn't care. I fed off his anger—that energy, it kept me going. And he encouraged me to keep up with my adrenaline-junkie ways." She looked off into the distance.

I stared at her throat, watched her chest move when she took in a breath.

"I lied about the motorcycle races in Peyson. I used to go to them all the time. Even participated in them. I was pretty good actually. Won a lot. I loved the danger of it all. Then I got a postcard from my mom." Her voice wobbled. "All it said was 'Don't make the same mistakes I made.' I think maybe my dad somehow contacted her and told her what a mess I was, but I never asked."

She wiped at her nose. "Doesn't matter because it worked. I realized that all the things I was doing were because I never dealt with her leaving. And it wasn't healthy. It made me want to change. This was last summer, at the end of junior year. I told Jared I wanted to get my act together, stop racing and stop taking my life for granted, stop feeding my anger, and make our relationship work. In order to do that, he had to get clean. Jared told me he was on board, that he knew he could do it with my support."

I knew that story too well. My mom lived through it herself with my dad. Jared wasn't all that different from the people he referred to as trash.

"But before that could happen, he wanted me to do one more race."

"Why?" I said.

"Because he made money off me. Every time I won, so did he. I agreed. And I won, like I usually did. We split the money and said it was the end of it. Then we went to an end-of-the-school-year party to celebrate. Jared promised he'd stay sober. He even offered to be my designated driver that night in case I wanted to drink. Which I did, but not that much. I was glad my boyfriend had been so thoughtful. Jared rarely thought about anyone but himself. He never did anything out of the kindness of his heart. It was always about how it benefited him."

That sounded familiar. Vance. X. Even my father.

"I'm guessing he didn't stay clean?"

Tessa shook her head. "I believed him when he said he was good to drive. I fell asleep in the car on the way back home. We were on the road to the lake. It was late; there wasn't anyone around. He ended up crashing it into a streetlight. I woke up with my head aching, body bruised, Jared gone, and me behind the wheel."

I froze. "He moved you?"

She nodded, sniffing, wiping the tears from her eyes. "He planned on telling the police that I stole his car after we got into a fight. That's what he told me the next day. I called him as soon as I woke up, completely panicked, but he wouldn't answer. So, I called Paige because I didn't know what else to do."

"What did she do?" I already knew the answer, but I had to hear it for myself.

"She said she would get there as soon as possible to help me get cleaned up. I was disoriented and tired and a little bit tipsy still. But a police officer got to me before she did. His name was Jenkins. I tried explaining what had happened, but he told me he was going to have to arrest me. I freaked out, and Paige showed up. She knew Jenkins because of my uncle Mike, and we ended up making a deal with him."

I didn't like where this was going. My palms were sweating, and I rubbed them on my pants.

"What deal?"

"I gave him my winnings from that night to keep quiet."

I let out a breath. "Shit." Bribing a police officer was a felony. Tessa was lucky the guy didn't turn her in for it. "How much?"

"Ten grand," she whispered. "I wasn't thinking. I couldn't stand the thought of my father finding out. I wanted to clean up my life, and I couldn't do that with a police record."

I didn't say a word.

"I know how that sounds, Corey. It was a selfish decision. I should have let him arrest me. I shouldn't have done something so stupid."

"What about the car?" I asked instead.

Tessa played with the ends of her hair. "We had it towed to Jared's. I called to let him know how it all played out and told him to stay out of my life. His parents found the car and figured he had crashed it and sent him away to a private school. I hadn't seen or heard from him until after graduation."

I processed her words, thinking it all over. "You weren't guilty."

Tessa crossed her arms and kicked her foot back and forth. "No. But I drank. Don't know if you remember, but it's illegal for people under twenty-one to do that. Even if Jared had stayed and taken responsibility for his actions, I would have gotten in trouble. And I bribed a police officer. I *am* guilty."

I held back a laugh. "You probably would have gotten a slap on the wrist, at most."

"Maybe. But my dad doesn't know what happened that night. I've had to keep it a secret from him, and it's killing me."

I decided to sit down on the log. I needed to think, to work out what was happening in my head.

"I was going to tell you," she said. "Tonight, actually. I thought you deserved to hear the truth from me." She paused. "Are you mad?"

I knew she was telling the truth from the way her eyes glistened and her voice wavered. "Yeah."

"I'm so sorry, Corey." She shifted closer to me.

"Is this why you decided not to turn me in to the police?"

Tessa nodded. "I thought if I helped you, then I would be off the hook for what I had done."

I rubbed my chest and dropped my hands to my lap. This whole night was a shitstorm.

"That's not how it works."

Tessa took another step and when I didn't scoot away, she sat down next to me. "I know, but I wanted to help you because you did something that I couldn't. You confessed. Corey, please." There was an ache to her words. It killed me a little.

I nodded. "You did what you had to do. You were scared. I don't get what the big deal is. Why did Jared do that?"

Tessa shifted, placing her hands under her thighs. "Because of who his family is. His grandfather is Thomas Wilson, the owner of the drugstore chain. They're big names around here. Mr. Wilson is pretty much a recluse and hates having attention drawn to him. Jared driving while high isn't exactly something they want all over the papers."

My whole body grew stiff. I couldn't move. The night got quieter, still and threatening. Tessa said something but her voice sounded muffled, like she was trying to talk to me through a window.

"Corey?" Time finally caught up with me, and I shot up.

"I have to go." I started heading back the way we came. At least I thought it was—I turned around because all the trees looked the same, every corner too dark and a stark contrast to the high-pitched squeal blaring in my head, shouting out a warning.

"What's wrong, Corey?"

I had to get out of there. Away from Tessa. From the way my chest grew tighter and tighter, like I was holding a breath that would never release.

"I'm sorry, Tessa. But we can't do this anymore."

Tessa came after me as I tried to finally figure out where the hell I was going. I followed the glow of the house and the sounds of the kids splashing in the pool. When I got out of the woods, the lights were too bright, and I blinked to clear the blur.

Tim sat in the hot tub with Libby and a group of girls. I headed for him, but Tessa jumped in front of me.

"What's going on, Corey?"

I tried to step around her, but she kept getting in my way. "Tessa. Please."

"Corey, I am so sorry for keeping everything a secret. I'm sorry if you feel used. I never meant for things between us to get to this point. I didn't expect to fall for you."

Her words finally got me to stop. The party around us kept going.

We were still on the outskirts of the yard, and no one paid any attention to us.

Except for Tessa's ex. Jared stood on the deck, zoned in on us. I narrowed my eyes at him. Now that I knew exactly who I was dealing with, I should have been afraid. Worried even. And maybe a part of me was those things, but mostly I wanted to knock the guy's teeth out of his mouth.

"I didn't, either, Tessa." I finally looked in her eyes. They were glazed over, and I wanted to reach out, touch her cheek, comfort her. "But we can't go any further."

"Why not? Is it because of what I did? I thought . . . I thought maybe you would understand. That you might be more forgiving."

"It's not that, Tessa. I'm the last guy who will judge you for what happened."

"Then what is it?"

Taking in a breath, one after another, I unclenched my fists and took that step toward her. I ran a thumb along her chin. "That guy, Jared, stay away from him. He's dangerous. And don't ever let him treat you like that again."

I moved away from Tessa and went to get Tim. Except he wasn't in the hot tub anymore.

I sent Drew a quick text, asking him for a ride, and scanned the area for my little brother. The need to escape wound its way around my lungs, constricting, heavy. Where the hell was Tim? I stalked around the yard, ignoring the guilt kicking at my stomach every time I pictured the look of despair in Tessa's eyes when I walked away from her.

Maybe I should go back to her. Find her. Explain. Except it wouldn't change anything. It would only make it worse.

I came around the side of the yard where the front and backyard connected and stopped in my tracks, clenching my fists when Jared stomped my way. Dragging Tim behind him with one arm and Tim's bag in the other.

"What the hell are you doing?" I charged at Jared. "Let go of my brother."

"Corey!" Tessa called out, suddenly by my side. "Jared, what are you doing?"

Jared smirked, yanking Tim to his side. "You and your druggie brother need to get the hell out of here."

I lunged at Jared, gripping his collar in my hand, pulling his face to mine. "You don't know what you're talking about," I snarled. The hold I had on my emotions evaporated in an instant. The night had peeled the layers away bit by bit until a thin skin remained, one I broke through too quick.

"Corey, no." Tessa jumped to my side, trying to pry us apart. Her hand went to my chest, and I instantly released Jared.

"What the hell are you doing?" Tessa turned to her ex, her back to me, arms out front.

"Tim, we're leaving." I didn't want to wait around and hear that prick make up shit about me and Tim.

Jared straightened his clothes. "No. Not until you know the truth. I caught this little shit trying to sell." He pointed to Tim.

"You're lying. Tim wouldn't do that," I ground out.

"You can't make accusations like that just because you're jealous, Jared," Tessa piped up.

I needed to get out of there. It itched at me and got worse with the crowd of kids watching the show growing by the second.

"Seriously, Tessa? You're going to believe them? I saw him," Jared said.

"That's enough, Jared. I think you're the one who should leave." Tessa stepped back to my side, placing a hand on my arm.

Jared shook his head in disgust. "You want evidence? Here it is." Jared held up Tim's bag. "Explain this." He tossed the bag my way and it hit my chest with a hard thud. I glared at him before unzipping the bag.

My hands started shaking, and I kept breathing too fast. My stomach dropped. The bags of drugs stared back at me, and no amount of blinking made it change. I whipped my gaze to Tim.

"Tim? Is this yours?"

Tim's eyes widened and the guilt there, all too familiar, made my stomach grow heavy like a rock sank inside of it.

"Tim?"

Tim's eyes shone. "I'm sorry, Corey," he whispered.

The air grew heavy, choking me. "Please say it isn't true." I stepped closer to my brother.

He winced. "It's true."

"Corey?" The question in Tessa's words was almost too much. I'd forgotten she was there.

"Don't worry, Tessa. We're leaving."

That look of triumph on Jared's face almost undid me again. "Probably for the best. Don't want to get the cops involved."

I thought about calling his bluff. Like hell he would call the police, but I narrowed my eyes and I grabbed Tim and we made our way to the front of the house. People whispered around us, giving us a wide berth, but I refused to hunch over like a criminal. I kept my shoulders straight and didn't look back when Tim and I started walking down the road.

I kept waiting, maybe even hoping that Tessa would come after me. I was dumb enough to believe that I could start something new with her. That my past wouldn't find me. But it had and now I knew the truth: I could never have anything new. The road ahead was paved with the same regret and sorrow as the one behind me.

"Let me explain, Cor," Tim whispered, sniffling.

We walked side by side; the only other sounds in the night were the crickets singing by the side of the road. I swallowed the hard stone that was lodged in my throat. "Who was it? Who approached you?"

Tim kept his head down and his steps were heavy. "Vance. I thought I could do it, but I chickened out. Then Vance got pissed and said if I didn't sell soon I'd pay for it. This party was my last chance."

Anger roared in my ears. "Fuck," I muttered under my breath.

I should have known; I shouldn't have been surprised. I thought X would keep his word and keep my little brother out of his business. That was one of the deals we made when I went to work for him. Clenching my fists, I tried to keep from losing my lid. My arms were shaking, and pain radiated along my muscles from the tension.

This was my fault. How could I expect my brother to be better than me when I kept fucking everything up?

Headlights in the distance grew brighter, and the sight of Drew's car caused relief to wash over me. Until I remembered what I had to do next. Fix everything. All of it. Whatever I had to do to keep my family safe, I would do it. I said a silent goodbye to Tessa Hopper and got into Drew's car.

TESSA

Corey left, and I did nothing to stop him. Paige said it was for the best, and I kept my mouth shut, refusing to argue.

A few kids came up to me to tell me what they saw, to prove that Jared wasn't lying. I pushed away from the crowd and headed inside, my head pounding.

"Tessa, wait," Jared called after me, and I made myself move faster. "Tess. You saw the truth about that guy. He's scum." His hand went around my arm.

I yanked it away and twisted around to face him. "Stay away from me, Jared. I'm not interested in anything you have to say."

Jared's face flushed red and the vein on his neck popped. "You're telling me you don't think what that guy did was wrong? Are you kidding me? After all the shit you've given me about my past?"

I shook my head. "I don't know what's going on right now. But I do know Corey isn't capable of what you think he is. He's not the guy you're trying to make him. I'm over this, Jared. Over arguing with you. Stay away from me."

He shook his head in disgust. "Whatever you want. Don't come begging when you realize that I'm right."

He stormed off and I stood staring after him, trying not to laugh at his words. Like I would ever beg him for anything.

People continued to stare at me, and I knew going inside and hiding out wasn't going to change anything. I had to get away. I had to go after Corey. I got in my car and drove off in search of him and Tim, but they were nowhere to be found. Guilt coated my tongue, splashed over my skin, doused my whole body. The look of utter disbelief on Corey's face told me he'd had no idea what his brother was up to.

I didn't sleep. Instead I stared at my ceiling. Corey had changed in the woods when I told him my story. In an instant. He gave me the benefit of the doubt in the beginning, told me it wasn't my fault, and then . . . then he walked away. The recognition of regret in his eyes turned to steel and fear.

I knew lying there wouldn't make sleep arrive any easier. Instead, I kicked off my blanket and decided to do something. I deserved an explanation.

I got my keys and headed outside to Beauty. Dad slept soundly in his bedroom and I didn't want to wake him, so I pushed her down the driveway and to the end of our street before turning her on.

Calm sank into my skin as I got onto her. I didn't know where I was headed when I started riding, but that didn't matter. The growling of her engine, the wind against my body, the vibration running along my bones brought me a sense of peace. After a few minutes, I changed direction from the back highway where I usually drove and went south. Toward the darker part of town. Toward Corey.

When I pulled up next to his apartment building, I turned off the engine and texted Corey to see if I could talk to him. It was late and too soon after he left for me to expect an answer, but I didn't want to wait. I was tired of waiting, of hiding.

A few heart-pounding minutes later, he still hadn't responded. I stared up at the building, squinting at the darkened windows, the shadows stretching across the side. Which one was his, I wondered, moving my gaze from window to window. Not that it mattered. I didn't plan on knocking on his front door like a stalker. I suddenly realized I was acting like Jared, driving to Corey's and demanding he speak to me.

I picked up my helmet and decided to head home. We both needed more time for things to work out. I placed the helmet on top of my head, ready to slide it down over my face when the headlights of a car blinded my eyes. I put my helmet back down and raised an arm to block the light.

The car pulled into the parking lot, and I stared at the familiar white frame. The same car I had seen with Jared and at the restaurant.

Frowning at the idling vehicle, I tightened my hold on the helmet. The passenger-side door pushed open, and I forced myself to keep in the gasp working its way up to my lips when Corey stepped out. He slammed the door shut behind him and ducked low to the open passenger-side window to speak to the driver.

A few seconds later, he slapped the roof of the car a couple of times and it took off. He stood there, staring after the car, hands in his pockets. He'd changed into sweatpants and a plain white shirt. The dark feathers of his tattoo peeked along the top of his chest. I forced myself to stop staring and get moving. Jumping off Beauty, I headed straight for him.

He didn't see me coming. Not until I was practically in his face.

"Tessa?" Surprise etched his face. "What are you doing here?"

I swallowed and looked in the direction the car had taken. "Who was that?" I asked. The frown on Corey's face smoothed over, turning to stone. "I've seen that car before."

"You should go." There it was again, that coldness in his voice.

I shook my head. "Stop pushing me away, Corey. I saw that car with Jared, then at Alex's restaurant, and now you're getting out of it. Do you know Jared?" I tried to pull all the pieces together, but none of them fit the way they should.

"No. Never met him before tonight." The distance between us grew, the chasm a void of darkness.

I took in a shaky breath. "What aren't you telling me, Corey?"

"Tessa, it's too dangerous. I'm trying to keep you safe."

A laugh, caught between disbelief and anger, let loose. "I don't need you to protect me, Corey. And if you had, you never would have let things get this far between us."

He stiffened and pursed his lips. "Tessa." The warning in his tone pushed me on.

"Earlier, when I mentioned Jared's family, you closed off. You never met Jared before tonight but had heard of him." The pieces came together.

I knew I had him when the tight coil around his shoulders loosened. "You're not going to let this go, are you?"

I shook my head. "No. I'm not. Are you going to tell me what's really going on?"

A moment passed. Quiet crested the space between us, climbing higher. The slow nod to his head released the pressure.

"Okay. I'll tell you everything. Tomorrow."

I shook my head. "Not good enough."

Corey took in a breath through his nose. "Tessa, I have to deal with Tim right now. I have to figure some stuff out before I can tell you what you want to know. I'm sorry, but you're going to have to wait. But only a little while longer. Then I promise to tell you everything."

"Fine," I relented. I wanted to touch him, hug him goodbye, but I turned around and walked away instead.

COREY

I paced the tiny hallway in our apartment. Twenty-three steps, back and forth. I kept counting. Mom was at work. I made Tim go over to a friend's house, promising him that I would fix everything.

My hands itched for a lifeline. A concrete piece of anything to keep me tethered to the present, because all my mind wanted was to wander the past. It echoed in my head, made it loud, painful. My dad. When I went to work for X. The moments that led me to last night when the ground beneath me started shaking and collapsing.

Running a hand over my face, I tried to wake myself up. It didn't work. I wasn't dreaming.

Tessa had texted earlier to let me know she had a shift at the vet's office and asked if I could come over to her place tonight. I guess Hopper was out of town for the weekend, and she had the whole house to herself.

Drew and I'd talked last night after we dropped off Tim. He'd gone to Vance for a job at the warehouse. I couldn't believe it at first, but when he explained his reasoning, that his family needed the money more than ever with Jaimie gone, I understood. We had to do what we had to do to stay alive.

I'd told him to be careful because even though Vance said X was trying to push me out, I didn't believe him. Why? Because if it were true, Vance would have killed me already. If he really thought I was the one thing standing in his way, then he would do whatever he could to get rid of me. But he hadn't. It had to be because X told him to leave me alone. Except all of it was conjecture when X refused to take my calls. I still didn't understand why he had left me floundering.

My head pounded louder every time I thought about it. My chest got heavier, and the world turned into a blur that made it impossible to see anything in front of me. I blinked and tried to focus.

I planned on seeing Vance tomorrow. Confronting him about my brother. Then offering him a solution.

I had to get out of the house. I grabbed some spray cans and rode to my favorite painting spot. At the edge of town, past the Chinese restaurant that Alex's family owned, stood an empty concrete building. Not like Vance's, hidden within the forest, but out in the open. Unshielded. People used to go there and break the windows on nights when it got too hot and claustrophobic to be inside.

I used to take Tim there, too. We'd grab as many rocks as we could find and watch the glass shatter when one of us managed to hit our target. All the windows were broken now. Nothing left but shards of glass, toppled concrete, and dust.

I pulled my bike to the back where the grass was overgrown, dry, and crisp. It crunched under my feet. I stepped inside, the sound echoing around me. Silence. Quiet. Everything I needed.

Taking out my supplies, I went to work. Guiding the cans, mixing the colors, letting myself not think about anything else but the painting. The sun started to set, the light sliding lower on the wall and the shadows growing deeper. My arm ached, my back felt tight, and then my phone began to ring.

Tessa.

I let it go to voice mail, wiping at the sweat dotting my forehead. She left me a message telling me it was time to come over. I stepped away from the wall, looked over my work. A giant spiderweb took up the space. At the center of it, caught in the trap, lay a man. The spider stood in the shadows, waiting to eat him.

My breathing got harder, faster. I stared for a few minutes, telling myself that it wasn't me. That the spider wasn't Vance. That he wasn't going to eat me alive. I grabbed a can and threw it across the building, letting out a scream. The one I kept in every time things went to shit. When I tried to hold it all together. Bending over, I covered my head with my arms. When my heart stopped beating faster than a moving train, I stood up, rolled out my shoulders, cleaned up my supplies, and headed over to Tessa's.

Night had crawled up the sky by the time I got to Tessa's. I rode my bike up the driveway and leaned it against the side of the house. My legs felt like lead when I took the steps up to the back door. A few knocks, with my arms feeling the weight of my day painting, and Tessa opened the door.

A soft wind wisped up her hair. We stared at each other. Me in my worn-out shirt and pants, her in a pair of shorts and a tank top.

"Hi," she finally said, stepping aside. "Come on in." Uncertainty colored her eyes when I brushed past her.

"Do you want something to drink?" She headed to a cupboard and grabbed a cup without waiting for an answer.

She filled it with water and handed it to me. My throat felt like a desert, dry and cottony, so I gladly accepted the water, chugging it down.

I placed the cup in the sink. This was familiar. Like a dance we had practiced many times. Tessa standing by the kitchen island, foot sliding back and forth. Me, moving around the side of the island, trying to keep my distance.

"So," she finally said. "You ready to talk?"

No, but she deserved an explanation. I followed her into the living room, and she told me to take a seat. I chose one end of the couch; she chose the other, bending a leg on top of the cushion to face me.

I didn't know where to start. How to explain everything to her. My voice got lost inside my head, and I didn't know how to make it work again. After clearing it, I finally started talking.

"Have you ever met Jared's grandfather? Thomas Wilson?"

Tessa frowned at me but nodded. "Yeah."

"Any other members of his family?"

She bit down on her lip. "Just his parents and his cousin Chloe."

I was stalling. My palms started to sweat, and I rubbed them on my pants. Tessa waited for me to continue, and all I could hear was my heartbeat roaring.

"There's a man that controls Branson and the gang. A powerful man. My dad worked for him and now I do, too. His code name is X. Only a few of us know his real identity."

Tessa crossed her arms. "Which is?"

"Thomas Wilson."

She stilled. Her eyes widened, crinkling in confusion. "What are you saying? That Jared's grandfather is some kind of mob boss?"

"It's not exactly a mob, but as close as you can get to one in Branson."

Time ticked by. Tessa started gnawing on her thumbnail.

"You didn't know Jared and he were related until last night?" she asked.

I shook my head. "No. He keeps his private life private."

Tessa moved so she faced the fireplace. I stared at her profile while she chewed on her lip. "How did you end up working for him?"

I met her gaze, the frown on her face growing deeper and more troubled.

"My dad. He was X's right-hand man in Branson. He kept things running in town. With him gone, it got harder to keep up with the bills, even though when he was alive most of what he earned he spent on getting high. Mom was going to school, and she realized that things were getting tight. She talked about dropping out and getting a full-time gig somewhere else. I didn't want that for her. She was finally doing something for herself. I worked at Stan's, the auto-body shop, but it didn't pay enough. So I did the only thing I could think to. I went to X."

I pictured that day in my head. Knocking on the door of Wilson's house. Dad had taken me a couple of times to pick up his pay, but I always waited on the porch steps. Wilson never allowed us inside. He made us wait outside for him. He was always friendly. Offered us drinks, even gave me candy. I wanted to piss myself the whole time, I was so scared. Alone. But I remembered what my dad said to me right before he died. That someday I might have to be man of the house, and when that happened, I had to make sure to take care of my family. So I did.

Sometimes I think he knew he was going to die but didn't do anything to stop it, and that made the resentment pump faster in my veins. I stared at the glass coffee table sitting in front of the couch. Clear of any smudges, shining like it was new. All I had to do was reach out a hand and press my fingers against the surface to ruin its perfection. I felt like that was what I was doing to Tessa. Leaving dirty marks all over her.

"I was fourteen when I approached him. He took me under his wing. Taught me the ropes. I did a lot of things I'm not proud of. Used Stan to help Vance figure out what cars to steal in town. I never dealt, but I worked alongside a lot of those guys. I was Vance's driver for a number of years, helping him make a quick getaway when he went after someone who crossed him. I've done everything I can since then to take care of my family, to provide for them. And it wasn't until I went to jail that I realized that I wasn't so innocent, that I couldn't use them as an excuse for making my own choices. But by then it was too late. I was in too deep. And now they're in danger because of me. Of what I did. Just like my dad."

Tessa shook her head. "That's awful, Corey. I'm so sorry."

"Look, Tessa, I only told you this to keep you safe. To show you that you deserve better. Stay away from Jared and his family. Don't tell anyone you know the truth. It's not safe for you. Things in my world are getting out of hand, and I don't want you caught up in my mess."

"What kinds of things?"

"My little brother, for one. I had no idea he had started dealing. I swear, Tessa."

She reached across and placed her hand over mine. "I believe you, Corey. What are you planning on doing?"

"Pay Vance back. Find a way to make things right." I gauged her reaction, watching emotions play over her face. Shock, sadness, maybe even pity. But one seemed oddly absent. Fear. Tessa didn't seem afraid. I cracked my knuckles, waiting for her response.

"I can't help with the house anymore. It's not safe. Would you tell your dad?" I started to stand up, thinking that was the end of it. Tessa grabbed my wrist and I paused. The feel of her skin against mine sent heat all over.

Tessa stood up and closed the distance between us. "Tomorrow you're going to try and clean up Tim's mess."

"I have to. He's my brother. I would do anything for him."

She licked her lips and let a breath out of her nose. "Think this through, Corey. There has to be another way."

The insistence in her tone caged in my emotions. "No. There isn't."

"Corey. Please. Don't go to Vance's."

I stepped in closer to her and cupped her cheek. "I want to thank you, Tessa. For letting me see what it's like to be normal. To have a real life. The night you taught me to ride your bike, our first date, even the pool party. Before it all went to hell. I've never had anything like that before."

It was hard to picture that version of myself. The one I became around Tessa. She gave me a taste of a life outside of the gang, and I almost gorged myself on it. Our texts, the simplicity of everything we did. I wanted it, I realized, the thought squeezing tight around my heart. I wanted everything I missed out on. And maybe someday I'd get it.

"Thank you for that," I said. "For giving me those nights. For showing me what it's like on the other side."

I stepped to the door. Ready to walk away.

"No. This is not how it ends. I'm not going to let you walk away without a fight, Corey." She wrapped her hand around mine, and I didn't want to let it go. I wanted to stay. I already had a plan. One that didn't involve Tessa. I had to keep her out of my plan. I had to keep her safe. And I would do whatever it took to make sure that happened.

TESSA

Corey's confession hit me in waves. One minute I thought it wasn't that bad; the next I remembered that Jared's grandfather was involved in the drug scene. He had a gang of boys doing his bidding. It made my vision blurry and unfamiliar.

"What would you do if you were out, Corey? Do you ever think about that?"

"I don't like to think about those things too much. It makes it harder not to be angry."

"I thought you were always angry?" I teased, remembering the night at the skate park.

He chuckled. "Isn't that the Hulk? And I don't remember saying that. A part of me will always be angry. It's what fuels me sometimes, but it doesn't color my entire life. It scares me a little when I think about it, if I allow myself to indulge in those fantasies. It's probably for the best if I don't anymore."

I shook my head and grabbed his hands in mine. "Corey, that future is possible. All you have to do is ask for help. I could help you. My dad can help you."

He pulled away from me.

"How, Tessa? By turning X over and spending the rest of my life in witness protection or on the run? Because that's what's going to happen if I do. If you go to your father, he'll be in danger, too. I can't do that. I shouldn't have said anything to you. I should have kept it to myself."

"No. I'm not going to accept that. What about getting rid of Vance? Is that possible? You could get out."

He rubbed his face and started pacing the room. "If Vance is out, then I'm the only one up for taking over the Peyson territory, which Vance wants. He thinks I'm in his way for it, and I can't do anything to make him suspicious of me, otherwise I'm screwed." The blood drained from my face. "This isn't your problem, Tessa. I can do it on my own. I'm not putting you or your father in danger any more than I already have. Let me figure this out, Tessa."

I didn't know whether to believe him. Maybe he did have a way to get out, but doing it on his own seemed dangerous. Lonely. I was never good at standing by and watching.

Corey walked over to me and placed his hand on my cheek. "Please. For my sake, stay out of this." Tension radiated in the air around him. His eyes cruised over me, and I felt exposed. "It's easier this way."

I stepped closer to him, until he had no other choice but to look me in the eyes. "For who?" He pursed his lips and flicked his gaze away from mine.

Corey moved forward, and his hand came around my waist. In one tantalizing breath, his face neared mine. His eyes held a hunger I felt pulsing through his fingers but clouded beneath his lips slipped indecision, and I stared at them, hoping to separate the truth from the lies he told me. His mouth descended, and my back pressed against the wall with my hands against his chest. I snaked my arms around his neck and held on as tightly as I could. He pulled away before I caught my breath.

"For you," he answered. So that was the lie. The truth still swam in his eyes but refused to show itself.

Tears pricked my eyes, but I held on to him. He didn't fight me. I closed the distance between us, a vast space opening its gaping mouth wider until it gobbled one of us.

He didn't push me away when I kissed him.

It was a sad kiss, an ode to a goodbye. Slow, wrapped in the arms of desperation. Tears pricked my eyes because there was the truth. In his mouth, in the way he kissed me. He really was leaving. I pulled away and stared at him.

This boy, who stood in front of me, holding my face in his hands, lips hovering over mine, sad eyes with an even sadder brow, undid me.

I wanted to beg him to stay, to let me help, but I knew he'd refuse.

My hands roamed the grooves and crevices of his skin, finding the places laid waste, forgotten and tender, from Vance and his thugs. The bruises and marks had faded, and all that was left was a lost boy, staring down at me with such tenderness it made me want to cry. It might be the last time I ever saw him. The thought struck an arrow through my muscles and heart, tearing it apart.

I thumbed down to his neck, feeling the curve, and with feather-light fingers skimmed over his shoulder, tracking faster until I held his hand in mine.

"Don't, Tess. This really is goodbye."

He squeezed my hand and walked to his bike without looking back. He got on and rode away, leaving me brokenhearted and burning for answers. I slumped to the ground and cried.

I didn't regret giving so much of myself to Corey. It was the first time I'd felt that way about anyone. After my mom walked out, I didn't think I'd ever be able to trust someone with that much of my heart. With Corey, it was instant. And dramatic. And beautiful. And tragic.

No. It didn't have to be. There was still a way out. Even if Corey had given up hope, I hadn't.

COREY

Mom was asleep when I got home, so I was lucky enough to have access to the car. I grunted. Lucky. Right. I sped along the back highway that led out of Branson and into Vance's territory, the memory of the night I rode Tessa's bike fresh and shredding into pieces.

My head felt like a sledgehammer was pounding the side of it. Vance going after my brother. Tim keeping it a secret from me. The suspicious inkling in the back of my mind when my little brother suddenly got a better wardrobe. The signs were there, but I'd tricked myself into thinking Tim was stronger than me. That he could withstand the temptation of a better life.

I couldn't wipe away the look of despair on Tessa's face before I took off. Her scent was on my clothes, clinging, unwilling to let me go. I ground my teeth and tightened my grip around the wheel.

I pulled into the dirt driveway in front of the building. Vance's guys were out front, standing guard. With a quick check in the mirror, I wiped away any traces of the worry I felt for Tim and shot out of the car, slamming the door behind me. The guards eyed me, threats posed in their stances, but they let me through.

The place crawled with lowlifes. The smell of rotting garbage permeated the fresh summer air. Every single guy in there had the same look in his eyes: dark, helpless, lost, angry. But worst of all, desperate.

A few guys wearing coveralls exited the building holding boxes. It couldn't be drugs. It wasn't the day for moving product. That was usually done on Sundays.

"What the hell is going on here?" I asked when I spotted Drew. He slammed the door to the black van.

His dark eyes shifted and he swallowed hard, stuffing his hands into his pockets. "Nothing, just getting some work done early." He pushed past me, steps quickening into the building. He gave me a small nod. We'd talk later.

The rest of the guys kept their gazes away from mine. I wondered if X knew. He had a very specific way of doing things, and if it changed without his knowledge, there would be hell to pay.

I hated how even with my body buzzing with fear for my brother my head couldn't stop working. My focus needed to be on Tim, not X or his business, but years of protocol couldn't be rewritten. It was hardwired in me.

I walked inside, where Vance hung out on his seat on the dais in the middle of the room. "Corey. Haven't seen your pretty face around here in a while. What brings you by?"

My haggard breathing flared through my mouth. "Why the hell did you go after my brother?" My throat felt full of gravel, and it made it hard to talk.

Vance's laughter echoed around the room, the quiet from the rest of the guys unnerving. "I needed a few new guys. He said he was up for the job. It would be rude of me not to let him into the family business."

I stepped forward, but one of his guards got in front of me. I thought back to last night. The way Tim's head hung low, shoulders slouched when he confessed everything to me. I was all too familiar with the helplessness that hung over him.

After Dad died, Tim started wetting the bed. The only time he didn't was when he slept with me. Two years straight that little kid snuck into my room and lay down next to me. I was so fucking stupid. How could I get my little brother dragged into this shit?

"How much does he owe?" I asked.

Vance cocked his head. His beady eyes bore into mine. I wasn't backing down. I'd do whatever I had to in order to protect Tim.

"Three grand. For starters. I gave him product to move and he didn't. Said something about not being able to go through with it. I lost business thanks to him, and my suppliers weren't too happy with the slow move, so I had to pay them extra to keep them off my ass. The price is now fifteen grand."

Shit. Shit. Shit. I rubbed my forehead, trying to think of something. I had some money saved up, but it wasn't enough. I planned on using what little I had to send Tim to college. No way was I going to give up on his dreams like I had on my own.

"I can pay it off."

Vance let out a bark of laughter. "With what money?" He stretched out his arms.

I made myself stay still, to get ready for what I said next. "I'll deal. I'll help out with whatever you want. Including your side business."

Shock and maybe even a little bit of respect lined Vance's face. He leaned forward, eyeing me up and down in the silence. "Seriously?"

I curled and uncurled my fingers. My heart sounded too loud in my ears, and my chest got tighter. "Yeah. I'll do it."

"All right, Fowler. You've got a deal. But try and screw me over, and there will be hell to pay. Got it?"

I nodded. "Got it."

TESSA

That couldn't be the end of it. Two days since Corey left. Two days of me lying awake at night, brainstorming ideas to help him. I refused to mope and wait to hear whether he was dead like that boy they pulled from the river a couple of weeks ago. I pictured the news story, how it would cause an uproar for all of five minutes before people started to move on with their lives. Corey deserved more; he deserved a life.

I figured work would be a distraction, but all it did was remind me of Corey and the day he spent volunteering.

"You have got to get it together," Paige informed me as soon as I got inside after spending a few minutes outdoors with our pet guests.

"Excuse me?" I walked Mr. Wiggles, a dachshund with a penchant for humping pretty much everything in sight, back to his crate.

"You're moping."

I shut the crate door and faced Paige. "I don't know what you're talking about."

I was not moping. I refused to believe it. How dare she?

"Look, I know you're disappointed with the way things ended with Corey, but you have to move on. The guy is bad news."

I hadn't told Paige anything about X and Mr. Wilson or how he was connected to everything.

"No, he's not. Am I not allowed to be upset about his life? Paige, you of all people should know how easy it is to fall into that trap." Our fathers talked to us about it all the time.

Paige leaned against the doorframe, her jaw set. "Yeah. I get it, but he made his choices and he needs to accept the consequences. I'm worried about you, Tess. Is Corey really worth all of this?"

I swallowed the angry words filling my throat, ready to spew all over her. Hadn't we made mistakes, too? Underage drinking, for one. Paige and Alex helped me while I raced my motorcycle. It was Paige's idea to bribe Officer Jenkins. We hadn't faced the consequences of our actions, so why did Corey have to pay for his? I wanted to shout those things at her, but alienating my cousin and best friend wasn't part of the plan.

Didn't she do those things for me? To keep me safe? Hadn't I gone along with it because I was afraid of the repercussions? I thought helping Corey would somehow balance the universe, make me feel better, but all it did was remind me that I had yet to own up to my mistakes.

"Yes. He's worth it." I walked over to her and wrapped my arms around her stiff body. "I love you for caring, but I can't not do anything."

Paige finally loosened her muscles and returned the hug. "I know. Be careful, okay? And tell me if you need my help."

Stepping away from her, I gave her a watery smile. "I'll let you know."

"Promise me, Tess, that if anything comes up you will come to me." Her stare pierced me and my heart grew full, ready to burst. I didn't deserve Paige.

"Okay," I said through the thickening in my throat. I didn't have time for tears. Not yet. I needed to get my head straight and finally do something.

On the drive home, I thought about telling my dad everything, but getting him involved would not only endanger him but complicate matters legally for Corey. I needed to keep him out of jail.

A plan started to formulate. One with plenty of risks, but with a payoff that could finally help Corey get out of the gang for good. But I couldn't do it on my own.

"I don't think this is a good idea," Tim said over the phone.

"Tim. I'm trying to help. Please give me the information I need. I promise you won't get in trouble."

A heavy sigh on the other end of the line told me I had won. "Okay. But be careful. Please."

The knots in my belly didn't loosen. They tightened instead. If this worked, it would require a level of stealth and finesse that I wasn't sure I possessed anymore. But I was ready. I just hoped Corey would get on board with it. If he didn't, then we were both in trouble.

COREY

The day smelled heavy and hostile with gray clouds hanging low, ready to burst with the oncoming rainstorm. An ache pricked my muscles, and my eyes grew heavy. I hadn't slept in almost two days. Hadn't been home for more than a few minutes. Just long enough to take a shower and put on some fresh clothes. Tim waited for me when I did come home, asking what happened, what I planned to do. Telling me that Mom was worried and asking questions.

I told him to hold tight, it would all be over soon. I'd stared at my art supplies with longing, fingers twitching with the need to get out and paint. I settled for my sketch pad and some pens instead.

Vance had me on the clock. He didn't want me to run. Not that he said that to my face, but I knew what game he was playing with me. I wasn't going to chicken out. I was in too deep.

"Hey, we've got some supplies coming in." Anderson's brown skin glistened under the sun, a sheen of sweat forming on his brow. He was one of the newest members of the crew and usually stayed back when Vance came around. Didn't say much, kept to himself.

"I'll be out there in a minute," I said.

We stood on the roof of the building. Not many guys liked to wander up there, the danger of it caving in and falling to your death too risky, but I needed an escape. The upper level of the building had a crawl space with a ladder that granted access. Vance never came up, another bonus. I stood on the edge of the building and stared down at the ground below. A dark van had pulled up a few minutes ago, and several members of the crew, now including Anderson, started placing boxes inside the back. Like they had the other day. And on another non-shipment day.

Vance had stopped hiding the fact that he was screwing over X. It happened in broad daylight. I took out my phone and snapped a few pictures. I would need them later. I didn't lie to Tessa when I told her I had the situation handled. I needed Vance to believe how upset I was about Tim. So upset that I wasn't thinking clearly. Meanwhile, I was planning. Once I had enough proof, I was going to X. But I had to get him to answer my calls first.

Putting away the phone, I picked up my pen and stared at the picture on my sketch pad. Tessa. Always her.

I dropped the sketch pad and pen next to me on the roof. It landed with a thud, and I squatted low, putting my elbows on my knees.

The sooner I forgot her, the better. If I lived through my plan, if I survived Vance and X, I'd go back. Apologize to her and her father. Then I'd run.

I continued to stare at the bustle below me.

I was about to go down and join the crew when the revving of an engine caught my ears. I shot up from my squat and hurried to the front of the building. It couldn't be. She wouldn't. And yet there she was. Tessa Hopper with the siren song of her motorcycle coming up the path, straight into danger.

"Shit," I muttered. Without thinking twice, I headed down the ladder, my pace causing me to slip. I caught myself before biting it and ran to the stairs.

Vance stood at the center of the building, talking to one of his main guards. I tried to get past them unnoticed. I had to get to Tessa before she came inside. I ducked my head and crossed the room, clinging to the walls, hoping they would keep me in the shadows. Lifting my foot, quietly, and placing it on the floor, gently.

"What's going on out there?" Vance called out when a couple of guys walked through the front door, their steps determined.

"There's a girl here," one of them said. "I think it's Hopper's daughter."

I stayed in the shadows, my whole body growing rigid, ready to jump out at any minute.

Vance laughed. "Tell me you're joking."

The guard shook his head. "She's asking for you."

Vance scratched the side of his face. "Interesting. Wonder if Fowler has something to do with that? Fowler?" Vance slowly turned to where I waited. "Come on out. Let's see what your girl wants together."

I stepped out of the shadows, heart thumping, fear wringing its hands around my muscles.

"Tell her to leave," I said, my throat getting tighter. "She doesn't belong here."

Vance darted his eyes to the open door and back to me, and that sly smile spread on his face, making my stomach sink deeper. "Nah, I think I want to see what she wants. Bring her in."

What the hell was Tessa thinking coming here? How did she even know where to find this place?

Two guards flanked Tessa, and I took an unintentional step forward. Vance caught my arm and forced me to hold back.

There was no way in hell Tessa would walk into Vance's place unless she had a death wish. I swallowed and clenched my hands. I was trying to protect her by leaving, and what does she do? Puts herself in even more danger.

"Are you Vance?"

Even though it had only been a couple of days since the last time I talked to her, hearing her voice comforted me. Then I remembered where I was, and any sort of comfort I felt went flying through the door.

"Tess, you need to get out of here." I yanked my elbow out of Vance's hand and started toward her. The crew surrounded me, blocking my way. I needed to get her out, to protect her from this world.

Vance stepped past me. The closer he got to Tessa, the more my ribs tried to stretch out of my skin. He got right in her face, looking down at her. She didn't flinch under his gaze, and I fell for her a little more.

"What do you want?"

"You're Vance?" She eyed him up and down and peeked over his shoulder.

Vance wasn't much to look at physically. But his eyes bore the sinister truth that controlled a room full of thugs. He shifted and blocked my view. "What. Do. You. Want?"

I needed to see her. Make sure she was okay, but three guys held on to my shoulders, and every time I moved, fingers dug into my skin.

"I'm here to make you an offer."

Vance turned and gave me a once-over, smiling, toying with me. "What kind of offer?"

"The kind where you end up making a crap ton of money and let Corey's debts go."

What was she doing? What could she possibly do to get us out? It was hard to think when all I wanted to do was grab her hand and get her the hell out of there.

"Really? I'm intrigued." Vance finally moved out of the way, and I got a better view of Tessa. No fear etched the outline of her face, only fierce determination.

Vance headed to his seat, taking his sweet time sitting down. He nodded to his guys, and they let me go. He waved Tessa closer.

As soon as they released me, I walked over to Tessa. She wouldn't meet my eyes, so instead I dared to grab her hand in mine and whisper in her ear, "What are you doing?" I wanted to scream at her to get out, but there was no talking Tessa out of something once she'd made up her mind.

She finally faced me, her features set hard. "Helping you."

"If you two are done sweet-talking over there, I'd like to hear what little Ms. Hopper has to say." Tessa's eyes jerked to Vance. "Did Corey tell you that I know about his little deal with your dad?"

Tessa didn't break eye contact with Vance. "No."

"Let me tell you something, Tessa Hopper. There's very little I don't know when it comes to the affairs of Branson."

Her hand squeezed mine, palms sweating. She wasn't as fearless as she made herself out to be. Good. She needed to understand the danger she was in.

"I know. That's why I'm here. You want your money, right? What if I could pay it back and then some?"

"I'm intrigued. Go on."

"Have you ever been to the drag races up in Peyson?"

Shit. No. I didn't like where this was going.

Vance's eyes sharpened. "And what would a girl like you know about drag racing?"

"A lot more than you would think. I used to race up there. Won a lot." She raised her head, stood up taller, and even managed a smirk.

"And how do you propose to get me my money?"

"I'm going to win it. The race. You're going to bet on me. In return, you let Corey out of the gang and forgive the debt."

Vance sat back against the chair, crossing his arms. He seemed to contemplate the idiotic idea. My heart rushed faster and louder, drumming in my ears and head. I had no idea how no one else heard it.

"No." I found my voice. I grabbed Tessa's wrist and pulled her back until we were face-to-face. "Tess, you can't do this," I pleaded. I refused to let her put herself at risk for me.

Her eyes glistened. Instinctively, I ran my hand across her cheek, ignoring the audience of criminals watching us.

"I can. And I am. You're not alone in this anymore, Corey." She moved away from me and approached Vance.

"Why would I want to let Corey out? Maybe I like having him around," Vance said.

I almost laughed at that one.

"No, you don't. If he's out, there's no one standing in your way to take over an even bigger market. I can make you enough money to do that. To show your boss that you're the guy for the job."

Vance rubbed the bottom of his chin. He wasn't really considering that asinine plan? No.

"Okay, let's see if you can pull it off, little girl."

TESSA

"Vance, this is crazy." Corey stepped forward. "There's no guarantee she'll even win."

"I'll try not to take that too personally," I mumbled.

Corey pinched the space between his brows. "You know what I mean, Tessa."

Vance stood up and dusted off his pants. My senses went on high alert, arm hairs standing on end. I didn't like the look of him, the way he watched me with hooded eyes. I could see the similarities between him and Jared. The way they walked, a cocky step in every stride, like no one would ever dare to question them. I swallowed the lump in my throat.

"He has a point. What happens if you don't win?"

"I'll owe you one."

Vance shook his head. "Not good enough. I want something more." He peeked over my shoulder, out the door. I followed his gaze and froze when I noticed what had caught his attention. "I want the bike. And Corey gets to pay off whatever debts you accumulate after the loss. Which means I get to keep him for . . ." He started counting on his fingers. "The rest of his life."

Corey's jaw twitched. He wouldn't even look at me. His shoulders were drawn low and stiff. I wanted to reach out and touch him but kept still.

"Deal," Corey answered for me. His gaze met mine, and his expression softened around the edges of his eyes.

"Good. When's the race?" Vance slowly circled me like a shark preparing to attack its prey. I felt him staring at my body, and I wanted to pull a blanket around myself.

"This weekend," I answered.

Vance came back around to face me. He stared for a minute before the smile that made my stomach sick returned. "See you then, Tessa Hopper."

I was dismissed. Vance turned away, and his guys walled me in again.

"I'll walk her out." Corey ground out the words. He held out his hand. I stared at it for a few seconds before taking it.

I blinked a few times when the sun hit us. The inside of the building had been dark and gloomy and smelled rancid. I was glad to be back outside. I took a deep breath and allowed myself to relax for a minute. We stopped in front of my bike, and Corey let go of my hand.

"Corey, I'm sorry."

He stared off out into the distance. His heartbeat pulsed on the side of his neck, and I waited while anxiety ran hot in my veins.

"We'll talk later." He walked away from me, and I was left with lingering doubts that clouded my vision. Or maybe it was tears. It was hard to tell. I pulled on my helmet and rode off on Beauty before I could figure it out.

<hr />

"Please tell me you didn't." Paige's eyes were wide with horror.

The day was warm and a slow breeze moved through the trees. The smell of freshly cut grass sank into the air. Alex was currently situated next to my bike, doing a tune-up, while Paige shot me laser beams.

"I did."

Paige squeezed the bridge of her nose and took a deep breath. "Okay. Why?"

"Because I want to help him."

"Tessa! You have to stop trying to save everyone. First your mom, then Jared, even your dad, and now Corey? What are you thinking?"

I sucked in a breath. Paige had no idea that I had the same thought not that long ago, that I wasn't able to save anyone. Having her throw it at me made me want to puke.

"I was thinking that I needed to do this for myself just as much as Corey. I need to make things right, Paige. This is the only way I can think to do that."

Paige shook her head. "I don't understand any of this. I can't stand by and watch you risk your life."

Jiminy whined by my side. He did not like conflict.

I wrapped my hand around her arm. "I'm not, Paige. No one is going to get hurt. But I can't do this without you there," I admitted. I really couldn't. Paige was my number one fan, my cheerleader, my best friend. If she didn't think I could do it, then maybe she was right.

Alex stopped tinkering with the motorcycle, his eyes moving back and forth between us. If she said no, then he'd most likely back out, too. Paige tapped her foot and the silence compressed around us.

"Fine. I will be there. But only because I love you and I know you're going to win. Not because of the whole 'approaching a drug lord and making a deal with him to buy your boyfriend's freedom' thing."

I jumped across the space between us and pulled her into a hug. "Thank you. You have no idea how much that means to me."

"Yeah, yeah," she grumbled under her breath. She pulled away from me but couldn't hide the little smile working its way up the side of her mouth. "So what next?"

Alex stood up and wiped his hands off on a towel. "The bike looks great. You're good to go." He put his arm around Paige's shoulder.

"Next I have to meet with my maybe boyfriend who is not too happy with me right now and try to convince him that it's all going to be okay." I checked my watch. "In fact, he's going to be here in a few."

Paige grimaced. "Good luck with that." She patted my arm. "Talk to you later?"

I waved goodbye to them and waited for Corey to show up. My whole body grew tight at the thought of what was to come. I hadn't raced in a year, but I knew I still had the skills to win. That didn't mean I wasn't afraid. Maybe Vance would back out of our agreement. Maybe I would lose. I grabbed the basketball from the garage and decided to distract myself. Whatever ended up happening, I needed Corey to know I was on his side. No matter what.

COREY

rew and I worked alongside each other in silence. The warehouse had more goods than I imagined. It was like walking into the stockroom of Wilson's. There were appliances and furniture along with drugs. I couldn't believe Vance had let us in. I thought at first he only wanted me to deal, but I'd been right about business being down on that end in Branson.

"What's his plan exactly?" I asked after we loaded up a van.

"He wants to save up enough to move to show X he's the right guy to run Peyson."

"By screwing him over?"

Drew scratched the back of his head while we approached his car. My body was finally starting to feel normal, but my arms and shoulders were aching from hauling everything in the warehouse.

"X isn't supposed to find out about that."

We got into the car, and Drew drove us back to town.

"Do you have any idea who X thinks stole the shipments?"

Drew shook his head. "He doesn't care. He got his insurance payout, didn't he?"

"Maybe this won't work. Maybe X won't care that Vance is stealing from him because he got his money."

"You really think X isn't interested in knowing his nephew is screwing him over? That he's lying his way into power? What's going to stop Vance from doing more? If I were X, I would be worried about that. Look, Corey, this shit is terrifying, but we can't quit now. We've come too far."

Drew was right. If we were going to get out of this, then I couldn't back out now. I couldn't let the fear immobilize me. I had to go through with this. Not just for my family, or Tessa, or everyone else that wanted out, but for myself. I had to try.

"You're right. I need to take care of things with Tessa first. Will you drop me off at her place?"

Drew sent me a smirk. "I still can't believe you got Hopper's daughter to enter a drag race for your ass. That's some impressive shit."

I held back a groan. "It's not impressive. It's dumb. I don't want her in this. It's screwing up the plan we came up with."

"Or maybe we can use it to our advantage." Drew turned onto the main highway.

"How?" I didn't buy it. I couldn't see how Tessa getting involved was good for anyone.

"I don't know. But we'll figure it out. Like we have before."

I leaned my head against the window and stared at the passing scenery. "We better or we'll all end up dead."

Mom texted me on the way to Tessa's to let me know she was going out with Stan. Good, she needed the distraction.

She still had no idea what was going on. I didn't plan on ever telling her about Tim's involvement with Vance. It was bad enough she had one son who constantly disappointed her; she didn't need another. Besides, Mom had finally interviewed for the new position at the hospital, and I wanted her to enjoy her moment. She hadn't heard back yet, but I knew she'd get it.

Drew pulled up to Hopper's, and I thanked him before walking up the driveway.

Tessa had a basketball in hand when I got up there. The basketball hoop over the garage sat rusted and the net was ripped in places. Jiminy ran up to me, and I bent down to rub his back before approaching her.

"Didn't know you liked to play."

She bounced the ball, her face set in concentration, before shooting for the basket. It went in with a swish before bouncing over to me.

"I don't. My dad and uncles do, but I'm sort of hopeless when it comes to anything athletic."

"That was just a lucky shot?" I grabbed the ball and took my own shot, using the backboard. It went in and the ball bounced off to the side of the yard. Neither of us made a move to grab it.

Tessa shrugged. "It was the first one I made in the last ten minutes." Her smile was off, not quite reaching her eyes.

"Why did you do it, Tessa?"

She tugged at the end of her shirt. "Because I want to help you."

"And I told you I was taking care of it."

"Really?" She took on a defensive stance. Shoulders back, arms crossed, eyes narrowed. "And what was it exactly? Deal drugs like your father, the one thing you refused to get involved with? Have it hang on to your conscience for the rest of your life? Or at least until it got you killed?"

I shook my head. "Vance is screwing over X. He stole from him, and I'm getting proof of it so I can finally get rid of him."

Tessa frowned and put a hand on her hip. "Where does that leave you, then? You're still in the gang."

"It's better than nothing." I didn't have anything else. Not without risking everyone in my life.

"What kind of proof are you getting?"

I filled her in on the situation with Vance. The stolen shipments, the warehouse, how Vance was gunning for the position in Peyson. She listened, her face playing over several emotions: shock, surprise, anger. After I finished she stood there wearing a contemplative expression.

"I remember the stolen shipments. It was big news around here. Jared freaked out because he thought Mr. Wilson was going to cut down his inheritance. It happened right around the same time as the accident. Another reason he didn't want the blame for the accident. Bad timing."

"That makes sense. X is all about appearances and those two events taking place back-to-back would have set him off."

Tessa rubbed her forehead. "There's one thing I don't understand. How are you going to get this proof to Wilson if he won't even call you back?"

"I planned on showing up at his place and making him listen."

"And get yourself killed in the process? Great plan. Look, if I've learned anything about Mr. Wilson, it's that he doesn't like intrusions in his life. He will not take kindly to you showing up out of the blue. What you need is someone to get through to him about what's going on."

"Like who?"

Tessa chewed on her lip and made a face that made my stomach sink. "Jared."

TESSA

"I don't like this," Corey murmured.

We sat in my car out in the back field. I'd called Jared and set up a meeting. The nape of my neck was sweating, so I pulled my hair up into a bun. The heat of the night was oppressive, and it made it hard to breathe.

"I don't, either, but do you have a better plan?"

Corey grumbled something under his breath and turned his attention to the window. A smile tugged at my lips.

"I'm sorry, I didn't catch that, what were you saying?"

Corey shook his head. "I said anything was better than involving your douchebag ex."

I let out a laugh. I leaned over and kissed his cheek. He let out a puff of air and dropped his shoulders. "It's going to be okay," I said.

Jared's car bumped along the field, stopping next to my car. He didn't seem very pleased to see us, his lips thinned into a straight line, his eyes hooded. Like Vance's. I shivered at the thought.

He put down his window. "What do you want?" he asked, killing the engine.

Corey and I exchanged a quick look. "We have some interesting information to share with you about your cousin."

He frowned. "Chloe?"

I shook my head. "No. Vance."

Jared flinched, and his face turned grim. "What about him?"

Jiminy whined at my side, probably sensing my anxiety. It sent ripples along the edges of my nerves. I sent a quick text to Paige and Corey before bending down to hug his soft coat.

"I'll be back. I promise," I whispered in his ear. It was the night of the race and my nerves were shot. It was always like this beforehand. The clenching in my belly and clammy texture covering my skin.

I was ready, though. After Corey and I told Jared what we knew about Vance, he seemed on board with helping us. I hoped he would come through this once, but the uncertainty of the situation held my muscles like a vise. With one last pat, I stood up and headed for the back door.

"You're going out?" Dad sat in the living room, watching a baseball game. It was the first time he'd been home in days, and we'd actually managed to have dinner together.

I swallowed. "Yeah. I'm meeting Paige and Alex."

Dad sipped his water. "Okay. Don't be out too late."

"I won't." I went for the door before he started asking more intrusive questions but stopped short. Dropping my hand from the knob, I turned around and headed to the living room. I leaned over and gave my dad a hug.

"What's this for?" he asked.

"Just because." I pulled away from him. "I love you, Dad." If tonight didn't completely fall apart, I would tell him the truth about last year. All of it.

Dad frowned, smiling. "I love you, too, Tess. Is everything okay?" He put his cup on the table.

"Everything's good, Dad. Don't worry about it. Just thinking about college and getting emotional."

"I'm glad to know I'm not the only one. Have fun tonight, okay?"

"Thanks." I hurried to the door and got on Beauty before tears could fully form in my eyes. With Beauty's growl beneath me, I headed for the highway.

The hour drive to Peyson went by too quickly, and before I knew it I was pulling into the drag strip. Crowds lined the sides of the road; cars filled up the grassy parking spots. The track that we used stood outside of Peyson in a less-than-stellar part of town. The buildings were crumbled, the sidewalk was broken in pieces, and the air was gritty. But no one bothered the racers out here.

I parked Beauty by the strip and took off my helmet. A few familiar faces surrounded me. They nodded their acknowledgment before turning back to their teams, and I searched the crowd for mine.

"Tessa, over here!" Alex waved his arms to get my attention. He stood with Paige over by the sign-in table.

My legs felt shaky as I walked over to them, but I kept my face neutral. "Is Corey here yet?"

They both shook their heads.

I stared out over the crowd again and my eyes landed straight on Vance. He smirked when our gazes clashed. I scanned the guys he'd brought with him, and I found another familiar face. The guy who had been with Jared out in the field a few weeks back. I frowned at him and turned my attention back to Vance. I gave a slight nod, hoping he didn't read the fear in my face, and he raised his hand in a mocking wave. I flared my nostrils and turned away.

"I'm sure he'll be here soon," Paige said. "But for now we need you to get signed in."

If I didn't, then my spot would be taken by another racer. Usually you had to reserve a spot weeks in advance to get in for a race, but Simon, the guy who ran the races, and I had a good relationship. He also knew I brought a bigger audience than anyone else. People loved watching a teen girl race. He'd advertised my return as soon as I called in, and I knew the bets would be high.

After I got done signing in, we waited for the races to start. It was a winner-take-all situation, and tensions ran high. The pot for the winners tonight was fifteen grand. That didn't include all the side betting, which was where Vance came in. He had already placed the money Corey owed him on the line. It all rode on me winning.

"There he is." Paige pointed to the entrance of the races.

Corey pushed through the crowd, and I practically ran over to him. He pulled me into a quick hug before placing a kiss on my lips.

"You made it."

"Wouldn't miss it for the world."

I smiled up at him and the waves of fear that had crawled up my spine settled down. "Everything taken care of at the warehouse?"

He nodded. "We're good to go."

"The races are about to start," Paige called.

We went over to them. Alex greeted Corey, but Paige only gave him a once-over before turning her attention to the track.

"How does this work?" Corey asked.

"There are different races depending on the power of your bike. Right now it's the fifteen-hundred-horsepower race. I'm in the one-thousand-horsepower one."

Cheering erupted around us. The sound rippled and shredded in my ears. The bikers took their places, and I squeezed Corey's hand. Even though I wasn't racing yet, my heart began to speed up, almost like I was already on my bike, taking my position at the line. The starting lights flashed red. Engines revved; the crowd reached a crescendo. The light turned green and the racers were off, tires squealing. I stood on my tiptoes to get a better view, holding in a breath. The road was a straight shot down a quarter mile and it went by in a flash, but at times it seemed to stretch into forever. The smoke cleared, and I let out my breath when the winner was declared.

I let out a whistle. "Wow, that was a good one."

Corey frowned. "That was it?"

I let out a bark of laughter when I got a look at Alex's horrified expression.

"Was that it?" Alex's face burned red. "Dude. It's much more than *it*. Just wait until Tessa gets out there. You'll lose your shit."

"Speaking of." Paige pointed to her watch. "You need to get ready."

My belly did a flip, and I stretched out my arms. Then my quads. My neck.

"What are you doing?" Corey looked me up and down.

"This is my ritual. I like to stretch out before a race."

Corey raised a brow but kept his mouth shut. "It's a nice ritual," he commented when I bent over and did a straddle stretch.

I stood up so fast the blood rushed to my head. "You're such a perv."

"You're the one who put her butt in my face."

My cheeks started to hurt from smiling. I missed this version of Corey. It made my heart flutter. Corey did a slow walk to me with a gleam in his eyes that made me want to crash my lips to his. Which is exactly what I did. Then I melted against him, a calm washing over me.

"Seriously, you need to get out there." Paige grabbed my elbow and pulled me to Black Beauty.

"Good luck," Corey called over the crowd.

Paige dragged me all the way to Beauty, and I straddled my motorcycle before turning it on.

"You ready?" Paige squeezed my shoulder.

"Of course." I slid on the smirk before putting on my helmet.

Driving Beauty to the starting line, I glanced over at my competitor. I couldn't see who it was through their helmet, but they were decidedly male. We exchanged a nod before I turned my attention to the drag strip. The stretch of road was lit beneath the floodlights. The quarter mile seemed so much longer laid out in front of me.

Only seconds to go and my pulse raced with the growling engine vibrating between my thighs. The sound of the cheering crowd faded to the background until it was a deep rumble of metal grinding on metal. There was a moment before every race when my mind finally emptied itself of all the weight it carried. When the pain of the past, the longing for change, the desperation for something I could never quite grasp finally let go.

And I felt free again.

No world, no troubles, just me, Black Beauty, and the road. My hand clamped on the handles, my feet itched to push the pedal. In flashing waves, the world lapped against the bubble that encompassed me. The beeping of the light sounded, blinking red one, two, three times before the green.

Beauty flared to life. Smoke puffed; tires screeched; engines roared. I couldn't see it, but in my mind Beauty took off like a demon rising from the smoke. Beauty told me what to do, when to shift, when to speed up. The boom of her engine was as familiar as Elvis. It soothed away the frayed edges of nerves biting my insides. The world disappeared into a mirage of phantom sounds until there was nothing but white noise. My mind went into overdrive, focused on the small quake the engine produced, the way my hands held fast to the handles all the way to my feet pressing against the pedal.

Everything grew sharper, more focused; I saw only asphalt I had yet to conquer. This was what I missed about racing. Flying high above the rest of the world. If I reached out my hand I'd feel it in the wind, shaping around my body, in my hair. The scent of the gasoline was intoxicating, pulling me deeper into folds of ecstasy.

My whole body tensed as the finish line drew nearer, time slowing down. I clenched my jaw, and we crossed over it, Beauty and I. And then it was over. Just like that.

I screeched to a halt, the pounding of my heart bellowing in my ears. I was out of breath, gasping for it, while my heart tried to regain a steady pace. I glanced over at the other racer, taking off my helmet and letting the cool night weave through my hair as I shook it out.

The cheering came back in a sudden flash. I dropped my arm and hopped off Beauty, turning toward the crowd. I didn't know if I had won. Not yet. I was afraid to look, afraid that I had let Corey down and that my plan had failed. I squeezed my eyes shut for a second and told myself to stop being a coward.

I pulled them open and saw the results. Time slowed again, tears brimming in my eyes. Vance stood by the spectator line with the group he brought, his face flashing with laughter. I moved over to my friends and spotted Paige and Alex, arms wrapped around each other's waists. Corey was gone. My heart settled in my rib cage.

I'd won. And he was gone. Just like we planned.

I ran over to Paige and Alex and jumped into their arms. "When did Corey leave?" I asked, fighting off a smile.

"Right after you crossed the line." Paige was beaming, and it made my body feel even lighter.

"Where the hell is he?" I was whipped around and Vance suddenly stared down at me. "Where'd he go?"

I yanked my arm out of his hand. "Who?"

"Don't play dumb, Tessa. I saw Corey run out of here."'

Paige and Alex pushed their way in front of me. "He was just here, man. Don't know what to tell you." Alex shrugged.

Vance stepped up to him, putting his face right in Alex's. Paige put her hand on Vance's chest and pushed him away.

"Back off. We told you we don't know where Corey is," Paige growled. "Are you going to start a fight out here?"

People had started to gather around us, drawn to the high tension stirring in the air.

"Is there a problem here?" One of the guards edged his way closer to us.

Vance took a step back and pointed his finger at me. "You better pray he isn't where I think he is. Come on, boys, we have to take care of something."

Vance and his crew headed for their cars while the crowd dispersed.

"I need to warn Corey."

"Tessa." The warning in Paige's tone did nothing to deter me.

"I need to get to him. Now."

I grabbed my phone and made the call.

COREY

atching Tessa cross the finish line was better than I imagined.

Alex was right: Her race seemed to go on forever. I stood on edge. My heart started beating so hard I started to sweat even though all I wore was a T-shirt and joggers. As soon as she was confirmed the winner I took off without looking back.

I sped back to Branson. My destination? The warehouse. If Jared kept his end of the deal, then X would be there, too. He'd see for himself what Vance was up to.

My phone started ringing not even a quarter of the way back, and I answered quickly.

"Tessa?"

"Vance knows you're gone. He's headed your way. Watch your back."

Shit. I thought the race would be enough to distract him from me. Enough to keep him away for the night.

"Okay. I'll deal with it."

"Be careful."

"I will. I promise." I ended the call and pressed harder on the gas. I had to beat Vance back.

Darkness covered the warehouse when I pulled up twenty minutes later. I got out of the car and checked my phone. Tessa hadn't called again.

Clouds covered the night sky, making it difficult to see. I waited in the car for a minute, waiting for my heart to calm down. Before I chickened out I finally exited the car and headed for the warehouse doors. I pulled them open and the sound of the empty room echoed around me.

"Hello? Anyone here?" My stomach sank when no one answered. "Shit." Jared had lied. He hadn't shown up.

I squeezed my eyes shut and told myself to calm down. It was going to be okay. Tessa won the race. We'd paid off the debt. I clenched my hands, nails digging into my palms. I had hoped that Jared would do this one thing for Tessa. Hoped that there was an actual way out for me. Hoped for a different future.

Car brakes squeaked behind me. I squared my shoulders.

Vance.

I spun to face him but found the headlights of a black town car instead. A bodyguard the size of Thor stepped out. I recognized him immediately. Sweat started to collect behind my neck. Thor stepped to the side and the back two passenger-side doors opened simultaneously. The cane came out first, then a foot. Mr. Wilson stood tall, staring over the door. Jared stood on the other side.

"Everything okay, Corey? You look worried." Jared wore a mocking grin.

"Corey, it's so good to see you." Mr. Wilson—X—approached me. Standing face-to-face for the first time in over a year, I realized that I was taller than him.

"Thank you for coming, sir. I know how busy your schedule is."

He waved a hand. "Think nothing of it. When my grandson explained the situation, I knew I had to see it for myself."

Thor stepped into the warehouse and flipped on the lights. Wilson and Jared brushed past me to check it out.

"This is interesting," Wilson said, casting a glance around the full shelves. "I have to hand it to Vance. I didn't think he was smart enough to pull this off."

"I'm sorry, sir. I tried reaching out and then Vance killed Jaimie and threatened my family. I didn't know what else to do."

Wilson placed both hands on top of his cane and nodded thoughtfully. "I'm afraid the fault is mine. My mind hasn't been the same lately. Old age and all that. Vance sought to take advantage of my health issues. He told me everything was well. The money came in on time. I didn't think anything of it. I had other things on my mind."

I didn't know why he felt the need to explain himself. X never shared his motivations with anyone. Ever.

"Why are you telling me this?"

"Because I want to apologize for the role you've played in everything. You told me you wanted out when you were released. I told you eventually it would happen. I didn't keep that promise. It's time that I did."

My body stiffened. "Are you saying what I think you are?"

"You're out, Corey."

It took a minute for his words to settle in my head. For me to realize he meant what he said. "Thank you, sir."

X nodded. "My men will take care of the warehouse. I'll take care of Vance." He patted my back. "Take care of yourself, Corey."

I stood in silence. Jared leaned against the car, messing with his phone. I waited for someone to tell me it was a joke, that I wasn't getting everything I wanted. My phone buzzed in my pocket, and Vance's name flashed across the screen.

"Sir," I called after Wilson, holding up my phone. "It's Vance."

"Answer it, and put it on speaker," he instructed.

I did as he asked.

"Did you really think you could screw me over, Fowler? After everything?" Vance's angry hiss echoed around us.

"It's over, Vance."

"No. It's over when I say it is. I have your little brother here with me. Come and get him, and we can actually end this." The line clicked.

"He'll be at his hideout," Wilson spoke up. "You should go get your brother."

"What do you want me to do?" I asked.

"Whatever you need to. I wash my hands of that nephew of mine."

"It'll get ugly," I answered. "The police will have to get involved."

X nodded. "Everything we need is in this warehouse. Feel free to call the officers."

I didn't wait for more approval and got my ass in the car and drove like hell all the way to Vance's.

The lights were on when I got to the building. Cutting the engine, I stepped outside and hesitated for a minute, staring up at the looming shadow of it. I slammed the door shut and entered. Vance sat at his usual spot. Drew on one side. Bucky on the other. And Tim in front of him, hands duct-taped together.

"I'm here."

"We had a deal, Fowler. So imagine my surprise when my surveillance camera shows you hanging out with X at my warehouse." He stood up, gun in hand.

"It's over, Vance. X knows everything. What are you going to do now? You have nowhere left to go." I tried to keep my voice even, but the thought of Vance turning that gun on Tim scared me shitless. I had to keep my brother safe.

"I'm using the money I made and getting the hell out of Branson. Taking Peyson for myself. X can't stop me. Not anymore." He pointed the gun at Tim's head.

I took an involuntary step forward. "No! Don't do this. Kill me. I'm the one you hate. My brother has nothing to do with any of this."

Vance raised his gun and let out a laugh. "You're pathetic, you know that, Fowler? I'm going to enjoy watching you watch your brother die." His aim moved back quick, but Drew was quicker. He pushed Vance out of the way before the gun could go off and threw himself on top of him.

Bucky tried to pry Drew off Vance, but they were rolling on the floor.

"Drew!" I ran for him, but he shook his head.

"Get Tim out of here!"

I changed directions, and Tim was already on his feet. I grabbed his tied hands and hauled him toward the exit, shielding his body.

"Get outside. Hide in the woods until it's all clear," I said through shaky breaths. The sound of police sirens drew near.

"Come with me, Corey." Tears stained Tim's cheeks, but I couldn't leave Drew behind. Not after everything he did.

I pulled him into a hug. "I love you, Tim."

I ran back to Vance. They were still on the ground, fighting for the gun. Bucky was nowhere to be seen. He must have heard the sirens and made a run for it.

Vance got the upper hand, gun in hand, and stood up, kicking Drew in the stomach. He pointed the gun and the shot flew through the air. Drew's gasping breath echoed around the quiet building, even more deafening than the gunshot.

"No!" I ran to him without thinking.

Vance moved the gun to me, and I skidded to a stop. My heartbeat rushed to my ears. The seconds slowed. I took in panting breaths. And then I waited. I refused to close my eyes. If Vance was going to kill me tonight, I was going to watch it happen. I wasn't going to be a coward and back out now.

Drew's hand shot up and wrapped around Vance's leg.

Vance stumbled forward and fell to the ground. Anger spiked through me and the seconds moved quickly again. I ran to Vance and kicked the gun out of his way before grabbing him by the collar.

"It's over. You're going to jail for a very long time. You understand?" I curled my hand into a fist and pulled it back and slammed it into his nose. My hand ached, the pain sharp and stinging, but I didn't care. One more hit. Then another. I let out all the anger I'd held in for so many years. Until I had nothing left to give.

"Corey!" Drew's cry broke me out of the red that colored my vision.

I let go of my grip on Vance and sat back on my heels, breathing hard, chest pounding. I crawled over to Drew to check on him. Blood covered the floor beneath him. Hot and slick. My hands hovered over his body.

"You shouldn't talk." I covered the wound on his shoulder with my hands. "The police are almost here." The sirens were right on top of us.

"You should get out of here." His breathing sounded off and he fought for each breath.

"I said not to talk." Drew closed his eyes, his breathing shallower. "Stay with me, man. Don't give up, Drew. It's not over for you."

Tears pricked my eyes and I closed them, saying a prayer of hope. Officers burst through the doors, and I stayed with Drew. It took them making me stand and show my hands to leave his side. An ambulance pulled up while they cuffed me. The clouds broke apart up above and rain started to prick cold droplets onto my head before the officer made me duck into the back of the cruiser. Tim joined me in there moments later, his face ashen. I wanted to reach over and hug him, offer him comfort, but there wasn't much I could do with the cuffs around my wrists.

"I thought I told you to stay hidden." I leaned my head back against the seat and closed my eyes.

"I didn't want to leave you," he replied.

I opened my eyes and looked over at my brother. He hung his head, chin touching his chest. The night wasn't over for the two of us, but at least we were still alive.

The car started moving, and I jolted backward. The rain smacked hard against the car, turning into a full-on summer storm. The officers took us to the police station, but I said nothing and neither did Tim.

They took us inside and made us sit on cold, plastic chairs. Blood stained my hands. I couldn't see them, but I knew it was there. I wondered if Drew was okay.

"I'm sorry you got dragged into this," I said to Tim while we waited to be booked.

"It's my fault. I never should have gone to him. You taught me better, and I didn't listen." His voice wobbled.

"Corey." Hopper walked down the hall of the brightly lit police station, looking haggard. The buttons of his shirt were off by one, like he'd hastily dressed. "I tried to get here as fast as I could."

"Mr. Hopper?" One of the police officers approached him. A squat-looking dude with a buzz cut. "Everything okay, sir?"

"No. It isn't. Can you explain to me why my clients are cuffed?"

"Your clients?" The officer looked back and forth between us. "I don't understand."

"I'm representing Corey Fowler and Tim Fowler. They are innocent bystanders in the raid that happened tonight. My client called me beforehand to tell me what was happening. Vance Higgins kidnapped his little brother and was holding him hostage. He's the one who called the police to tip you off. You should be thanking him for his cooperation. Uncuff him now."

I had to hand it to Hopper—he could be scary as hell when he wanted to be. Tim had even straightened up during the exchange, watching in fascination.

"Of course, sir. Sorry for the mistake." The young officer uncuffed us, and I rubbed my wrists.

"Thank you, sir," I said as soon as the officer left us.

"Mind explaining to me exactly what happened tonight?" he asked.

"I will but can we head to the hospital first? I need to check up on my friend."

Hopper sighed and rubbed his temples. "All right. But you tell me everything. Got it?"

I nodded. "Yes, sir."

I went to the bathroom and washed my hands before we grabbed our things at the front desk. Mom's car keys and my phone.

I'd share my part. Keep Tessa out of it. It was up to her whether she wanted to come clean. Knowing her, she probably would. Tessa. Shit. I needed to get in touch with her. Give her an update. She was probably worried sick.

"Do you mind if I make a quick phone call?" I asked.

Hopper raised a brow but gave me a stiff nod in response. We stepped outside, and the cool night air helped ease the tightness coiling around my muscles. The rain had stopped. I got my phone and stepped aside to call the girl who had risked so much for me. I hoped she still thought I was worth it.

TESSA

"He's not here," Jared said as soon as I arrived at the warehouse. I'd ridden like a bat out of hell to make it there. My thoughts only on Corey's safety and whether Jared had come through.

"Where did he go?"

Jared checked his watch. "By now he's probably at Vance's hideout."

My heart shuddered. "What did you do, Jared?" I held up my helmet, ready to knock him over the head with it.

Jared stepped back, hands up in surrender. "Nothing! Holy shit, Tessa! Vance kidnapped his brother, and he went to get him back. Corey called the police before heading out there. Told them everything."

I dropped my arm and almost sank to the ground. "I can't believe it. After everything. He's going back to prison."

Jared had the decency to look regretful. "I'm sorry." He approached me slowly and wrapped me in a hug that I couldn't return.

"I need to get to him." I stepped out of the awkward embrace. I suddenly realized how unfamiliar Jared's touch felt.

"And do what exactly? The police will probably be there soon. You can't get caught in the middle of that."

My shoulders slumped forward. "I hate this. I hate that I can't do anything."

"You should go home and wait until you hear from him."

I sighed in defeat. He was right. I got on Beauty and drove home where it was quiet and dark. Dad wasn't anywhere to be seen and Jiminy waited by the front door. I paced my living room floor, Jiminy following me back and forth, and called Corey. Over and over.

An hour later, my phone started ringing.

"Corey? Where are you?"

"On the way to the hospital. Drew was shot. Vance is in jail. Your dad is taking me over there. Will you meet me?"

"Of course. I'll be there soon."

I hung up and made another call.

"Tessa? Everything okay?" Jared's voice held the worry from earlier.

"Corey called. He's headed to the hospital. Vance was arrested. I thought you would want to know."

"Okay. I'll let my grandfather know."

"Thank you for coming through, Jared. I hope you have a nice life."

"You too, Tessa."

With that, I hung up and walked out to Beauty once more and rode her toward the hospital, ready to see the boy I'd fought so hard to keep.

───

Corey sat in the waiting area, elbows on thighs. Tim wasn't with him. And neither was my dad.

"Corey!" I ran down the hall to him.

He stood up and opened his arms to me. I melted against him, my arms around his waist, his around mine. I took a steady breath and listened to the sound of his pounding heart.

"Are you okay?"

"Yeah," his voice rumbled in my ear. "Your dad is taking Tim home. My mom is around here somewhere. I didn't want her to see him right now."

I pulled away and looked up at him. Dark circles hung at the bottom of his eyes, his expression weary and tired.

"What happened?"

Corey explained everything that went down at Vance's hideout while I tried to keep myself together listening to the story of how close he got to losing his life.

"I'm glad you're still here. I'm glad you're safe. But how did my dad end up bringing you here?"

"I called him right after I called the cops. Told him what had happened. I hired him as my attorney."

I blinked a few times, grateful for everything my dad had done.

"I didn't tell him about your involvement. Figured it wasn't my place."

Corey pulled me down, and we sank into the faux leather chairs. "I need to tell him. About everything. The night of the accident. The racing. And about us."

"That's a good plan."

"What about Mr. Wilson. I mean X? What do we do about him?"

Corey slumped. "He told me I was out. I'm free. In a way. My past will still be a burden I have to carry, but I'm going to spend my future making up for it."

"I can't tell him about X, can I?" I leaned into Corey, resting my head on his shoulder. "In order to keep him safe."

"It's up to you, Tessa. I'm not going to tell you what to do. I'll support whatever decision you make."

I contemplated my options. If I told Dad, then not only was my life going to be affected but Corey also would be brought into the crosshairs. There was Jared. His entire family. Their empire. They wouldn't give that up without a fight. They were powerful, and I knew opening my mouth would endanger too many people.

"I can't. It's too dangerous."

Corey pressed a kiss to my temple. "I know. I'm sorry I burdened you with the truth. You don't deserve this. You deserve better. If you want to walk away, I'll understand, Tessa."

I sat up straight. "You're not getting rid of me that easy, Fowler. I just drag raced to save your ass. You think I do that for just anyone?" I joked, but his eyes were serious and desperate. I dropped the smile from my face.

"I mean it, Tessa. If it's too much, you need to get out now. Because if you don't, I might not be able to let you walk away."

I leaned in closer to him, eyes drifting down to his lips. "Then don't let me." Our lips brushed, tentatively at first, like it was the first time we were kissing all over again. Then suddenly I was falling into him, and the heat rose inside my limbs.

"Tessa?"

Corey and I jumped apart. Panic zoomed through me. "Dad. Hi." I stood up and met my father's furrowed gaze.

"I think we have some things to discuss." He crossed his arms and cleared his face. I called that the lawyer look. It was the one he put on every time he entered the courtroom and it was the number one indicator that I was in trouble.

"Yes. We do."

Dad and I headed down the hall, his steps thumping along the floor. I sent Corey what I hoped was a reassuring smile over my shoulder.

Dad found a quiet corner at the back of the hospital while my feet practically dragged to the spot. He turned to me, holding the exact same stance from earlier, and I stared up at him with my face flushed with guilt. I cleared my throat.

"I should start at the beginning."

"That's probably best." His voice was hard.

With a deep breath, I spilled everything. About the accident. The aftermath. Then Corey and how we came to be. And the role I played in helping him get out of Vance's clutches. All the while my father stood silent, his brows heavy with an expression I couldn't place.

"I'm sorry. I shouldn't have gone behind your back."

Dad didn't say anything for a minute. Maybe less. It felt like an eternity.

"Let me get this straight, just to be clear, because I want us to be on the same page. You dated that prick Jared even though I hated him, then you started drag racing illegally, bribed a police officer after getting into an accident that was clearly not your fault because he was high and you had been drinking, and then went to a drug lord and made a deal with him because you started dating Corey behind my back. Did I get everything?"

My throat closed up. When he laid it all out there like that, well, I could see why he might never forgive me. That was a lot. I didn't understand how my father was still standing. "How are you feeling?" I asked. "Is your heart doing okay?"

"My heart is fine. My blood pressure, on the other hand, not so great."

"Well, your blood pressure and heart are sort of connected."

Dad raised a hand. "I'm going to stop you right there because I will definitely lose a gasket if you say anything smart." I clamped my mouth shut. "I love you, Tess. I gave you a lot of freedom. And it's partly my fault that you're in this mess. If I hadn't been so involved in my work life, maybe I would have seen the signs that things were off. But I raised you to know better, and I'm disappointed."

My stomach dropped with those words. "I know, Dad. I'm sorry. It'll never be enough, but I promise I'll make it up to you." Tears pricked my eyes, and I wiped them away before they dropped.

Dad wrapped me in a hug. "We have a lot to discuss. I'm guessing you don't want to head home yet with Corey being here."

"You're not forcing me to go with you?" I stepped out of his embrace and wiped my nose.

"No. He needs you. As mad as I am at the both of you, I can wait a little longer until dishing out your punishment."

"Thanks, Dad. I love you."

"You better be home before I wake up for work in the morning. Got it?"

"Understood." I held back a smile, and he gave me a squeeze before leaving.

I called Paige to let her know what had happened after missing fifty phone calls from her and explained that I had confessed everything to my dad, which meant her dad would be hearing about it soon. She told me she understood why I did it, and we made a plan to meet up later. Then I went back in search of Corey, ready to start a future with a boy who finally had his freedom.

COREY

rew's family showed up at the hospital a few minutes after Tessa and Hopper went to talk. I gave them a quick update before making an excuse about needing a drink in order to get away.

Tessa hadn't returned. I hadn't lost her, though; I knew that for sure. From the look in her eyes, I knew nothing could keep her from me. I slowly realized that nothing could keep me from her, either. She was a part of my life now, permanently etched into the picture of my heart.

I walked the busy hall of the hospital, the smell of disinfectant making my stomach roll and the fluorescent lights burning my retinas. It wasn't until I found myself standing in front of the coffee machine that I realized I didn't have my wallet and couldn't get the drink.

"When exactly were you planning on telling me you were here?" Mom's voice burst the heavy cloud hanging over my head.

She stood behind me, hands on her hips, hair up in a tight bun, eyes heavy with worry.

"What happened, Corey? One of the nurses said that the police were here and that Drew was admitted with a gunshot wound." Her hand rested on my shoulder. "Are you okay? Did you get hurt?"

I stared at her for a full minute. Unable to speak. The burden life placed on me crumbling around me.

"Corey?"

Instead of speaking I started to breathe heavy. I leaned into my mom, wrapped my arms around her, felt her return the hug, and I cried.

⁓

I told Mom about Tim. Her shoulders slumped, and her neck bent forward while the tears streamed down her face. A lump formed in my own throat, and I pulled her into a hug.

"It's not your fault, Mom. It's mine. He followed my path."

"It's neither of your faults," Mom said. "You were a kid, Corey. You didn't know what you were getting into. All you've ever done is try and protect us. I'm glad you're safe, that you took care of your little brother, but I'm also so angry with you. What if you had gotten shot instead? What if you had died? Don't ever think you have to put yourself in that kind of situation for us again. Do you understand?"

I nodded and apologized. Then Mom told me she officially got the promotion at work. The good news softened some of the pain that had bruised my body because of that night.

"I'm sorry, Mom, for being just like Dad."

Mom shook her head. "No. You're not. You're so much better, Corey. I hope you finally see that and give yourself a chance at a new life." She kissed my forehead.

"Corey?" Tessa's hesitant voice made Mom step away. "I'm sorry, I didn't mean to intrude."

Mom stared at her for a moment as recognition filled her eyes. "You're the girl from the picture." She stepped forward and wrapped Tessa in a hug. "It's nice to finally meet you."

Tessa stared at me, wide eyed, over Mom's shoulder and I hid a smile. "Thank you. It's nice to meet you, too, Mrs. Fowler."

Mom let her go and rubbed my arm. "I better head home and check on your brother. Don't stay out too late, okay?" Mom kissed my cheek and left us alone.

"Your mom is beautiful." Tessa lingered unsteadily near me.

"Yeah. She is. What did your dad say?" I reached over and took her hand in mine, hoping it would ease the uncertainty in her stance.

She sighed and finally leaned into me. "Well, he didn't forbid me from seeing you. Yet. But I think we have a ways to go before he'll trust me again."

"I'm sorry."

"Don't be. I made my decisions. They're on me."

Our hands, still clasped, hung between us. "You want to get out of here? Spend some time together before your dad does decide to forbid you from seeing me?"

Her familiar bright smile made an appearance. "Yes. I'd like that very much."

I gave her a quick kiss and marveled at this girl who risked so much for me. Risked pretty much everything so I could be free to live a life I wanted. A life with freedom and choices. A life that allowed me to finally be who I wanted to be and start fresh. A life where I could be with the girl of my dreams without having to look over my shoulder.

I squeezed Tessa's hand, and we walked outside together, an endless road of possibilities ahead of us.

TESSA

One month later

My shoulders were killing me.

"You missed a spot over there." Paige pointed to a section of the siding that I had painted over three times already.

"You're so not helping." I shook my paintbrush, and she screeched and jumped away to avoid getting paint in her hair.

"Hey, you're the one who got me into this mess, remember?" She indicated the overalls she wore that were already splattered with paint.

After my dad told Uncle Mike everything that had happened, they got together to think up a punishment before we both headed to college. Apparently, painting the graffitied siding was the top choice.

"If you two are done chattering over there, I'd really like to continue my work in peace," Corey chimed in, keeping his brushstrokes even and perfect. He was a master at not just spray painting, but also actual painting of houses.

I stared down at him from the ladder. "Hey, buddy, watch it, I'll get you next."

Dad had also decided to let Corey continue his community service. He figured forbidding us from seeing each other would only entice us more. And despite everything, I think he sort of liked having him around.

"You drop any paint on me, and there will be no kissing for a week."

"Gross," Paige groaned.

"Yeah, let's see how well that threat holds up," I said.

Corey did a slow look up at me. "You're right. No way could I last a whole hour with you throwing that puppy-dog look at me."

"Oh, isn't she so good at that?" Paige said, smiling. "She has been using that look on me for years."

"I wouldn't use it if it didn't work so well. And will you two stop discussing me like I'm not here?"

Paige and Corey exchanged a look and instead of annoying me it made my heart burst. They were finally getting along and I couldn't be happier.

After we finished the newest coat on the house, which my dad had made us paint ten times already, we washed off our brushes, and Paige headed out with Alex, and Corey waited for me so we could spend some time together before he went to work at Stan's.

A lot had changed over the last month. Drew was out of the hospital and had managed to avoid jail time. Corey's mom had me over for dinner, and she and Corey even tried to teach me how to cook Indian food.

Tim was currently in counseling, still dealing with the aftermath of his kidnapping and the shoot-out. Corey worried about him all the time, but things were getting better and the two of them had started spending more time together.

Corey and I walked down the driveway to his car. I leaned back against it, and he placed his hands on either side of me, caging me in. A piece of his hair fell forward and I reached up and tucked it back.

"Did you just pull a romance-novel move on me?"

I bit back a smile at the memory of our night at the skate park.

"So what if I did?"

Corey's smile brightened my life. I loved seeing it every single time.

"You must really like me, Tessa Marie Hopper." He pressed his lips to mine and moved his face to the side of my neck and I sighed.

"I signed up for a couple of fall classes at Randall," he said, kissing the spot right behind my ear.

I pressed my hand to his chest and pushed him back. "Really?"

"Yes. Really."

"I'm so proud of you, Corey."

"I figured it was time to take a chance on something." The sun shone over us. The sky was a pale blue with small wisps of clouds. Pretty much perfect. "Like some crazy biker chick did with some punk who ruined her dad's car."

I pulled him so we were nose to nose. "You are so worth it, Corey Fowler."

ACKNOWLEDGMENTS

It takes a village to raise a book. And I definitely have a lot of villagers to thank for helping me raise mine.

First off, I have to thank the amazing team at Swoon. Thank you to my editor, Kat Brzozowski, for your enthusiasm for IYOK and your willingness to talk to me on the phone while I tried to work out how to tackle a round of edits. Thank you to Emily Settle and Andre-Naquian Wheeler for your insightful notes. Thank you to Jean Feiwel, Lauren Scobell (and another thanks to Lauren for her thoughtful notes as well), Starr Baer, Kim Waymer, and the rest of the Swoon team. Thank you to my talented cover artist, Kasi Turpin, for bringing Corey and Tessa to life, and of course my creative cover designer, Liz Dresner, for coming up with the concept.

Thank you to the Swoon Squad. I cannot imagine what this journey would have been like if it weren't for all of you. I am so proud to be a Squad member. Thanks to Vicki Skinner for being my "big sister" of sorts when I was selected. Lillie Vale, thank you for always answering my messages and for being an awesome BookCon roomie. A special shout-out to Aiden Thomas and Natalie Williamson. I'm so glad we were selected together. I cannot thank you enough for the messages we've exchanged and your friendships.

Shannon Doleski, Jenny Elder Moke, Liz Lawson, and Jeff Bishop: you all helped make a hard life moment better. I cannot thank you enough for being there for me. Love you all.

Thanks to Molly E. Lee, the first reader ever for IYOK (back when it was titled *Fading!*). I have loved watching your career grow and am so grateful for the time you took to give me notes. Soni Wolf, thank you for your helpful critiques, along with Salena Casha and every other person who has ever offered me a critique on this book. I'm sorry if I forgot you!

Thanks to the Pitch Wars 2014 group and to my mentor, Monica Bustamante Wagner, for choosing me as an alternate, and to Susan Gray Foster, my amazing Pitch Wars sister. Thank you to Amy Trueblood for selecting me not once, but twice, to be on her team for the Sun vs. Snow pitch contest. Both contests helped me learn so much and made my pitch and pages that much stronger.

Thank you to everyone reading this book. I hope you all love it as much as I do.

I'm going to end by saying a thank-you to my family, the most important people in my life. My mom and dad for always believing in me. My brother, Anmol, and sister, Sumedha, for just being there. My extended family, for being so colorful and fun. To my mother-in-law, Vicki, who is the greatest cheerleader anyone could have. To the rest of the Pickett and Dauphinee clans, you guys rock.

And of course, my fab five: Logan, Dylan, Adhira, Sameera, and Soren. You are the greatest gifts in my life.

No, I'm not going to forget you, Cam. Saving the best for last, duh! Thanks for always encouraging me, for dreaming with me, for lifting me up, for always making me laugh, for supporting our family while I pursued this wild and crazy dream. Love you always. What can I say—we're meant to be.

Check out more books chosen for publication by readers like you.

DID YOU KNOW...

readers like you
helped to get this
book published?

Join our book-obsessed community and help us
discover awesome new writing talent.

1 Write it.
Share your original YA manuscript.

2 Read it.
Discover bright new bookish talent.

3 Share it.
Discuss, rate, and share your faves.

4 Love it.
Help us publish the books you love.

Share your own manuscript or dive between the pages
at **swoonreads.com** or by downloading the **Swoon Reads app**.